WINDSWEPT

Titles by Patricia Ryan published by Severn House

WINDSWEPT

WINDSWEPT

Patricia Ryan

This first world edition published 2014
in Great Britain and the USA by
SEVERN HOUSE PUBLISHERS LTD of
19 Cedar Road, Sutton, Surrey, England, SM2 5DA

British Library Cataloguing in Publication Data

Ryan, Patricia, 1946-
  Windswept.
  1. Vacations–Caribbean Area–Fiction. 2. Murder–
  Fiction. 3. Romantic suspense novels.
  I. Title
  813.6-dc23

ISBN-13: 978-0-7278-8357-5 (cased)
ISBN-13: 978-1-84751-504-9 (trade paper)

All Severn House titles are printed on acid-free paper.

Severn House Publishers support the Forest Stewardship Council™ [FSC™],
the leading international forest certification organisation. All our titles that
are printed on FSC certified paper carry the FSC logo.

MIX
Paper from
responsible sources
FSC® C013056
www.fsc.org

Typeset by Palimpsest Book Production Ltd.,
Falkirk, Stirlingshire, Scotland.
Printed and bound in Great Britain by
TJ International, Padstow, Cornwall

To my sons – John, Hugh and James
For their support and constant good humor
And to John – thank you for being who you are

ACKNOWLEDGEMENTS

To those who have shared the journey and given advice along the way, Anne Keary, Eileen Twomey, Kathleen Behrens, Una Glennon and Robin Metcalf, many thanks. To all those at Severn House, especially Sara Porter, my editor, thanks for taking the chance. To my agent and friend, Meg Ruley, for her insight and encouragement, her able assistant, Rebecca Scherer, and everyone at the Jane Rotrosen Agency, this never would have happened without you.

PROLOGUE

Emily had only gone a few steps when she began to regret her choice. She'd been so preoccupied trying to get to the beach barbecue. In spite of her unease, she had to chuckle at the thought of the usually sedate guests 'getting down to boogie' to the reggae beat of a steel band. It was about as uninhibited as things got at Island Bluffs. Somehow the 'hot . . . hot . . . hot' vibe seemed beyond this crowd.

She should have let Annie send someone down from the main house. It was surprising how dark it was, the high clouds occasionally blocking the moon. She couldn't even remember which way the path turned – was it right first, then left, or . . . And the steps, three sets or two? It was hopeless. There was no choice but to take the ocean path which hugged the steep cliff. There were a few lights there; hopefully they would be enough to guide her.

She had taken this path during the day, loving the sound of the pounding surf and the spray of saltwater which accompanied the mild sea breezes. But at night it seemed considerably less pleasant. Emily, quickening her pace on her revised route, was soon startled by a distant, muffled voice calling out.

'Help me. Please, someone help me.'

Shaken, she ran on, peering into the darkness on the side of the path and fearing what she would find, but she could see no one. Was she imagining things? It was darker now, the moon totally shrouded by the clouds. The path was becoming narrower as it wound its way up the bluff.

'Oh, God, someone please help me,' moaned the faint voice. At first, the sound seemed to come from somewhere among the gullies. But no, it was up there, from the deep crevices that lined the cliff face near the top. Or was it just bouncing off the wall of rock?

'I'm coming! Hold on, I'm almost there,' Emily cried, forging ahead in spite of her confusion, trying to climb faster.

She cursed the flimsy sandals which were no protection from the jagged rocks. At every step she had to reach out to the rock face to steady herself. There was no avoiding the scrapes and bruises. She wanted to turn back but she was drawn on by the desperation in the voice.

When she reached the top of the bluff, however, there was no one there. Emily looked around. Down below, she could see the flaming torches from the beach barbecue. Shadows shifted as people mingled. She could hear faint traces of laughter. But there were no human sounds up here, just the roar of the waves. She was frightened now. She turned to look back at the dark, lonely path, hoping desperately that someone else might have chosen this route. Of course, no one had; her isolation was complete. Too late, she realized something was terribly wrong as she felt the sharp blow to the back of her head.

For a moment everything went black, and then she felt her body being dragged along the rocky ground. Oh, God, the cliff edge – someone was dragging her toward the cliff edge. She tried desperately to think but her head roiled with confused, broken images.

That voice . . . someone was talking. '*Sorry, Emily, but I can't take the chance that you'll remember.*' Remember . . . remember . . . Oh, God, remember.

'*I'm afraid you played a dangerous game.*' A game . . . a dangerous game . . .

'*Why couldn't you have just stayed out of it? It was none of your business. You hardly even knew him. I didn't want this to happen, but it's too late now. Everyone will think your fall was tragic, but the darkness, the slippery rocks and those shoes . . .*'

Rough stones battered her back and head . . . the sound of the surf was closer now. She had to do something. Scream – she had to scream. It was her only chance.

Emily struggled against panic. She waited for the momentary silence, that brief interlude between the roars of the rhythmic waves. Steady, she thought. Concentrate on the timing. Soon. The next one. Now. But just as she opened her mouth, the stillness of the night was shattered by the opening salvos of the steel band . . .

ONE

Emily wakened slowly, snug under the weighty comforter, her body still warm and soft with sleep. Her mind resisted the pull of dawn. Thank God for Saturdays, she mused, as she reached out to gently wrap her arm around Michael.

'Damn,' she muttered, throwing the covers back and jumping out of bed. 'Damn, damn, damn.' This was the second time in a week that her phone alarm hadn't gone off. Today was Wednesday, a bitter, cold February Wednesday, not Saturday. Michael was in London, not New York, and that incessant buzzing was the intercom.

'Yes, Eddie?' she called, pressing the button.

'Oh, Ms Harrington, I was getting worried. The car is here to pick you up and you weren't answering the buzzer.'

'I'm so sorry, Eddie. I overslept. Could you explain to the driver? Tell him I'll be down in a few minutes.'

'No problem. And Hector hasn't left yet. I'll send him up and he can help you with the bags.'

'You're a lifesaver, Eddie. I don't know what we'd do without you.'

Like many New Yorkers, Emily and Michael were highly dependent on an assortment of urban caretakers. Their compact two bedroom co-op in a pre-war, red-brick elevator building was the envy of all their friends. The neighborhood was one of those unique to New York – a couple of square blocks of low-rises on dead-end streets adjacent to some major landmark (in this case the United Nations) that actually managed to feel like a community.

They knew the names of their doormen and their doormen's children. Their laundry and cleaning were picked up and delivered. The local pharmacy was open twenty-four hours and no medication was dispensed until Howard was sure that you understood the doctor's instructions and potential side effects. The hardware store, which had somehow managed to survive on the same spot for the last sixty years, acted as a referral source for local handymen, everyone properly 'vetted' by Joe before the name was passed on.

As she waited for Hector's knock, Emily ran around the apartment, throwing some last-minute things in her suitcase, pouring a glass of water on her two straggly plants and checking she'd packed her passport and ticket. Her eye strayed to the brochure on her night table – white sand, blue water and bright, bold sun. She sighed contentedly as she threw it into her carry-on. No time for those pants I was going to press, she thought, as she struggled into a pair of jeans lying on a chair. No matter, these and a shirt would do.

A last-minute call to Jack, her assistant at the New York State public advocacy program she ran, and she'd be on her way. But Jack didn't pick up. Emily realized he must be in a subway tunnel so she left a detailed message. 'Jack, it's Emily. I'm heading out but I wanted to tell you that I left a folder on my desk for the city council meeting on Friday. That day-care center is scheduled to close next week so we don't have much time. There are three letters of support in there that you have to get into the record. They'll try to stop you but be persistent. There are also the names and phone numbers of the seven people we have lined up to speak at the meeting. Check in with them before Friday and make sure they're ready. It won't be easy to get in touch with me but I wrote the resort's main number on the folder just in case. I'll try to check in with you, but remember – give 'em hell.'

Although thirty-one, Emily's youthful face often left her mistaken for someone much younger. She was tall and slim, with soft red hair and bright blue eyes that were quick to laugh and smile. But her easygoing exterior belied what was a tenacious, sometimes stubborn spirit. Born Emily Claire Harrington, her early years were lived on bustling New York City streets where she spent summer days pursuing her two greatest loves, stoopball and stickball. A freckle-faced tomboy with a fierce desire to win that was never diminished by losing, she would join any game and accept any challenge. Climb down the fire escape from the seventh floor? No problem. Squeeze through the cemetery fence at dusk to check out an open grave? Easy.

Jump on the rear bumper of a moving bus? Well, maybe next time.

When she was twelve her family moved to a Hudson Valley suburb, where Emily spent her teenage years like a perennial out of season, her brains and her beauty hidden under a baseball cap. She was happiest on the soccer field and the basketball court, or fishing on nearby Carson's Lake with her father, whose passion for history resulted in her reeling in more knowledge than fish. And although suburban life had some charm, Emily never lost her love for the city.

Bzzz.

That would be Hector. She hoped she had everything, but as she opened the apartment door she realized that would've been a long shot even if she had gotten up on time.

'Sorry, Hector, but I have all these bags – Michael's and mine. How's the weather outside? No more snow, I hope.'

'No, not last night. It's just cold – really cold out there. I held the elevator, so I'll take these two and come back,' Hector said, picking up the two largest suitcases.

'That's OK, I've got the rest. Oh, Hector, I forgot to ask, how did Miguel make out on the exam?' Miguel was Hector's oldest son, a high-school sophomore struggling with English composition. Emily had found a free tutoring program on the west side that Miguel had been going to for about a month.

'Good – well, better. The teacher, she said he did better and she says the tutoring is helping. But you know the English is hard for him.'

'Hey, I remember a time when the English was hard for me.' Emily laughed. 'He's a good kid; he works hard. He'll get there.'

As they rode down in the elevator, Emily made a mental note to call the tutor when she got back. Maybe one session a week wasn't enough; she'd push for two.

A blast of frigid air hit her as soon as the front door opened. 'You must be goin' away for a while,' the driver commented as he helped with Emily's bags.

'No, just a week, really. Some of these bags are my fiancé's. He's stuck in London . . .' she started explaining until she realized that the driver was already getting behind the wheel.

She and Michael had met in college, and although they'd fallen head over heels, the road to romance had not always run smooth. Emily was fiercely independent and committed to any number of serious causes, but her dedication was enlivened by a zany sense of humor and a generous touch of irreverence. Michael, on the other hand, was reserved, but he was also earnest and supportive, every future mother-in-law's dream: conscientious, intelligent, and obviously going far.

For three years they had dated on and off. Rarely would Michael join Emily at a demonstration or on a picket line – more often, she would track him down in the library stacks, sometimes at midnight, smuggling in forbidden sodas and snacks. There they would sit for hours, with Emily telling funny stories, complete with outrageous imitations that were often brutally honest.

By senior year he was Phi Beta Kappa and she was student body president. For months at a time they would be inseparable, and then either his gravity or her flippancy would strain the relationship and they would break up. Life would temper these tendencies, but not before they graduated and, for a while, went their separate ways.

The driver pulled away from the curb, his back wheels spinning and squealing as he tried to get some traction. 'Two, three, four bags . . . you gals are all alike. My wife, she says to me all the time, "Al, you just don't . . ."' the driver droned on as Emily watched out the window. As she tried to settle herself, she decided to give Michael a call. Let's see, five hours ahead . . . that would make it almost noon in London. It was worth a try. But when she fished in her bag, she realized she had left her phone charging on the kitchen counter. 'Driver . . .' she uttered, thinking of going back for it. 'Oh, never mind.' What difference? she thought. There was little service where she was headed.

It was hard to imagine that she and Michael had been living together for almost two years now and, until recently, had been more than satisfied with their sometimes frenetic lives. Michael, tall, dark and dimpled, with rugged good looks, had followed in his father's footsteps after college, heading for law school in Boston. The son of a Midwest lawyer, not rich but comfortable, he had a sense of security that enabled him to see life in a straight line. And although doted on by his mother and two older sisters, he was more satisfied than spoiled.

He had been on the fast track since his graduation from law school, where he was first in his class and on law review. Now, as a junior partner at a 'white shoe' New York law firm, he devoted most of his waking hours to the betterment of Michner, Dawkins, Harris & Smith. Whatever time the firm did not demand was given over to Emily, but there had been less and less of that lately. That was one of the reasons Emily was so looking forward to this vacation. It would give her and Michael a chance to slow down, to talk, maybe figure things out.

The sidewalks were still piled high with snow and the occasional patch of ice made driving difficult. Yesterday's white blanket had already started to turn dirty, and sprays of blackened slush threatened walkers as cars and buses jockeyed for the lead in the race to the next red light. Car horns blared, drivers cursed and the dull crunch of a dented fender was an invitation to shouted threats and gridlocked streets. Emily had to admit that her driver was skilled, if a little more daring than one might have hoped. If pressed, she might even have corroborated the necessity of his driving on the sidewalk on East 51st Street. Still, she was relieved when they reached their destination in one piece.

The airport was packed, just as Emily had imagined it would be. Bitterly cold temperatures and the city's sixth snowfall this winter had made the luxury of a Caribbean vacation almost a necessity. At this point, desperate New Yorkers were booking any flight available.

But Emily's reservations had been made well in advance. This was no spur-of-the-moment vacation. She had spent months pouring over travel guides and brochures; well-worn copies of *Caribbean Travel and Life* had long ago replaced the stack of books on her night table. Eight days of pampering at a luxury resort, a different sort of vacation for her and Michael. It would be their last fling, really, before they started making important decisions about their future.

Both of them believed it was time for a change. Marriage

had just been an assumption until a couple of months ago, but Michael's promotion and a surprise engagement ring on New Year's Eve meant that assumption was becoming reality. Michael felt it was time to legitimize their relationship. 'I'm a partner now . . .' was his introduction to more and more of their conversations. They were both anxious to start a family, but Emily was already overwhelmed with the inevitable changes to come. She had a million questions. What to do about her career? Where and how to raise children? What would Michael's role and availability be in childrearing? And the more she thought about these things, the more she found herself thinking back to her own mother. The warmth and closeness of their relationship, her mother's openness and enthusiasm – how Emily missed those things. Sometimes she would imagine conversations that would never be, but would still search for advice in remembered wisdom. So many questions, so many possibilities. Yet days could go by and she'd barely see Michael, and there were times when she felt all alone. Was that really what she wanted from her marriage?

The skycap dropped Emily's bags at the end of a very long line of very short-tempered New Yorkers. Although it was early morning, flight delays had already been posted as runways were cleared and planes de-iced. Families, some with small children, had planted themselves in corners and against walls. Mothers attempted to soothe crying infants and rambunctious toddlers as fathers dragged or pushed piles of bags along the line.

While Emily waited, her mind wandered. It was over ten years ago, she thought . . . graduation weekend. When her parents arrived at Cornell, younger brothers and sisters in tow, Emily could tell that there was something wrong. Her father seemed distracted and unnaturally quiet. Her mother, always energetic and spontaneous, seemed wan and pale. And although the kids seemed their rambunctious selves, she sensed an edge to their laughter that wasn't usually there.

Six months later Emily's mother was gone, a victim of breast cancer, and Emily was trying desperately to replace her irreplaceable presence. Their big old Victorian house, rambling and spacious, with its open porches and secret crannies, had always been filled with life and laughter. It was comfortable and welcoming, and friends would often congregate there, watching TV in the family room, talking for hours on the side porch or partying in the backyard. Emily's parents had always been easygoing and open, supportive of almost everything the kids did, and proud of their every achievement.

The oldest of this ragtaggle crew of four siblings, Emily was determined that the house should remain as it was. She knew this determination was her own denial of her mother's loss, yet she spent the better part of the next three years wiping away streams of tears, opening furiously slammed doors, settling fierce arguments and sharing late-night conversations that would often stretch into morning. During the more difficult moments she would yearn for Michael's steadfastness and support.

Although they had left college as good friends, swearing that they would keep in touch, Michael and Emily had eventually grown apart, their lives too different to accommodate a long-distance relationship.

It was a busy time in her life and, although filled with responsibilities, not without its rewards. By the end of it, Brian had managed to earn the high-school diploma which for some months had been in doubt; Jane had gotten the lead in the junior play; Kate, the baby, was in high school; and her father had emerged from his grief-induced sabbatical, spent primarily in the upstairs study, with a publishable manuscript and an intact sense of humor. The house was once again a lively place with an army of friends who raided the refrigerator, tied up the phone and, on occasion, danced till dawn. Emily had added strength and resilience to her character, but also a nagging sense that life could be fickle and rob the unsuspecting of joy at a moment's notice.

She was more cautious now, careful to observe the world around her, watching for signs of trouble. She would read people like books, noting a shift of the eyes or twitch of the mouth. She could sense uncertainty or anger or approval, and although it made her good at her job, she sometimes missed the carefree young girl she used to be.

'Lady,' a man said sharply while poking Emily in the

shoulder. 'Lady, you're next. Come on, lady, wake up. You're next.'

'Sorry,' Emily mumbled, moving her bags forward. She had been so caught up in her thoughts she hadn't even heard the ticket agent calling her. Luckily her flight was straight through and she would soon be rid of these bags. She was starting to agree with the limo driver – she couldn't possibly need all this stuff.

'Checking in everything?' the agent asked as Emily put her bags on the conveyor belt.

'Just these three. These two I need to take on the plane with me.' Even though she had sworn she wasn't going to take work with her, with Michael's delay in London she'd grabbed a couple of pressing files just before she left.

Emily loved her job but, as she hoisted the two bulging bags on to her shoulder, she wondered whether the demands were just too much. That city council meeting she was sending Jack to cover would probably last until midnight, as most of them did. Emergencies always seemed to happen after five or on weekends, and Emily was usually the first one on site and often the last to leave. But what was the alternative? She couldn't just give it up; she had worked so hard to get there.

By the time she arrived at the departure gate she had only minutes before boarding the plane. She considered trying to organize her stuff, but quickly realized it was impossible and so she just stood, lost in thought, waiting to be called.

It wasn't until her youngest sister, Kate, had entered high school that Emily had begun to focus on her own life. The choice of what to do was almost inevitable. She had always been politically active, and since coming home she had devoted what little free time she had to local politics. She believed that individuals could make a difference in a community and she'd put her heart and soul into it. She'd gained skill and knowledge, and her ability to deliver her often strong opinions in an easy, sometimes humorous manner made her a valued spokesman for certain issues. She was able to motivate others and her own enthusiasm for a job, be it the clean-up of a local stream, the opening of a soup kitchen or new zoning regulations for the main street area soon rubbed off, making her a real asset for getting things done. It wasn't long before she caught the eye of local and then statewide elected officials and, although she was often sought for campaign work, she'd realized her heart was more in the issues themselves than individuals. After spending three years working for community groups, she was hired by a state-wide public advocacy program. Two years later, she was running it.

It would be another year before she and Michael would meet again, on the No. 6 train of all places, and although it had been over seven years since they had left Cornell, it was as if their last phone conversation had been the day before. Certainly, some things had changed, but their emotional attachment was still there, safe beneath the details of their lives. Their relationship quickly became serious and in no time they moved in together.

Emily hardly looked the picture of someone anticipating eight days of serenity and luxury as she struggled with the carry-on bags and boarded the American Airlines flight for the island of Aruba. Disheveled, she struggled down the airplane's narrow aisle mumbling 'I'm sorry' to those she inadvertently bumped into until her litany was interrupted by a distinguished-looking elderly gentleman who tapped her on the shoulder.

'Excuse me, but I think you dropped this.'

'My passport!' she exclaimed as her furrowed forehead was replaced by a radiant smile. 'I'm afraid I'm rather disorganized. This trip hasn't had the easiest beginning. I don't know what I'd have done if I'd arrived at the airport without this. Thank you so much. You're a godsend.'

'Please, it was nothing. As a matter of fact, it looks like you could use a little help getting to your seat. Martin Maitland,' he said, extending his hand. 'Here, let me take this small bag.'

'Emily Harrington,' she responded, protesting that he was too kind and she could manage. Her protests were short-lived, however, as passengers behind them started to complain about the hold-up in the aisle.

When they arrived at Emily's row, they discovered that Martin was to be her seatmate for the trip. He seemed delighted, commenting on the good fortune of having such a pleasant traveling companion. Emily, however, moaned inwardly, fearing she would have to talk to him the whole time. But then, feeling guilty, she offered him his choice of seats. He chose the window, settled in, quickly took out a notebook and started to scan its pages. She was much relieved, and soon opened her magazine and began reading.

The two exchanged only smiles as the flight attendant went through the familiar instructions and emergency procedures. Then Emily settled back, closing her eyes during take-off. A short time later the stewardess came to take breakfast orders. It was obvious she knew Emily's seatmate.

'Good morning, Mr Maitland. I didn't expect to see you so soon. Coffee?'

'Yes, thank you. I could use another cup. You people certainly are busy this morning. I guess it will stay like this till the end of the month.'

'At least. And with the weather we've been having it'll probably be like this till the end of March. Coffee, miss?'

'Yes, I'd love some,' Emily responded. As the stewardess moved on, she turned to Martin with some curiosity. 'You must travel quite often.'

'More often than I'd like, really. I live on Aruba and business frequently brings me back and forth. In fact, I was quite lucky to get a seat on this flight at the last minute. I hadn't planned on coming back until next week but a matter . . .' He paused for a moment, frowning slightly. 'Something important has come up.'

'I'm certainly familiar with that problem!' Emily said, explaining what had happened with her vacation plans. 'My fiancé and I are supposed to be spending eight days at this really exclusive resort, but at the last minute he had to extend an important business trip in London. There was nothing he could do about it, but still . . . Hopefully, he'll be meeting me there tomorrow.'

It was Michael who had actually chosen Island Bluffs. 'It's the perfect spot, Em. One of the partners told me about it. It's really beautiful and he said there are good contacts to be made there. Don't you see, it's perfect for us.' Emily had agreed, even though she was frustrated but not really surprised that Michael was thinking about work when the whole point was to leave that world behind for a few days. Still, the more she read about the Bluffs, the more she liked it – beautiful, great food and all the extras. She'd just have to hope there weren't too many 'contacts' to be made.

'Ah, then your misfortune is my good fortune,' Martin mused. 'I must owe my seat to your fiancé.' As he sympathized with her, he said, 'Perhaps I can find a way to thank you.'

Emily excused herself and headed toward the restroom, not at all sure where this conversation was going and hoping to beat the breakfast cart. She knew that everything was timing now. She had once spent almost half an hour trapped in a narrow airplane aisle, the coffee cart on one end and the tray cart on the other.

As she neared the first-class section of the plane, she was surprised to hear angry voices. A gruff man's voice was spewing a litany of complaints: 'This is ridiculous, having to wait for a drink . . . I've never had such lousy service . . . Travel just isn't the same any more . . . There are no damn standards.'

And a younger female voice chided, 'Roger, please, give the girl a break. The plane is barely in the air. You've become so impatient, never satisfied, always finding fault, always complaining.' The voice paused for a minute; then a muffled sigh before it continued: 'It's beginning to show in everything you do . . . I read that review, by the way – the one you did on Blue Water. I guess we won't be having dinner there. It was pretty mean. And that's not the only one. If you keep that up you won't be welcome anywhere.'

'Hah,' he laughed harshly, 'don't be so naive. They all know my power, and frankly, my dear, if you think they fawned all over me when my byline led *The Experienced Traveler*, wait until this new travel show debuts. They'll be tripping over themselves trying to please me.'

The voices quieted down as a harried stewardess exited the first-class cabin. Emily, intrigued by this exchange, attempted to peek through the curtains, almost colliding with the ruddy face of a heavyset man looking harshly in the direction of the departing stewardess. Startled, she quickly opened the restroom door and slammed it shut behind her.

The rest of the four-hour flight passed uneventfully. Emily dozed, read her magazine and shared a few pleasantries with her seatmate, who continued to be charming but busily engaged. As they approached Reina Beatrix airport, Martin explained that a car would be picking him up and offered to drop Emily off on the way. 'It's the least I can do.'

After only a moment's hesitation Emily accepted gratefully, realizing that she would soon have to retrieve both her and Michael's bags.

The warmth enveloped her as she walked across the tarmac. Emily was struck by the color that surrounded her – bright blue sky, low green bushes, trees and brightly-colored flowers. It was a welcome relief from Manhattan's winter grays.

The task of deplaning and going through customs was amazingly easy with Martin's help. He was obviously a man of some influence, for they were whisked to a special line and waved through with barely a glance at Emily's passport. In minutes they were entering the back seat of a waiting black limousine. As they settled in, both Emily and Martin were distracted by the same angry voice Emily had overheard on the plane. 'What the hell . . . I don't understand this. Martin said someone would be here to meet us.'

Martin quickly closed the car door and said to the driver, '*Bon tardi*, Johnno. Thank God you're here. Oh, dear, we'd best hurry.' Then, turning to Emily: 'We'll have to skip the ride along the coast to the resorts, my dear. It's a favorite of mine, but it seems we had best take the shortest route today.' He spoke to Johnno again: 'I take it everything is all set, Johnno, and someone is on the way. Sounds like Roger is in rare form already.'

'We're all set, Mr Maitland; the place has never looked better.'

With that, Emily realized just who her traveling companion was. 'Martin Maitland! Forgive me, I thought the name sounded familiar but it wasn't until just now that I realized

why. I've read so much about you. And here I am headed for
Island Bluffs . . . I feel so foolish.'

'No reason to feel foolish. Few first-time visitors to Island
Bluffs recognize me, but those who return almost always return
as friends. Now let me tell you about the Bluffs. Since you're
vacationing with us, you must already know a little bit about
the place . . .'

TWO

E mily actually knew more than a little bit about Island
Bluffs already, thanks to various articles and features in
travel and style magazines, not to mention the society
columns. Martin Maitland, although obviously modest, was
probably the best known of all the Caribbean hotel owners.
His story had a certain romance to it, particularly for Emily.
He and his wife, Annie, refugees from the public relations
business in New York, had relocated to the islands some thirty
years ago with the idea of opening a small inn. For the first
two years they had spent their time moving from island to
island, sometimes staying only days, sometimes weeks,
depending on their feelings for the place. Martin was intent
on finding a place where he and Annie would be content not
just to work but to call home. His choice of Aruba was
revealing.

Not the most beautiful of the Caribbean islands due to its
arid climate and relentless trade winds, Aruba was nonetheless
unique. Because sugar cane could not be grown there was no
history of slavery, making the relationships that evolved
between the indigenous and outsiders considerably more
harmonious than in most of the Caribbean. This mattered to
Martin. Always a man of strong opinions, he was often
overheard commenting on his desire to be a member of a
community, not an overlord.

'Aruba is the only place in the whole damn Caribbean where
owners and employees truly work together,' he once told a

reporter, much to the anger of other owners. But in many ways, what Martin said was true.

He and Annie had settled there in 1982. They'd bought an old villa perched not far from a rocky bluff that overlooked the ocean on the northwest corner of the island. This large house, in need of a great deal of work, was to be the heart of their burgeoning plans. Renovated over the next six months, it housed six large, airy guestrooms, all with a private bath, a small dining room, a parlor and a library, all for the use of their guests. The only private living space that Martin and Annie reserved for themselves was the tiny attic.

Perhaps it was this beginning which led them to treat their guests as visitors to their home rather than customers. Even now, three decades later, when the resort consisted of a series of buildings containing some sixty rooms and suites which could accommodate over one hundred guests, Martin and Annie had a reputation for knowing each person who came through their doors by name, if not when they first arrived then certainly within a day or two. This club-like atmosphere soon spread among their regular guests. Many of them made fast and long-lasting friendships which were particular to their Island Bluffs vacations. They would return the same time each year, looking forward to seeing each other again and spending their time sharing news and catching up.

Emily was so caught up in her own thoughts that she almost missed Martin's description of the Bluffs and the places they passed on route.

'We will bypass Oranjestad today, the main town on the island, but you must be sure to visit it while you are here, my dear. Wonderful architecture, vibrant colors, a real mix of its Dutch and Spanish roots but with a Caribbean flavor. And, of course, great shopping. But up ahead is Aruba Aloe. Their fields stretch out here and further on is the factory. We have very little industry here on the island, so some are quite dependent on this. I'm sure you know of the healing properties of the aloe plant. Many people keep a small plant in their home gardens. It's so soothing.

'Now, we're about to enter the district of Noord. The Bluffs is actually in Noord, but in the quieter area. If you head toward the coast, you will see several of our most well-known beaches and the high-rise hotels and casinos that line them. Very popular, although a bit garish for my taste, but still a great source of revenue. The town of Noord is lovely though, and in this inland section you will see some beautiful Aruban-style homes.'

Martin continued pointing out places that might interest Emily, and she was so caught up in this informal tour that she was taken aback when she heard him say, 'Well, here we are. The front gates are just around the bend.'

Emily's first glimpse of the Bluffs was breathtaking. It was nothing like the dry, arid areas that surrounded it. Bordering the front drive were cultivated lawns and gardens awash with deep emerald greens, vivid reds, startling yellows and intense purples. Masses of hibiscus, bougainvillea and frangipani lined walkways and entrances. The white stucco and wood buildings were accented with the soft pastels and deeper hues that were the earmark of the Caribbean. Jutting out from the land, Island Bluffs formed a narrow peninsula bordered on one side by a sheltered turquoise bay and on the other by the deep sapphire-blue ocean. Both had wide sandy beaches, but the bay was usually calm and the ocean could be quite rough.

Directly in front of them was the resort's main house, a single-story white building with a vaulted roof, surrounded by palm trees. The entrance portico with its marble floors was awash with potted plants. Waiting to greet them on the front steps was Martin's wife, Annie. Slim and lovely, with graying jet-black hair and high cheekbones, Annie was known for her grace and warmth.

'Martin, thank God you were able to make it back. The thought of facing Roger Stirhew alone was more than I could bear. Nelson has gone to pick them up. They should be here any . . .'

Noticing Emily for the first time, Annie quickly switched gears. 'You must be Emily Harrington. Welcome, we're so glad to have you. I'm so sorry to hear about the disruption to your plans. Your fiancé called just a few minutes ago and I told him not to worry, we'd take good care of you. Come join us in the main house; we'll get your registration completed

and then get you settled,' Annie said, leading Emily in through
the wide mahogany front doors. 'Now, you look hot and tired.
What will it be, a rum punch or a piña colada?'

For a moment, Emily was too overwhelmed by her surroundings to answer. The dark rattan furniture covered with white
cushions and piled with pillows in vibrant hues was perfectly
complemented by the lush hanging plants and vases overflowing
with dazzling cut flowers. These and the four sets of open
French doors created a seamless flow between the outside and
the interior.

'Now,' Annie said, 'while Penny handles the registration,
why don't you relax outside . . . and shall it be a rum punch?'

Sitting on the sun-dappled patio and sipping her punch,
Emily observed both staff and guests. Everyone smiled readily,
and the staff were quick to respond to any need or want. Emily
was amazed by the sense of comfort and familiarity which
permeated the place. Guests greeted each other and the staff
by name, commenting on the day's activities: 'Brilliant ninth
hole, Tom.' 'Thought for sure Ed and Sarah would take that
first set.' 'Perhaps Susan and I will join you for tomorrow's
sail.' Everyone appeared thoroughly at home.

In fact, soon after Emily sat down she was joined by a
woman who immediately welcomed her as warmly as the
Maitlands had. Although the woman looked vaguely familiar,
Emily could not imagine that they had actually met before.
She was reed thin, with an aristocratic-looking face heavily
made up to deny the obviously advancing years, and a crane
neck that seemed to swivel as she talked. In her dark cat-eyed
sunglasses, flowered silk kimono and white feather cap, she
appeared to be a caricature of an aging Hollywood star. Like
Nancy Reagan playing Norma Desmond, Emily thought,
smiling.

With a practiced intimacy, the woman quickly engaged
Emily in what turned out to be a mostly one-way conversation.
Before Emily realized it, the 'Now my dear, you must tell me
a little about yourself,' had turned into twenty questions and
Emily had shared an overview of herself, her life with Michael
and her present predicament, but she had yet to even find out
her companion's name.

'Marietta, there you are,' said a pleasant-looking woman in her early fifties, approaching them from the reception area. 'I've sent the fax and picked up some more of that sunblock you like, so we should be all set.'

'Thank you, Nora, whatever would I do without you? Now come and meet a new guest, Emily Harrington. Emily has had the most unfortunate disappointment. Her fiancé has been detained on business.' Turning, she placed her hand on Emily's arm. 'I must insist to Martin that you be seated with us at dinner, my dear,' she said. 'Nora, you must remind me to speak to Martin before we go back to our room.' Then, turning back to Emily: 'That way you won't be too lonesome. Well, Nora and I are off to the beach; perhaps we'll see you there.'

Emily was still wondering what had hit her as Marietta and Nora waved from the path. Perhaps she could get to Martin Maitland first, before her dinner plans were made for her. Although she had enjoyed talking to Marietta, she wasn't sure if she would be up for such enthusiasm this evening. Oh, but she would seem mean spirited and ungrateful and, after all, everyone was just trying to be nice. What did it matter, anyway? It wasn't as if she had other plans.

'All set, Emily,' Annie called, heading out of the office. 'Come, I'll do a brief tour and then show you to your room.'

Annie led the way down the brick path which encircled the main house and radiated outward to the various parts of the complex. 'The layout of everything is fairly simple really. In the main house you'll find the reception area, several offices, a gift shop and the patio lounge where you were just relaxing. There's also a small but surprisingly interesting library. We have a number of authors who stay with us regularly and they've been kind enough to share their works. My favorite spot here is the restaurant, Pepperhearts. Dinner is served every night, except Friday's, of course, as that's barbecue night. There are a series of terraces leading off the restaurant which wend their way down to the sea wall. Although all the terraces have views of the ocean, you can actually feel the sea spray from the lowest one. On a really hot afternoon it's perfect. The tennis courts and the bay beach are over this way to our left . . .'

While Annie pointed out the extensive facilities – almost everything one could ask for, from water sports to tennis and golf – Emily enjoyed observing her fellow guests. Almost all of them appeared to be couples. Even those sitting alone were accompanied by the telltale extra book or pair of sunglasses. And although there were a few brave souls battling with gravity on skis or windsurfers, there didn't seem to be any great rush to take part in any of the activities. In fact, for most of the sun-worshippers the battle with gravity had long been abandoned in favor of hammocks and loungers. The weather, of course, was sultry and a piercing sun made the shade and the gentle breezes especially welcome.

Emily, still harboring a New York chill, gloried in the heat and could hardly wait to get to the beach. As she and Annie walked down the rambling garden paths that meandered through the resort, all bordered by a profusion of flowers, she learned the basics of life at the Bluffs.

The resort itself was situated on a hill, which gave it a remarkable view of the surrounding area and the sea. The entrance to the main house, in the center, faced the road, but the rest of the resort was oriented to the bay and ocean which swept away to either side. On each side of the main house were paths which led to the resort gardens, guest rooms situated on the bay and ocean beaches, the beach bar and restaurant, tennis courts and a spa. Annie and Martin's house, Cliff House, stood alone overlooking the bluff. So heavily landscaped were the grounds that Emily could hardly see the house, only glimpses of its whitewashed walls glistening in the sun.

The bay beach was the site of most of the watersports: skiing, paddling boats, kayaks and snorkeling, which provided plenty of activity for those who were so inclined.

'And don't ever worry about getting hungry or thirsty on the beach,' Annie pointed out. 'Right down there is the beach bar and restaurant. It's open from midday onward and you can get lunch or light snacks. Watch out, though – each day the bar highlights a beverage of the day, usually a rum and liqueur-spiked concoction of blended fruits and juices. They're sweet . . . and delicious, but don't be fooled, they're pretty potent.'

As Emily watched, a tall, muscular man raised a small red flag on his umbrella. 'Oh, yes.' Annie pointed. 'If you find walking over to the bar too taxing, simply do that and you'll summon a waiter who'll be only too happy to bring you your heart's desire. As you can imagine, the atmosphere here is usually pretty festive, although I understand that the occasional business deal is a not uncommon occurrence. Now, let me show you the ocean beach.'

They turned around and walked back in the direction they had come from. 'There are two ways to get there. You can come this way, past the main house, as we're going – the garden path, we call it. Most people do that because they want to stop in the main house for something on their way back to their rooms. Just go through here, down the steps and past that small building up ahead. The path will curve and open up on to the ocean beach and rondovals.'

For those who craved serenity and peace, the ocean beach was magnificent. Deep blue waters bordered by a stretch of white, powdery sand provided a peaceful setting where the only sounds were the chirping of birds, the swishing of palm leaves and the rolling of the surf. Emily was delighted to see that the rondovals – round huts with bamboo cone-shaped roofs that would house her and, hopefully, Michael for the next week, were only steps off the beach.

As they stood on the brick walk that bordered the sand, Annie pointed out which rondoval would be Emily and Michael's. 'The last one down at the end is yours. This side of the place is pretty quiet anyway, but that's certainly the most secluded spot in the complex,' Annie said pleasantly as she opened the door.

The very private, secluded rondovals were the most exclusive accommodation available. Each housed a small suite of rooms decorated in pure whites with splashes of bright Caribbean color and natural wicker. Original local art adorned white stucco walls and louvered windows invited cool ocean breezes. The gleaming tile and marble bathroom opened onto a private solarium; a wall of glass separated it from the double tub with facing headrests. As travel weary as Emily was, thoughts of romantic evenings under starry skies began to surface. For a moment she worried about how long she would have to wait for those evenings to come.

'The other path – the ocean path – is over this way to your left. This one eventually leads back in the direction we've come, but by going up around the point there.' Annie pointed to the hilly path. 'Those buildings that line the lower part of the path house our executive rooms and suites. They don't have direct access to the beach like the rondovals, but they have lovely balconies, big windows and incredible views. Once you round the point, the path winds down to the bay beach below the main house. It's rocky, though, since it winds so far up the bluff you need to be in pretty good shape to take it. But you get a magnificent view of the water from up there, so it's well worth it.'

'I'm in pretty good shape,' Emily said. 'I'm a runner back home. Maybe you could suggest some trails – although not today, I'm exhausted already.'

'I imagine you must be. Maybe you should try to get some rest. I'm heading back up to the office. The rooms have no phones but the intercom connects to the main house. If there's anything you need just buzz. Penny's on the desk this afternoon and she'll be able to help you. If you're hungry, the beach bar is open, tea is served at five in the patio lounge or there's always room service. Don't eat too much, though; Martin and I are hoping you'll join us for dinner. It'll give you a chance to meet some of our other guests.'

For a moment, Emily thought of mentioning Marietta, the woman in the white feathered cap, but quickly stopped herself. The thought of dining with Martin and Annie was such a pleasant one and she'd like the opportunity to make some acquaintances. 'I'd love that, Annie.'

'Wonderful. See you at about seven-thirty for cocktails. Enjoy the rest of your afternoon.'

Emily's eyes were drawn to the queen-size bed coolly dressed in crisp whites, and she was tempted to stretch out and take a short nap, but the sound of the surf was impossible to resist. She unpacked quickly, allowing herself only a few minutes to appreciate the comforts around her, from the soft down pillows to the ultra-thick white terrycloth robes and the toiletries heaped in a large shell. Then she grabbed her bathing suit, changed and was out the door.

The bay beach was almost empty now. Most guests were resting in their rooms in preparation for the evening, but a few souls had chosen to nap in the softly swaying hammocks hanging crisscrossed among the palms. Emily, denied the sun for so long, chose a lounge chair that was fully exposed to the sizzling rays and sat only inches from the tranquil, turquoise water. One lone snorkeler paddled along in front of her, but other than that there was nothing but a distant white sail on the horizon.

What peace! Emily thought as she picked up the page-turner she had brought with her. After only a few minutes, though, the sun and the heat overcame her. Whatever fleeting interest she had in the book's earnest young lawyer quickly dissipated as the bestseller fell gently from her lap and her eyes closed.

When she was roused by the buzzing of a small fly around her right ear, she was unsure how long she'd slept. Looking around, she saw that the beach was empty except for a young couple engaged in an earnest conversation as they walked along the shoreline. Watching them, Emily felt as if she had woken in the middle of a magazine ad. Both were fit and trim, mid to late-twenties, he with slicked-back blond hair, while she was windswept and dark. Their washed-out cotton clothes and shoeless feet made them look as if they *lived* on the beach. As they got closer, however, Emily could see they lacked the carefree expression she had expected. Their conversation was more serious than earnest, and he sounded pained as they passed.

'I honestly don't know if I can sit at the same table with him, Sarah,' he was saying. 'I despise his smug, superior attitude. He loves to watch everyone grovel. Well, I won't do it, and I don't care what he says about me. It can't get much worse anyway.'

Emily was intrigued as she heard the equally unhappy Sarah respond, 'Just tonight, Jon . . . please. Mom and Dad are awfully anxious about this. Oh, I guess everyone's anxious after those recent . . .'

Their voices trailed off, and Emily wondered what dreaded

event could cause such distress. It was hard to imagine anyone taking life so seriously in such an idyllic setting. Not me, she thought as she picked up her few belongings and headed back toward her room.

This time Emily took the ocean path. Annie was right, it was rocky, but her legs, strong and supple, had no difficulty negotiating it. And it was magnificent. As she walked, the water below her was a deep sapphire blue and the rolling waves were bearded with foamy white caps. The face of the bluff was jutted and creviced, with occasional slabs where you could sit to watch the ocean. The path was quiet and peaceful; the only sounds were the crashing of majestic waves and the cries of distant seabirds.

She sat for a few minutes on one of the outcroppings. The sun had warmed it and she rolled her towel and rested her head back on the smooth face of the bluff. Her thoughts turned to Michael, sighing as she imagined his long, muscled body stretched out next to her, his hair ruffled by the breeze, his hand reaching out to hers – a fleeting image soon replaced by a picture of him walking briskly on London's cold, damp streets, briefcase in hand, a determined look on his face. His work face. She had seen it often – leaving the apartment in the morning, relating the bones of a case he was working on, heading to a firm event called 'social,' but never really that. 'Now remember, Em, Dawkins is the real power in the firm. When you meet him, well, his stories are boring as hell but you need to seem really interested, engrossed. He . . .'

Emily would try to remember names and characteristics but they all sounded similar and it was hard to keep them straight. 'Oh, Michael, I hope I don't . . .'

'Don't worry so much, Emily. It's a party; it's supposed to be fun, and my standing in the firm isn't going to depend on the impression you make at a party.'

'You're right, Michael. I know how much they think of you.'

'You'll do fine. You're a charmer, Em, you always have been. It's one of the things I love about you. One more thing: if I don't introduce you to someone, it means I can't remember their name, so just jump in and introduce yourself.'

And Emily would jump in, and try to look engrossed by Dawkins' stories, and she would be a charmer. But the firm's presence in their lives had started to worry her. Not just the hours and Dawkins' boring stories – they were bad enough – but Michael's obsession with the partners. In fact, just two weeks ago they had had a real row over Michner. Emily had wanted to contribute to a local political campaign. It was run by a young guy earnest and committed to the issues that mattered to Emily – the closing of a day-care center to make way for a big box store, a proposed change in rent stabilization laws, a shuttered soup kitchen.

'Em, I think we have to be careful here. I mean, I care as much about these things as you do, but you know Michner, he's very conservative – the whole firm is really – and contributing to this, I mean, they might think . . .'

'They might think what, Michael? Come on, these are local issues and this is someone who wants to do—'

'I'm just saying, Em. Political contributions are public and they watch these things. It's taking a chance and maybe . . .'

Of course, Emily had contributed anyway and Michael had accepted it. But the argument had been a serious one and it had left Emily disturbed. It didn't help that Michael had come to terms with it by saying, 'I guess that contribution will be in your name; they'll never know about it.'

Emily's mood turned melancholy and she decided to move on. As she headed down the rocky path, her thoughts returned to the young couple she had seen walking on the beach. In truth, although she didn't envy them their obviously heavy hearts, their evident caring and closeness made her feel lonely, and she found herself questioning her own relationship again, wondering if Michael's 'emergency' had been resolved and how long it might be before he could join her. Not even the champagne and plate of fresh fruit that welcomed her when she got back to her room could lift her spirits; and when she saw that she had two hours before dinner, she decided a nap was definitely in order.

THREE

Emily awoke feeling rested and refreshed. Her earlier melancholy had passed and she was looking forward to dinner. She took a quick shower and, as she dressed, treated herself to a glass of champagne.

Dinner was considered an event at Island Bluffs and guests were asked to dress up. Michael had loved the idea from the start. 'It sets a certain tone, Em. It will be something different.' Emily, on the other hand, wasn't so sure. She had little opportunity to dress up at work, since her job could have her at a homeless shelter in the Bronx at nine, a housing office in Brooklyn at eleven, and checking out a problem on the Henry Hudson Parkway at two. On weekends, she and Michael enjoyed a casual lifestyle, more comfortable in jeans and corduroys than cashmere and silks. But once she'd got used to the idea, she'd decided Michael was right. Dressing for dinner would make the evenings seem special, and so she'd spent weeks searching for the perfect wardrobe.

As she stepped into her navy silk dress, she paused to look in the mirror. The light, soft fabric skimmed her body as it floated softly to the floor, the only adornment a beaded clasp at the single shoulder. It's lovely, she thought. The saleswoman had been right. Her red hair, already brightened by the sun, was pulled back into a loose twist at the nape of her neck and with a touch of sadness she fastened her mother's dark blue sapphire earrings to her ears.

She wondered who else would be at the Maitland's table this evening. She was probably seated there because of Michael's absence, or perhaps Martin and Annie made a habit of dining with new guests on the first night of their stay. Either way, there was a sense of adventure to the evening which Emily had not experienced since her pre-Michael days and, although she wouldn't want this as a steady diet, for tonight it seemed like fun.

As she walked along the softly lit path, the moon hovered just above the horizon. Almost a perfect circle, it cast a silvery glow on the still water and powdery sand. She took the garden path tonight, crossing the wide green lawn and savoring the sweet smell of the bougainvillea. Even from here she could see the twinkling white lights that draped the small trees at the entrance to the main house. A number of guests had already arrived and were enjoying cocktails on the terraces, their soft laughter the perfect counterpoint to the lapping of the bay beach's gentle waters.

Mounting the steps, Emily searched for a familiar face and immediately spotted her companion from this afternoon. Marietta had undergone a rather amazing transformation. Gone were the white-feathered cap and the cat-eyed sunglasses. In their place was a perfectly coifed hairdo and meticulously painted face, highlighted with iridescent eye shadow and luminescent lips. Her incredibly thin frame was draped in a deep magenta gown that was banded at the neck in gold, giving her a regal look. Although she was involved in a spirited conversation, she was quick to pause when she spied Emily's entrance.

'Ah, my dear, don't you look lovely. I see you got a little sun this afternoon. You must be careful of that, you know. It makes your face turn to leather eventually. I can't tell you how many women I know now regretting those "to-die-for tans" that marked their youths. Wizened, that's what they are. Now, you must meet a . . . um . . . fellow guest. Emily, this is Roger Stirhew.' She turned to the man standing next to her, paused, looked at him for a moment then turned back to Emily. 'I'm sure you recognize the name. Everyone does these days. Of course, some more than others, and often for very different reasons.' A slight roll of her eyes. 'Isn't that right, Roger?'

Emily was taken aback to see the man from the first-class cabin of the plane. He was standing almost directly in front of her. Amazingly, though, he also appeared totally changed. Gone were the red face and gruff expression. With a softened complexion and a pleasant smile he looked almost friendly, and she quickly realized this was a face she recognized.

She had often seen his column in travel magazines, in which he reviewed resorts, hotels and restaurants in some of the world's most fascinating places – big cities and small remote towns, and his opinions carried a lot of weight. Just last month she had read an in-depth interview with him. It seemed that Roger Stirhew, at fifty-eight years old, was considered the travel expert of the moment. A writer and food critic, he had recently been approached by a major cable company with an offer to produce and star in a weekly primetime show. Roger was interested from the start but in his own words in a recent article he 'had played out a long string and pulled the cable company along until the offer was one that no one could possibly refuse.' Between his monthly column and the much-awaited show, he was now considered a powerhouse in the industry.

The article had painted a picture of a self-made man who knew resorts and travel from the ground up. The only child of immigrant parents, he boasted that he had 'done every damn job in the business – from bellboy to busboy.' He was know-ledgeable and often humorous in his comments, but there had been an underlying arrogance in the piece that clearly came through. And although the bones of the story were true, it did not reveal the other side of Roger's rise, the side few people, let alone Emily, knew.

By the time he was sixteen years old Roger had been emotionally indulged for many years. Physically somewhat gawky, he nevertheless was very sure of himself, and that summer he had taken a job as a busboy at a Catskill Mountains resort. He knew the area well, since every year his parents rented a small, basic bungalow not too far from Monticello. And while Roger hated the dank bungalow, he loved the glamour and opulence of the nearby resorts and was deter-mined that he would one day share in that lifestyle.

Busboy was the first step in his quest and those first two summers were a time of tremendous learning and change. Gawkiness gave way to an athletic, dynamic grace as he learned to play tennis and handball, dance a comfortable foxtrot and a mean tango, and banter with the lonely middle-aged ladies who soon began to seek him out as a handsome, exciting antidote to their boredom. Before long, Roger was promoted from busboy to waiter and by the end of his second summer he was making enough in tips to finance his first semester at City College.

Always looking ahead, Roger would use his winters to 'prepare' for summer. Movies, Broadway shows and TV were always enjoyable topics for the ladies in his 'fan club' and what he couldn't see, he would read about. Although he couldn't afford to play tennis, he was a regular customer at the Y, where he could swim and play handball. And he would start working on his tan in early May, so that by the time he returned to Koch's he looked as if he had never left.

His big break had come at the beginning of his third summer there.

Danny DeNardo, who had been Activities Director at Koch's for the past three years, suddenly up and left one Saturday after lunch with little notice and no explanation (although it was rumored that Mrs Klein's husband had been searching the place for him all morning). The senior Mr Koch, expecting an overflowing crowd, was in no mood to 'meet and greet' the new arrivals, with the kitchen short staffed and a possible leak in the pool. Desperate, he surveyed the assembled staff until his eyes rested on Roger.

Perfect, he thought. In fact, this might even turn out to be a bonus. Koch had noticed the way many of the guests would greet Roger, pleased to have him as a waiter, and more than pleased to have him as a dancing partner. Hopefully, Koch thought, this one would be smarter than Danny, or at least more careful.

'Stirhew, you're promoted. Get out of that monkey suit; you're the new director of activities. Here's the schedule for this week – memorize it and get ready to welcome the guests. Won't Mrs Berger be delighted.'

In fact, Mrs Berger was not the only one who was delighted. It was almost as if Roger had been made for this job. He never tired of greeting, chatting, arranging and, most of all, smiling. And if the demands of some of the more overbearing guests annoyed him, he never showed it. He was cheerful from the moment he appeared in the dining room at breakfast, chatting up the day's events, until his final 'See you in the morning; don't forget, early to rise,' ushered the last guests to their rooms. And he was constantly coming up with new ideas to amuse and entertain, one of which actually set Roger on his career path.

Koch's Chronicle started out as a single-sheet reminder of the different activities scheduled for the week, but it was not long before amusing anecdotes, special events, guest profiles and reviews started appearing. Often Roger would be his own toughest critic as he evaluated everything from the evening's band to the theme party and the schedule of events itself. This, of course, encouraged guests to add their opinions, often writing glowing reviews of the different activities and, most of all, of Roger himself.

It was a guest's review of an event attended at a neighboring resort that gave Roger the idea of expanding the *Chronicle*. By focusing on what was happening, not just at Koch's but at the different area resorts, the *Chronicle* could become an informal link between them and their guests, who even if they did not directly know each other, always knew someone who knew someone who . . . etc. By the following summer, the newly titled *Catskill's Chronicle* was a six-page weekly, under-written by four major resorts, and Roger had himself the beginnings of a career.

The trip from the Borscht Belt to luxury resorts like Island Bluffs had been quite a ride, filled with daring risks, manage-able disappointments and exhilarating triumphs, but never self-doubt or self-recrimination. Roger knew what he wanted and where he was going, and would allow nothing to stop him. His wit was sharpened by an acerbity that could be benign or biting, and his charm could camouflage a numbing indif-ference or an intense dislike.

It was a shame that with each new achievement he found they meant less and less since, early on, he had taken great pleasure in his success. But, unfortunately, his professional acclaim hadn't translated to personal friendship. He was invited to all the best parties, but rarely to the casual, intimate dinners where people tended to be themselves and enjoy each other.

He had hoped that marriage would change that, or perhaps change him, but his first marriage had ended in divorce and this one might be heading in that direction. Roger didn't quite know what love was, and in the end each of his wives had become just another acquisition.

As the years went by, his drinking had steadily increased until it started to affect his work. Roger's opinions had become more dogmatic and his words sharper. It hadn't hurt him professionally, not yet – his charm and wit in front of a TV camera or a magazine editor still shielded him but, personally, it was a different story. Those who knew him well were more guarded in his presence – more wary – and his relationship with his second wife continued to deteriorate. His acidity was worse in familiar places where he tended to feel more comfortable and reveal more of himself, and he had been coming to the Bluffs for almost twenty years. It was one of the first places he had done a major review of, and it had been glowing. At one time, Martin Maitland had even considered him a friend, but friendship wasn't Roger's strength.

He turned from Marietta to Emily and gave her a dazzling smile. 'Pay Marietta no mind, my dear. She's beginning to speak as she writes – all inference and innuendo. But she always did have an eye for the loveliest creature in the room. I'm sorry, was it Lilly?'

'Emily – Emily Harrington. I just arrived today.'

'So did I. Now, you look familiar, my dear. Might I know you from somewhere? Have you been to the Bluffs before? Or perhaps it's from some other resort? In my line of work I do manage to get around and I'm almost sure we've met. I never forget a beautiful woman. Let's see . . .'

Just as Emily was becoming concerned that Stirhew might remember their encounter on the plane, the conversation was interrupted by a striking blonde.

'I said I'd only be a few minutes, Roger. I thought you would have waited for me. Marietta, it's so good to see you, and tell me, Roger, whom have we here?'

Jessica Stirhew's voice lacked warmth as she turned to face her husband, and it was quite obvious these two had a marriage that was held together by something other than love. Although exactly what was difficult to tell.

'This lovely creature, my dear, is Emily Harrington who just arrived at the Bluffs today. Where are you from, Emily?'

'I was born in New York City, in the Bronx, actually, and even though we moved to the Hudson Valley when I was twelve, I was always a city girl. I moved back years ago.' And, in deference to the undertones in the conversation, Emily was quick to add: 'My fiancé, Michael and I have an apartment on East 43rd street.'

'Emily and I had the loveliest conversation this afternoon, right after she arrived,' Marietta interjected as Roger, having lost interest in the conversation, turned and walked away. 'She came in on the twelve-thirty. The Keegans were on that flight, and the Andersons. You must know them, Jessica. Margaret Anderson is on the board of the MOMA and he's made a mint on Wall Street.'

'I'm afraid I don't, Marietta,' Jessica responded. 'But I'm sure Roger does. I've heard their names. She's Mary Anne, right? Roger attends most of those New York parties. I'm afraid I find them kind of boring.'

'Well, some certainly are. But we all have to tolerate a certain amount of boredom if we want to get invited to the best parties. Well, anyway, poor Emily . . .'

Marietta went on, explaining the disruption in Emily's vacation plans as waiters circulated with trays of champagne and hors d'oeuvres. Emily was dazzled by the scene before her. Glowing candles lit the night, and white linen and vibrant flowers adorned the tables as elegantly dressed couples chatted and smiled. The average age was slightly older than Emily expected, although it probably took that many years to earn enough money to afford an extended stay here. She and Michael would certainly be considered the 'younger set' and, of course, there were no children in sight. During the high season they weren't permitted.

'You must be so disappointed.'

With a start, Emily realized that Jessica Stirhew was commiserating with her. Now Roger had gone, her voice had become warmer and more sympathetic.

Before Emily could answer, Marietta launched into a long and complicated story that garnered little interest from either Emily or Jessica. Jessica was too absorbed in following Roger's progress around the room and Emily was transfixed watching her. She was very pretty, with light brown hair showing off soft blonde highlights, large round hazel eyes and full, sensuous lips.

She was younger than Emily had first thought – late twenties, maybe early thirties – and, at unguarded moments like this, she seemed vulnerable. The expression on her face was softer, until Roger's voice and laughter became louder, piercing the sultry air of the terrace and drawing curious eyes.

Roger seemed to love the attention, making sweeping gestures with his arms and punctuating his statements with directed pointing and dismissive waves. His audience, middle-aged and matronly, chuckled and gasped in turn.

'Roger seems to be playing the rapscallion this evening, how quaint,' Marietta commented slyly. 'But of course, it's early yet and the audience is fresh.'

Emily could actually see the physical change in Jessica. Her shoulders stiffened as she turned her back to the room. Her face had lost all trace of softness, her eyes narrow and her lips taut. It was a harder face now, older and bitterly wiser as she said, almost to herself, 'He certainly does love playing to an audience, particularly an adoring one. The only problem is, the better you know Roger, the . . . I'm sorry, where were we? We were talking about Emily . . . her trip . . .' But Jessica was interrupted by a glum-looking Annie Maitland.

FOUR

'Sorry, bad news,' Annie said as she led Emily toward the edge of the terrace. 'Michael called. There are some complications. He left a number and asked if you'd call him. Unfortunately we've been having some trouble with the phone lines and I don't think you'll be able to get through right now.'

'I could tell from your face that it wasn't good news, Annie. Maybe it's only a brief delay. But whatever, there's nothing I can do about it. I won't let it spoil dinner.'

Emily was disappointed by Annie's news but not really surprised. Ever since Michael had mentioned the emergency in London she had feared that this would happen. She had seen it before – a problem that would be straightened out in one day suddenly stretches out to three or four. Would she and Michael ever get round to sorting out their own problems? Maybe she should pay a bit more attention to her dinner companions, she thought – she might be spending a good deal more time with them.

'Everything looks lovely, Annie. And so far the company is interesting. Tell me, Marietta looks so familiar – where would I know her from?'

'Does the name Marietta St. John ring any bells?'

'St. John, of course. I should have recognized her. Although the picture that appears with her society column must have been taken some time ago.'

'I'll say,' Annie smiled. 'Marietta's been coming here for the last twenty years and that same picture graced her column the day I met her. She's a dear, but between her and Roger Stirhew the whole staff will have earned a vacation by the time the week is up.'

'I was wondering about Roger. When I saw him on the plane I didn't realize who he was. But just now, on the terrace, I knew immediately. He looks so different this evening. Is his visit business or pleasure?'

'It seems little with Roger is pleasure anymore. Although in the past he's been very good to Martin and me. His reviews were always more than favorable. But recently . . . I suppose it does no good to complain, but . . . Oh, never mind. Let's try to enjoy ourselves. Dinner should be interesting, to say the least.'

Emily and Annie headed back just as a young man and woman joined the group. Emily was surprised to see it was the couple from the beach that afternoon.

'Sarah, Jon, let me introduce you,' Annie said as Roger rejoined the group. 'Everyone, this is our youngest daughter, Sarah, and her fiancé, Jon Peterson. Now, you two already know several of these people . . .'

'Some of them a bit too well, Annie,' Peterson interrupted cryptically. 'But it's always great to see you, Marietta. And here's a new face.'

'This is Emily Harrington,' Marietta said, delighted to be launching into Emily's story yet again. 'It's her first time here. She and her fiancé Michael were to be staying for the week, only Michael's been delayed in London.'

'Which is putting a little crimp in the trip,' Emily laughed. 'But Aruba is certainly an improvement over New York.'

'And we promised Michael we'd take good care of her,' Annie continued. 'Now . . . where was I? Oh, yes, Sarah, I don't know if Jon's ever met Jessica Stirhew, Roger's wife.'

'No, I've never had the pleasure,' Jon responded warmly. 'Nice to meet you, Jessica,' he said. Was it only Emily who heard him comment, sotto voce, 'Although under the circumstances perhaps I should be offering my condolences.'

'Will Nora be joining us, Marietta?' Annie asked, perhaps a little too loudly. 'I don't see her.'

'Oh, she'll be here in a moment,' Marietta replied, straining to keep track of the conversation. 'I forgot my pills again and she's gone back to the room to get them. I don't know what I'd do without her.'

Roger rolled his eyes just as Martin appeared with a tray of champagne glasses.

'Ah, perfect timing,' Annie announced, handing Roger a glass. 'This is something new Martin is trying. Tell us, Roger, what do you think?' she said quickly, steering him away as Martin passed around glasses to the others.

'Yes, Roger,' Martin prodded. 'You certainly are the most experienced of us. What do you think? I hear the vineyard is . . .' he continued as the group followed Annie and Roger into the dining room.

Quickly, Annie dropped back to walk with Emily. 'On second thought, perhaps "interesting" was an understatement!' she whispered as Jessica Stirhew joined them.

'Everything looks lovely, Annie, as always. It's good to be back.'

'It's been almost a year since you've been here, Jessica. I guess Jason keeps you busy.' She turned to Emily. 'Jessica and Roger have a young son, Jason. Is your mother minding him back in Connecticut, Jessica?'

'She is. She just adores him. She's always disappointed when she hears I'm not travelling with Roger. If she could, she'd spend all her time with him.' Changing the subject, she continued, 'I didn't know that Jon Peterson was dating your daughter, Sarah. How long has that been going on?'

'They got engaged at Christmas, but all plans have been put on hold since Roger . . .'

'I'm sorry, I didn't realize. I'm amazed he was willing to join us tonight.'

'Please don't feel uncomfortable, Jessica. It's part of the business, although we did feel the review was rather harsh. Jon is a wonderful chef,' she continued, turning to Emily, 'and a couple of months ago he opened Blue Water, a restaurant near town. It's right on the bay with one of the island's most beautiful beaches at its doorstep. He's put everything into it and he and Sarah have worked so hard.' For a moment her voice faltered. 'It was doing amazingly well until . . . But Jon is young and talented. He'll survive.'

'Rather harsh? What a kind way to put it.' Jessica glared in Roger's direction as he made his way grandly to the table. Emily sensed that Jessica understood only too well the effort it took Jon Peterson to dine with them tonight. Somehow, Emily doubted that being Roger's wife saved her from his verbal taunts.

Emily noticed Jessica's eyes narrow again as she turned back to Annie. 'It's not just part of the business, Annie. Roger has been angry with Martin for some time, ever since Martin backed Willem DeVries in that disagreement they had last year. Oh, he didn't dare disparage Martin, but Jon was a convenient substitute. It's just like him to even the score with Martin by writing a scathing review of Jon's restaurant.'

As they reached the round table in the center of the room, Annie effortlessly and diplomatically arranged the seating. 'Emily, why don't you sit here between Martin and Roger? They always enjoy sharing their unique views of the island with a newcomer. Marietta and Sarah are to Martin's left. Jon, I promised Nora that you would share that wonderful salmon recipe with her, and Jessica, you must come and sit beside me. We haven't seen you in so long and I want to hear all about Jason.'

Emily didn't know whether to be pleased or dismayed with the seating. She was delighted to be next to Martin, but Roger Stirhew made her uncomfortable. He had been more than pleasant to her this evening, but between her view of him on the plane and some of the comments she had heard so far, she was wary of what the dinner conversation might be like.

For the moment he and Martin were caught up in an in-depth analysis of French vineyards, so Emily afforded herself the opportunity to take in her surroundings. Like most island restaurants, Pepperhearts was an open-air seaside pavilion. This one, however, was surrounded by a series of graduated terraces. The lighting was subtle and romantic with glowing candles and twinkling chandeliers. Pristine white linens were set with Christofle and Limoges, and the only color came from the burst of tropical flowers which formed the table's centerpiece.

The chef, Jean-Pierre Rozan, was known for the subtle blending of French, Caribbean and Asian flavors. He was said to have a near perfect hand with fresh herbs, aromatic vinegars and the occasional touch of soy. The menu was overwhelming. There were traditional island specialties like *sopi di mariscos*, (a seafood soup), and *kreeft stoba* (lobster stew), along with more European dishes like the carpaccio of duck and ravioli filled with lobster and boletus mushrooms, to say nothing of the extensive desserts. Emily was having a hard time deciding and was pleased when Martin came to her rescue.

'If you don't mind, Emily, may I choose for you? Jean-Pierre makes everything well, but I do have my personal favorites and I'd love to share.'

'That would be perfect, Martin,' Emily replied.

'Yes,' Roger chimed in, offering what sounded more like a challenge than a request. 'Order for me also, Martin. Let's sample the kitchen's best.'

'How did that chicken dish turn out, Martin?' Jon asked. 'I was planning to try something similar at lunch tomorrow. I know how busy you are, but if you get a couple of hours free why don't you come over and try it?'

'I promised Marietta and Nora that I'd drive them to that small gallery that just opened. I doubt I'd be back in time, but perhaps Annie and Sarah will want to drive over. I'm sure Annie could use a break after this last week.'

'I'd love to, Jon,' Annie joined in. 'I haven't seen the new table settings yet, either. Are you sure you'll have room? There's a ship in tomorrow, you know.'

'Oh, I'll have room all right. Things have slowed down considerably in the last few weeks.' Jon stared pointedly at Roger, who appeared unaware of the comment but immediately launched into a none-too-subtle story about a recent trip to a New York restaurant.

'Martin, did I tell you I visited young Andanno's restaurant? Just opened in Soho. Wonderful-looking place, but he'll never be his father, that's for sure. Of course, that's the trouble with young people today. They want it all, right away. They're not willing to put in their time, learn the ropes. Andanno never should have let him on his own so soon.'

'I have to disagree with you there, Roger,' Martin ventured. 'I haven't had a chance to visit the place, but Angelo Andanno has been working in his father's restaurant for over ten years. Sal himself told me that the kid had done every job from dishwasher on up. We can't expect this younger generation to wait forever, now, can we?'

'If it was up to Roger we would,' Marietta joked, joining the conversation. 'In fact, Roger, I've noticed something of a pattern in your recent reviews, only the, shall we call them, "well-seasoned" seem to meet with your approval . . . and I'm not talking about the food.'

'Well, you should know, Marietta – you're more well-seasoned than most.'

Marietta looked taken aback by Roger's taunt, but Nora leapt to her defense.

'You can be an awfully mean-spirited person when you want to, Roger, and . . .'

'Ah, the ever-loyal Nora Richards. How is it that someone can command such loyalty?' He looked piercingly at Marietta, then turned back to Nora and chuckled. 'There must be some mighty generous hidden perks to your job, huh, Nora? Some people say . . .'

Alarmed by the look of anguish that twisted Nora's face, Emily quickly jumped in. 'Roger,' she interrupted, as if unaware he had been speaking, 'Annie mentioned that you have a young son. How old is he?' She couldn't have picked a better topic. For a few minutes Roger was back to his charming demeanor, telling her all about Jason.

The exchanges at the table had been brief but brutal, and while Roger was talking a few of the guests took a moment to collect themselves. Marietta, her face so drained that her rouge was now two clown-like spots on her pale cheeks, asked for a moment to 'get some air,' while Nora and Jon both headed to the restrooms.

When Emily excused herself a few minutes later, she was surprised to find the three of them sitting in a dim corner of the bar. Unnoticed, she eavesdropped for a moment.

'I'm so sorry, Nora. Thank you for trying but I guess neither of us is any match for Roger.'

Nora sat flushed and flustered, beads of sweat on her brow, hands twisting and knotting around each other, recriminations echoing in her mind. 'I should never have come to dinner,' she whispered frantically. 'Not when I heard that he was coming. He knows. Oh, God, I know he knows, and it's only a matter of time before he tries to . . .'

'Marietta's right, Nora,' Jon nodded in sympathy. 'You're much too decent. You're no match for him – look at how he toys with people. He's a master when it comes to others' vulnerabilities – he just watches and waits. But, I'll tell you something, Nora. One day Roger Stirhew is going to meet his match, and I only hope I'm there when it happens.'

And to think, they haven't even served the salad yet, Emily mused.

FIVE

B y the time they were eating their entrées, Emily had given up. Although the food was delicious and the service impeccable, the conversation was halting and often strained. Emily was perplexed by the level of antagonism that poisoned the atmosphere.

Roger was certainly at the center of it. He purposely provoked the others and, as the wine bottle got emptier, he got nastier. It was impossible for Emily to ignore, and since she was seated next to him she felt responsible for trying to improve the situation.

'Tell me a little about what you do, Roger. From the outside, it seems like there couldn't be a more enjoyable job but I'm sure, like everything else, it has its drawbacks.'

'Hah.' Roger waved his hand dismissively. 'At one time it had lots of drawbacks – always having to be smiling and scraping to every damn fool blue-haired matron who needed an escort for the evening because her "big-time executive" husband couldn't bear to listen to her inane chatter and simpering giggle for another evening. But I'd listen, listen and more if they wanted. And soon . . . soon I was going to as many society parties as Marietta, and I didn't have the St. John name to open any doors for me, either. I did it like I've done everything in my life . . . on my own.'

After several similar attempts Emily realized that it was hopeless. Roger was determined to be unpleasant and she

was running out of things to talk about. Luckily, Martin came
to the rescue.

'I thought we'd have coffee and dessert on the terraces. We
have a small band this evening, a jazz group, and they do
some soft Caribbean music. Perfect for a little late-night
dancing. Come, Roger, perhaps you can show the rest of us
some of those famous steps of yours.'

'Dancing? I'm not in the mood for any damn dancing. I
want some action. Come on, why don't we all head over to
the Hyatt's new casino? I haven't reviewed the Copacabana
yet, and I hear they have the band suspended from the ceiling
in a birdcage.' His voice had gotten louder as the dinner wore
on. 'This way I can kill two birds with one stone. Hmm . . .
birds with stones and a band suspended from the ceiling,
sounds like an interesting evening,' he said, laughing at his
own joke. 'Let's have some fun.'

'Oh, I'm afraid it's an early morning for us,' Martin and
Annie said in unison. 'But, if anyone else is interested, we
can arrange a car.'

'No, thanks,' Jon responded, not even bothering to make an
excuse.

'Nora and I have to be up early too,' Marietta said hurriedly.
'Remember, Martin, you promised to take us to that new
gallery.'

'Roger, it's been a long day,' Jessica implored. 'I think we
could all do with a good night's sleep. I'm exhausted. Why
don't we just head back to the room and call it a night?'

'Oh, please, Jessica. Don't use that patronizing tone with
me. And don't bother heading back to the room for my sake.
It's been a long time since that held any appeal. I'm going to
the bar. The rest of you can do what you want.'

For a moment Jessica looked stunned, her veneer of sophis-
tication slipping away. But years of practice quickly came to
her rescue as she smiled and turned to Martin. 'Dessert on the
terrace sounds perfect, Martin, and I know you do a mean
foxtrot.'

As everyone made their way to the terrace, Emily excused
herself, needing a break and thinking she would try to find a
phone. But as she headed for the front desk she realized the

time difference. Oh, damn, she thought, it's much too late to call Michael. He must have gone to bed long ago. It wouldn't be fair to try to reach him now. I'll have to wait till morning. She couldn't bear to go back right away, so she decided to explore the lower terrace.

The night was beautiful, clear and cool. The moon was high, myriads of stars sprinkled the sky, and Emily could just make out the distant lights of a passing cruise ship. Maybe Michael and I should have taken one of those luxury cruises, she was thinking, when her thoughts were interrupted by the sound of whispering voices.

'Oh, God, what will we do? He knows about us. He'll destroy you. Perhaps I should take the first flight out tomorrow. You can say I got sick or there was an emergency at home.'

'Don't be foolish, Nora – nothing so simple would dissuade Roger from his present course. I'm afraid I made a fatal mistake with that comment in my column.'

Emily could just make out the two figures on the path below the terrace – Nora, who that afternoon had seemed so capable, was leaning dejectedly on the railing, while Marietta stood with a protective arm around her hunched shoulders.

Emily quickly headed up the stairs to the upper terrace, embarrassed that she had overheard Nora and Marietta's conversation. But she certainly was intrigued by what little she had heard. It explained the snide remarks Roger made at dinner, and the fear and pain he brought to Nora's eyes.

'Emily, we're over here,' Annie called as Emily reached the upper terrace.

'Oh, Annie, I took a few minutes to explore. It certainly is beautiful down there, so quiet and peaceful. There was a ship passing in the distance – it was so ethereal, mysterious almost . . . The band is wonderful. Are they local?'

'Of course. Martin prides himself on having the best local talent. Can I interest you in some coffee or dessert? Now that Roger is gone, people have stayed and I think you'll find everyone's mood greatly improved. The menus are there on the side table. Come and enjoy yourself and, fair warning, Martin is waiting for an unsuspecting dance partner.'

No sooner had Annie spoken than Martin was at Emily's side.

'Wonderful! I was afraid you had abandoned us. And I've been waiting for a new victim; I've worn Annie out already, unfortunately,' he said with a smile. 'Although, I remember the days when she'd dance all night, even if we did have to get up at six in the morning.'

'Oh, I'm not finished yet, Martin Maitland,' Annie laughed. 'Just taking a break and placing the dessert orders. After all, someone has to work around here. But I'll be back, so save room on your dance card.'

Emily was amazed at how the group's mood had changed. Even Nora and Marietta, who had just returned, started to relax and enjoy themselves. When she and Martin finished dancing, Emily joined a now effusive Jon Peterson, who was sharing some New York stories.

'You really had to be there,' he was saying. 'Just picture this. Here I am scouring flea markets and second-hand stores to furnish this tiny studio on West 98th street. This was several years before Sarah and I met. Now you have to understand, I didn't have two nickels to rub together at this point. When I said this restaurant didn't pay well but was great experience, I wasn't kidding. And I didn't care what I slept on, but what I cooked in, now that's a different story. So when I saw this ad, 'Contents – Upper East Side Apartment For Sale', I was one of the first in line. I headed straight for the kitchen and right away I spied this mixer. It was old but good, and I figured I'd get it cheap. But I needed to find out if it worked. So I wandered into the dining room to find someone to ask, and ran into this obviously harried matron who was heading into the roped-off library. And, get this, when I asked her if the mixer worked, she says, "My dear man, I wouldn't have the slightest idea. In my vocabulary, cook was never a verb!"'

Marietta delighted in sharing a harrowing tale about her dentures and a not quite warm enough caramel sauce, and Jessica told some funny stories about Jason. Even Emily was caught up in the high spirits, admitting that her cooking experience wasn't so far from that society matron and wondering out loud why they even bothered to put ovens, those ancient artifacts of an earlier generation, in New York kitchens when microwaves heated just as well.

The stories and the laughter continued and, although Emily was enjoying herself, she soon realized that the excitement and exertion of the day was catching up with her.

'I'm afraid I have to call it a night,' she said, trying to stifle another yawn. 'I'm just exhausted. But I must say, in spite of the disappointment and missing Michael, it's been a wonderful day. Thanks so much, all of you.'

'Yes, my dear, you must be exhausted,' said Martin. 'I'd forgotten what a long day it's been for you. Can I have anything sent back to the room for you? A nightcap?'

'No, thank you, Martin. Nothing, really. I'm fine. I'll be asleep before my head touches the pillow.'

'Sleep late in the morning,' Annie added. 'Breakfast will be available whenever you come down, in the dining room or on one of the terraces.'

'I think I'll call it a night too,' Jessica said. 'If you don't mind, Emily, I'll walk back with you.'

Emily and Jessica walked along the ocean path chatting about the evening and chuckling over Jon's New York stories. They made plans to meet for breakfast and visit Sarah's crafts cooperative in the morning, although they both agreed not to meet too early. The night couldn't have been lovelier, and it certainly seemed an enjoyable ending to what had started out as a disastrous evening. But as they approached Jessica's rondoval, Emily sensed a mounting tension.

'I imagine Roger will be asleep,' Jessica commented, just before the door to her hut opened a crack and the florid face of Roger Stirhew peered out. Startled, Jessica quickly slipped into the rondoval and pulled the door shut behind her, but not before Emily heard the sound of breaking glass and Roger's gravelly voice.

'You slut!' he yelled. 'You don't for a minute think that I . . .'

Whatever vile words followed were lost to Emily, but she felt an overwhelming sense of sadness for Jessica – sadness and confusion. She seems so trapped, Emily thought. I can't imagine how she puts up with it. Or why, for that matter. What twisted sense of life or self led Jessica to believe that she had to take that abuse or, even worse, deserved it? Emily worried about what ugly things were happening inside that beautiful rondoval.

Suddenly the night had lost its loveliness. The path seemed darker and not so much peaceful as lonely, almost sinister. Just my state of mind, Emily reasoned, but she was happy to reach her own rondoval, just two down.

Emily was drifting off to sleep when the quiet was shattered by the screech of a car's wheels and Roger's voice yelling outside. 'What the hell . . . you almost hit me. Who the hell drives a car like that on these paths? Martin . . . Martin, some idiot just . . .' he screamed, although Martin was nowhere nearby.

'Roger,' Jessica's worried voice interrupted Roger's tirade. 'Roger, what's wrong? Are you all right?'

Emily could hear her running out of her hut. 'Roger?' Emily quickly turned off the lamp and peered through her darkened window. She could see Roger just getting up from the grass. He was unsteady on his feet, a combination of the drinking and the close call, Emily imagined. In fact, watching him now, it seemed entirely possible that it was *Roger* who had hit the passing car. He pushed Jessica away as she reached out her hand.

'Oh, please, Jessica. Yes, I'm all right, but I'm heading up to the main house. Some idiot almost hit me. Driving a Jeep like that on the path. Probably some service boy heading out for the night. Well, I'll get to the bottom of this. I'll have his job. Martin needs to do something about this.'

'Wait, I'll go with you. You're in no condition to . . .' Jessica called out as Roger headed up the garden path.

'Jessica, just go to bed!' he yelled back at her.

Emily's first reaction to this scene was to head outside to see if Jessica was OK, but as she reached for the doorknob, she paused. What if Jessica didn't want any help? What if she didn't even want to see anyone? She surely must be embarrassed, even angry at Roger's behavior. Emily pulled her hand back. Probably best to stay out of it. She'd listen in case anything more happened but, for now, she really needed some rest.

As she laid her tired head on the soft pillow, however, Emily was suddenly wide awake, struck by a thought. 'Oh, God,' she moaned. 'I hope Roger isn't going to join us in the morning.'

SIX

Emily woke to the soft cooing of a mourning dove. Although she felt rested, she savored the few moments just lying in bed listening to the sounds of Island Bluffs awakening. The ocean's roar was muted now – softer, almost soothing. Another dove answered the earlier call and Emily imagined the two of them with their broad elliptical wings and long tapered tails flittering back and forth among the palm trees outside her window. She had read that mourning doves were monogamous, and that both parents incubated and cared for their young squabs. Just the way it should be, she thought.

She heard the swish of a broom and looked out her window. There she saw an older man with a dark, craggy face and bright, almost black eyes, sweeping sand from the path. A young girl carried a basket of red flowers, stopping outside each room and dropping a few into the small pools that bordered the doorways. '*Bon dia*,' they called out as they spied her. 'Is a beautiful day.'

'*Bon dia*,' Emily called back. 'Yes, it is. It's lovely.'

Emily showered and dressed quickly. She could not believe she was actually hungry after the huge meal she had eaten last night but she was, and happily made her way to the main house. Thankfully, there was no sign of Roger.

'Morning,' called a busy-looking Annie. 'How was your night? I hope you slept well?'

'I sure did. It actually took a while to fall off,' Emily said, wondering if Annie would mention what happened with Roger.

When she said nothing, Emily continued, 'I'm usually a light sleeper, but not last night. I slept like a baby.'

'Well, you had a long day. Traveling takes a lot out of you. I know it does me. I used to go with Martin to the States all the time but I can't anymore. It's just too much. I'm exhausted by the time we get back and I think lately it's starting to take a toll on him too. Michael called earlier. He insisted I not wake you. He should be calling back any minute.'

'Oh, great, maybe he's wrapped things up and is on his way.'

'I don't want you to get your hopes up, Emily. Unless he's calling from the airport, I don't think he can be getting an afternoon flight out of Heathrow. But there's the phone now; that must be him. You can take it in the office.'

Emily walked into the large, light-filled room and grabbed the phone. 'Michael, oh, it's so good to hear your voice. I tried to reach you last night but I kept missing you . . .'

'I called there before you arrived,' Michael said, disappointment in his words.

'I know. Annie told me. I guess you're not calling from the airport?'

'Sorry, Em, really. This thing just got so damn screwed up. That jerk Bixley – I can't imagine the firm is even considering *him* for partner. Every time he gets involved in one of these things he ends up making it worse, but I think we're close to a deal here. You're right, though, I'm not calling from the airport. We still have some stuff to work out. I'm sorry, Em. I wish there was something I could do. How are things there?'

'It's just beautiful, Michael, just what we dreamed of. But it isn't exactly a singles place, and although everyone's been great, it's not the same being here by myself.'

'I know, Em, and I promise I'll make it up to you. Maybe we'll make some progress this afternoon. I'm trying my damnedest. And you know the firm. They'll make amends for this. If only Bixley would just stay out of it! Let's see where we are by the end of the day. I'll be out of here the minute I can, Em. I promise.'

'OK, hon. I know you're as disappointed as I am. And I guess I shouldn't complain.' Emily tried to sound positive.

'Actually, this is a lot better than freezing in New York and I certainly will have had time to unwind by the time you get here. Meanwhile, I'll explore the island a little. And Michael, there are the most fascinating collection of people here. You know that woman who does the society column in . . .'

'Sorry, hon, I've gotta run. They're ready to sit down at the table and I want to get started right away while they're in the mood. I can't wait to see you. I'll call you later. Love ya.'

Emily hung up the phone quickly. She was more than disappointed but she didn't want to make Michael feel bad. After all, it wasn't his fault, was it? And he was in London where it was cold and damp and she was here in the warm sun. She shouldn't really complain. She'd just have to make the best of it.

'You were right, Annie,' she called, coming out of the office. 'He won't make it this afternoon. So it looks as if you'll have to put up with me for the day.'

'No problem for me. Actually, it's kind of nice having some "unattached" company for a while, if you know what I mean. Why don't you grab a cup of coffee and I'll bring you a breakfast menu.'

'Sounds good. I can't believe I'm actually hungry after that meal last night. Shall I sit anywhere? I'm supposed to be meeting Jessica. Although I wouldn't be surprised if . . . I'm afraid I was witness to a pretty nasty scene between Jessica and Roger last night and then . . .'

'I've heard those can be brutal. I haven't seen Roger like that, but more and more . . . He came up to the main house late last night – it must have been after that – screaming at Martin about some car. I could barely understand what he was talking about. Anyway, he stormed off and I don't know where he ended up.'

Emily remembered the sound of breaking glass and Roger's slurred voice. 'I don't know how Jessica stands it. Have they been married long?'

'It must be almost eight years now. Jason is seven already and he was born soon after they married. It was a pretty strange courtship, from what I've heard. No one really knows much about Jessica before she met Roger. They met in Atlantic City, of all— Oh, I think I see Jessica coming now.'

'Good morning,' Annie called as a somewhat somber-looking Jessica entered the terrace. 'How was your night? You look a little peaked. I hope you slept well.'

'Are you feeling all right?' Emily added.

'I'm fine, really. Just a stupid accident,' Jessica said as she removed the sunglasses hiding the bruise on the side of her face. 'It looks much worse than it is.'

'Oh, Jessica, how did you . . .' Annie exclaimed. 'Please, you must have it looked at! We have several doctors staying with us; I know one of them would gladly take a look.'

'No, Annie, that's not necessary. Really. Let's just drop it. It will be fine. It's my own fault . . . Now, I'm starving, what's for breakfast?'

'I was just getting a menu for Emily. Will Roger be joining you?'

'No, Roger never made it home last night. He probably stayed at the Copa. You know what kind of shape he was in when he left here.'

'Would you like me to call there to check?' Annie asked.

'No, Annie. Thanks anyway. I'll call later. To tell you the truth, I don't really care right now.'

Although Jessica had been quick to claim responsibility for the bruise, Emily couldn't help but wonder. She had seen the murderous look in Roger's eyes last night and he certainly seemed capable of inflicting a blow or two. No wonder Jessica wasn't anxious to look for him.

As they ate, Jessica and Emily talked about the day ahead. They were both looking forward to visiting the crafts cooperative. Jessica was really interested in local art and made a point of searching it out whenever she traveled with Roger. Emily was keen to pick up something for her dad and her sisters and brother, and she could look for some gifts for Michael's family too. By the time he got here, he wouldn't want to waste any of his time shopping. Today would be the perfect opportunity.

'I'd love to join you,' Annie said, 'but Martin is going to be out this morning and I have some paperwork to get done. Sarah and I were going to go to Jon's for lunch today, though. Why don't the two of you join us? I could drive over to the co-op at about twelve and we could all go to Jon's together.'

'Sounds great!' they responded in unison.

'Good, it's all settled then. Nelson will drive you into Oranjestad – he has some business to do in town – and I'll pick you up at noon,' Annie said as the three of them headed for the front steps. 'Be sure to have Sarah point out some of the other shops to you. And don't miss the galleries. There are some wonderfully talented people on the island.'

The drive to town was pleasant and informative. Nelson pointed out the local sights and it gave Emily a chance to get to know the island a little better. It was quiet and rural where Island Bluffs sat, its face to the sea, but it wasn't long before the landscape changed. Magnificent estates dotted the shores of Malmok Beach, home to some of the wealthiest families on the island. Not far beyond this they came to Palm Beach, a far cry from the tranquility of the Bluffs.

'This is where most of the resorts are located,' Nelson explained, indicating the lavish strip of hotels – complexes, really – which lined the expanse of white sparkling beach. As they drove along the seven-mile stretch of L.G. Smith Boulevard, he named some of the most notable. 'Up ahead is the newest, the Marriott. It has an eight-story atrium – incredible. Over there is the Hyatt, with its waterpark: pools and slides and even a lagoon; and the new Hilton, over four hundred rooms and the ladies love the spa.'

'It's so opulent, I can't believe it. Why, there must be twenty hotels here!' Emily exclaimed.

'At least,' Nelson answered. 'Tourism is the biggest, almost the only business on Aruba. Ever since the oil refinery closed it's what the people look to for jobs. And the industry has thrived.'

'I can see that. With all these hotel rooms there must be a lot of tourist dollars spent here.'

'It's a goldmine. It's not without its critics, though,' said Nelson, pointing to the strip. 'Some people complain that it's too much, too fast; that we are sacrificing the beauty of our island for these high-rise hotels and casinos. Too much of the profits go to the owners and not enough florins make it back into the pockets of the people. As with most things, the truth is somewhere in between.

'Now off the coast here is one of the sights that you might want to explore with your Michael when he comes,' Nelson continued, changing the subject. 'It's the wreck of the German ship *Antilla*, scuttled in nineteen-forty. It's a popular spot for divers, especially at night when the polyps of the brain coral that cover its hull pulse open. People say it looks like a ghost ship; some think it is haunted. Even if you are not much for diving, you can still see our beautiful coral reefs. There is actually a submarine that will take you down below.'

'Several years ago Roger and I visited a beautiful spot here on the island,' Jessica added, joining the conversation. 'I don't remember the name of it, but it was very hard to get to. We went by horseback.'

'Ah, that would be the Natural Pool,' Nelson, whose knowledge of the island was obviously exhaustive, explained. 'Another spot you must not miss, Emily. It is indeed quite hard to get to. It is full of stones and boulders, and the waves crashing against the rocks are fierce, but the tranquility of the pool is good for the soul. The town is not much further now. This here is Manchebo Beach where our more daring sunbathers like to go. Up ahead is Oranjestad.'

Emily was charmed by her first view of the bustling town. The streets were lively with visitors, both local and tourist, and the stores were busy with shoppers. People were friendly, smiles frequent, and the lilting sounds of Papiamento, a blend of English, Dutch and Spanish, could be heard everywhere.

It was here in Oranjestad that the island's Dutch influences were most in evidence. Gabled facades, done up in a rainbow of colors: candytuft pink, buttercup yellow, bright tangerine and cool lime, lined the main streets. Nelson pulled over so they could view the harbor with its bountiful market and a small mall full of chic shops and trendy restaurants. It seemed both festive and industrious. An elderly woman carrying a basket of fruit approached the car.

'*Bon dia*, Nelson!' she called out, offering him several small mangos.

'*Danki, danki*,' Nelson answered, handing her several florin from his pocket.

Beyond the harbor was Fort Zoutman, one of the oldest

buildings on the island; the Willem III Tower, named after a Dutch king; and just outside of town, a huge red windmill that had been turned into a restaurant – all spoke of the island's Dutch heritage.

Sarah's co-op was located on Caya G.H. Betico Croes, the main shopping street in town. She shared the space with a painter, a potter and a sculptor, and it seemed they were all benefiting from the cruise ship that had come in that morning. Tourists, cameras dangling from sunburnt necks, seemed to love her creations, 'oohing' and 'aahing' over the unique combinations of fabric and the vibrant island colors. Emily also found Sarah's clothes enchanting, sort of funky too, and she could not resist a colorful sundress adorned with red, yellow and lime-green flowers. A pair of matching lime-green slides caught her eye and she quickly slipped her foot into them. Perfect, she thought.

She wandered along the side aisle, browsing at the colorful scarves. The fabrics were light and soft and she considered getting one for Michael's mother, but quickly changed her mind – the colors were just too vibrant. Jane, she thought. The purple print would be perfect for her, and at the last minute she threw in a pink one for herself.

Then it was on to the other stores and galleries along the main street. The shops were full of Dutch porcelain and cheeses, fine hand-embroidered linens, European fashions, Swiss watches and Italian leathers. Jessica and Emily split up since they both had spent so much time in the co-op and still had some serious shopping to do. Jessica was looking for something special for Jason, of course, and Emily hadn't found anything for Michael's mother or sisters.

There were a number of places to choose from and Emily found herself going from one to the other trying to decide. The pieces were all lovely, fine gold and silver, pierced and painted tin, shell, coral and carved wood. She quickly decided on a coral necklace for one of Michael's sisters and a shell one for the other. Perhaps a burled bowl for his mother or maybe she should reconsider a scarf? Or maybe one of those straw purses instead? It was almost impossible to decide.

It was on her third trip to look at a painted tin necklace that she thought would be perfect for Kate that Emily saw Jessica again. She was standing in a little jewelry shop on a quiet side street, talking to a tall, athletic man who was very good-looking, wore dark sunglasses and sported a neatly trimmed beard. Late thirties, early forties, Emily thought.

Jessica looked up as Emily approached. 'Emily, I'd like you to meet Nick Marino. Nick owns a restaurant back in Connecticut, a wonderful Italian place in Westport. One that even Roger approves of.'

'Not that he wouldn't like to take a shot at me . . . literally!' Nick said with a crooked smile. 'Only joking,' he added, although his words didn't ring true.

'It's nice to meet you, Nick. Did you arrive on the cruise ship or are you staying on the island?' Emily asked.

'Oh, God, not the cruise ship,' he responded. 'I get sea sick in my bathtub. No, I'm staying on the island. By a lucky coincidence, I'm also at the Bluffs. One of my favorite places. Wouldn't stay anywhere else.'

'How nice. It's the first time I've been there. It's wonderful,' Emily added.

'Emily and her fiancé were supposed to be enjoying a long-anticipated vacation,' Jessica shared sympathetically. 'Only he got delayed in London on business.'

'That's great. Oh, sorry, wrong response. It's just that my girlfriend had to back out at the last minute. Family emergency. And you must have seen how it is at the Bluffs. Talk about third wheels! I'm only here for a few days so maybe you and I could team up for a bit, at least until your friend arrives.'

Nick seemed to be more smooth than charming, easygoing and confident. Emily was unsure how much she wanted to be 'teamed up' with anyone, so she was careful in her response. 'Perhaps we'll run into you later this afternoon on the beach,' was all she said.

'Great. Glad I met up with you, Jessica. Can't wait till Roger hears I'm here! Enjoy the rest of your shopping.'

Jessica seemed very uncomfortable as Nick was leaving the store and it took her only a minute to offer an explanation. 'Nick's a great guy,' she said with some fondness, 'and he runs a great restaurant back in Connecticut. It's just that he and

Roger don't get along at all. It's a little strange, perhaps, but Nick seems to enjoy it. He's so laid-back; he takes everything – including Roger's snide remarks – in his stride. I'm sure most of it just goes over his head, really. He loves poking fun at Roger, you know, for being pompous and all. It really drives Roger crazy, but Nick is so funny when he does it that everyone else finds it hilarious. And that only makes things worse. Nick isn't trying to be mean, he's just having some fun, but you know Roger.'

'Nick certainly seems very friendly,' Emily added, not really knowing what to say. She certainly understood Jessica's predicament. Although she seemed pleased to see Nick, she hardly needed anything else to shorten Roger's fuse.

'I guess we should head back to Sarah's – it's getting late. I'm just going to pick up this necklace for Kate. Did you find anything for Jason, Jessica?'

'I did – the most wonderful sailboat, wooden with real canvas sails. I know he'll love it. He's dying to learn to sail. We've promised to take him out and teach him. So that's all I need for now, although I'm sure this won't be my only shopping trip.'

Annie was already there by the time they arrived at Sarah's and in no time they were headed to Jon's for lunch.

'What's the restaurant called?' Emily asked as they rode along. She knew Annie had mentioned it but she just couldn't remember.

'Blue Water,' Sarah replied, 'because of its location. Jon spent almost a year fixing it up. He did a lot of the work himself to save on expenses.'

'Wait till you see it,' Annie added. 'It's really beautiful. Very lush. Like many parts of the island, the plantings have to be carefully nourished to survive, but it's surrounded by palm trees that shade the terrace tables. There are flowering vines that cover the roadside entrance and huge pots of hibiscus that frame the ocean view.'

Emily guessed that there might have been other spots of similar description, but she spotted Blue Water from a hundred yards away. 'It is beautiful, Sarah. Jon has done a wonderful job. The white stucco is so crisp-looking and those splashes of bright color really make it cheerful. And it's so open, look at that view. It's magnificent. The perfect backdrop. Jon must be a wonderful gardener; everything's so lush and vibrant.'

'Actually, the garden and the flowers are Sarah's handiwork. She's her father's daughter like that,' Annie said proudly. 'She could grow anything. Not like me, the original black sheep.'

'Perfect timing,' Jon said as he emerged from the kitchen.

'It doesn't look too bad, Jon,' Annie commented, noting the few guests lingering in the dining room and on the terrace.

'No, not too bad today. The ship helps. Not what it was two months ago, of course, but better than last week, I think. We'll survive.'

'We'll do more than survive Jon,' Sarah said. 'It'll just take a little longer, but already we're recouping some of the damage. Oh, I'm sorry, Jessica, I shouldn't have mentioned that in front of you.'

'And I had no right to make those comments at dinner last night either, Jessica,' Jon added. 'I'm really sorry. It's one thing to want to stick it to Roger, and believe me there's no one who wants to more than me, but it's unfair to make you uncomfortable. After all, you're not responsible for what Roger says.'

'I know you didn't mean to make me feel that way, Jon, but you're right, let's just drop it. Even though I'm not responsible, it does make me uncomfortable. I can't help it. So . . . the setting's great, but how's the food?'

'The best on the island,' Sarah said with obvious pride. 'Ooops, sorry, Mom. Jon's made that new chicken dish for us. It's wonderful.'

Lunch was every bit as good as Sarah said it would be. Emily tried the new chicken dish and was amazed when it arrived at the table. The chicken, lightly grilled and garnished with orange and lime slices, sat on a bed of mixed greens. Why, it's as colorful as my new sundress, Emily thought. It had a hint of spice that complemented the citrus.

'It's delicious, Sarah,' Emily said, savoring the subtle flavors. 'Is it marinated?'

'For hours,' Sarah explained. 'Jon marinates it for at least ten. There's orange and lime juice, wine, vinegar and a bit of tabasco. Even I don't know all the spices that he puts in.'

'I definitely get a hint of cilantro. It's wonderful, so refreshing.' And as Emily finished every last bit she had to agree with Sarah. If the rest of the food was this good, Blue Water actually might be better than Peppercorns. The service was impeccable, the setting was charming, and Emily was enchanted watching the tiny bananaquits alight on nearby tables trying to steal tiny grains of sugar.

By the time they finished their entrées the restaurant was almost empty, so Jon was able to join them and resume his stories of New York. Emily only needed to watch him and Sarah together for a few minutes to realize how much in love they were. When they left the table to show Jessica a small gallery next door, she had a chance to share her observations with Annie.

'They're very lucky, those two. They clearly love each other very much.'

'Isn't it wonderful? It's a shame that their plans have gotten screwed up. They were supposed to get married this spring but that awful review Roger wrote has really damaged the restaurant. I try not to be too down about it, especially in front of them, but . . . Martin was enraged, of course. He was actually going to tell Roger that he wasn't welcome at the Bluffs, but we all talked him out of it. It wouldn't have helped, and might have made matters worse. But enough of that; how was your morning in town?'

'It was wonderful. Sarah's shop was great and I couldn't resist a sundress and pair of floral slides. She's very talented, Annie. And then I found this great jewelry shop where I got a very unusual painted tin necklace for my sister, Kate.'

'And how did Jessica make out?'

'She seemed to do OK too. She got a great sailboat for Jason and . . . Oh, Jessica met someone she knew. He's also supposed to be staying at the Bluffs – Nick Marino?'

'Ah, yes, Nick. He owns a wonderful Italian restaurant, Lago di Como. It's very in these days. It's near where they live in Connecticut, so I'm sure they've crossed paths, though I've never asked . . . From what I hear Nick travels in pretty different circles from Roger, at least in public.'

Emily was surprised by this. 'Jessica seemed to know him.

And it sounded like Roger was well acquainted with him too, although from what he said . . . Anyway, he was very friendly.'

'Nick's OK. He just sometimes seems a little full of himself, and he always has a new girlfriend in tow. He only arrived today, a short time before I left. I hadn't realized he had headed into town, but now that I think of it, he was asking Penny about some gallery. I don't know if he mentioned it, but his girlfriend wasn't able to make it at the last minute, so he's sort of at loose ends too. Perhaps we'll have him join our group for dinner.'

'I don't know about that, Annie. It sounded like he and Roger don't get along very well, although it also sounds as though Nick handles Roger's nasty streak better than most.'

'He does, and if we only had dinner with people who got along with Roger these days we'd be eating alone. But you may be right. Martin also mentioned something about Roger and Nick. It's strange – there was still no sign of Roger when I left for town. I'm beginning to think we'd all be better off if he was really miffed and decided to stay at the Copa. Now, we should get Jessica and head back. I'm sure you'll want to get to the beach and I have to start getting ready for the barbecue tomorrow night.'

But when they went to find Jessica, they found out that she had decided to stay in town for a while.

'She said she wanted to do a little more shopping,' Sarah said.

'And she hates the beach!' Jon added, obviously finding that hard to believe. 'Can you imagine? Anyway, she knew you'd be anxious to get back, Annie, so she said she'd take a taxi back to the Bluffs later on.'

'Well then, it's you and me, Emily. Lunch was wonderful, Jon, as always. Will you be heading back to the shop, Sarah?'

'Yes, as a matter of fact, I should get a move on. I told Junaida I'd be back in an hour and it's way after that. I'm sure everyone will be in a last-minute shopping frenzy before they head back to the ship. At least, I hope they will.'

'Thanks so much for lunch, Jon,' Emily said. 'Your place is really beautiful and Sarah may be right about your rivaling Pepperhearts. But I guess I shouldn't say that within Annie's hearing. At least, not until I've gotten my ride back to the Bluffs.'

'I'd be careful if I were you, Emily. Annie might make you pay for that remark. God knows, she might sit you next to Roger again at dinner tonight,' Jon said, laughing as he waved them out the door. Although there was humor in his voice, each mention of Roger's name seemed to bring a dark veil of anger across his bright eyes.

SEVEN

The ride back was pleasant and relaxing. Emily was tempted to mention the conversation between Marietta and Nora that she had overheard the night before, but she was too embarrassed to admit to Annie that she had overheard it. Instead, she listened as Annie talked about her girls – what they were like growing up, so different and yet so close. Alex, her older daughter, independent and cosmopolitan, with a quick mind and a searing wit, was determined to make it in New York. She had joined a big fashion house last year and already some of her designs were being recognized. Alex had drawn Sarah to New York, about four years earlier, but Sarah could never be happy there with the pace and the people. She would never be happy anywhere but on her beloved island.

Emily spoke of her desire for children and her concerns about the changes that lay ahead. She talked about her mom and the loss which still played such a role in her life, and about her brother and sisters. It seemed hard to imagine really. They were all grown now. Brian had finished his residency at Columbia and rumor had it he'd be engaged by the summer. Jane had just gotten her first small role on Broadway, and Kate, sweet, gentle Kate, had married the boy next door. It was strange, in some ways, that their lives seemed so settled and it was Emily who was so unsettled, so unsure about where she was heading. For the hundredth time Emily found herself thinking, *If only Michael were here. We need to talk about these things together. Make some decisions, some plans. Oh, well, no sense in ruminating on it, if wishes were horses . . .*

'Let's take a small detour here, Emily. There's a spot I'd like you to see,' Annie was saying as Emily's attention returned to the present. 'It's just a few miles inland. It will only take us a minute.'

Very shortly, they came to a small stone church, simple and unadorned except for a beautifully carved oak altar. 'It's the Church of Santa Anna,' Annie said. 'Lovely, isn't it? I always think it presents a wonderful counterpoint to the hotel strip, so different and yet only minutes away. It's almost like a reflection of the island as a whole. Now look over there.'

Emily was amazed at what she saw – a small graveyard with brightly painted tombstones. 'It's lovely,' she said. 'It seems reverent yet whimsical. I've never seen anything like it. But why the bright colors?'

'That's the really distinctive part,' Annie explained. 'Each tombstone is painted the color of the deceased person's house.'

'Oh, what a lovely idea. It's so comforting in a way, isn't it? Makes it seem more like a home than a grave.'

'It does. I think this place gives you a wonderful glimpse of the people of Aruba, much more than the tourist areas. I wanted to be sure you didn't miss this as a lot of people do. Now, we'd better move on or we'll never get back.'

Emily watched out the window as they drove, enjoying the sights and asking Annie about different scenes along the way. 'What a spectacular picture, Annie. Look at all those sails – the colors are magnificent.'

'That's Fisherman's Hut. It's just about the best place on the island for windsurfing. Aruba is really known for it, you know. It's the constant tradewinds – they make the trees bow down and the sails stand up. You should see this place when they have the international windsurfing competition back there on Eagle Beach. It's a madhouse.'

'I'd love to try it. It looks so free, and easy, actually.'

'Well, I don't know how easy it is but try your hand at it when we get back. If you go down to the beach house, Hendrick will help you. He's a great teacher, even managed to get me up on one of those things. No mean feat, I'll tell you that.'

'I'll do that. I'm not great in the water, but I'm feeling kind of daring today, as long as I have a life belt on, that is,' Emily said as they neared the Bluffs. 'Thanks so much for the invitation to lunch, Annie. It was perfect, really. Just what I needed.'

'I'm glad. Now, enjoy your afternoon and tell Hendrick I said to take good care of you.'

Emily headed straight for her room, anxious now to get to the beach. The windsurfing sounded like fun and it would certainly distract her. She changed quickly and grabbed her straw bag, speaking aloud to herself as she gathered her things together. 'Let's see, sunglasses, sunscreen, hat, book . . . Oh, I won't need that. Hmm . . . maybe I might. Windsurfing could be a lot harder than it looks.'

EIGHT

The bay beach was much livelier in the early afternoon than it had been late in the day yesterday. Emily quickly settled in an empty hammock, swaying slowly between two sturdy palms. From here she could watch the windsurfers and the wannabes, and hear the soft reggae beat coming from the beach bar. In fact, she wasn't there two minutes when a waiter appeared urging her to try today's special. 'A Strawberry Delight – it's paradise,' he crooned to the tune of 'S Wonderful'. Oh, what the heck, Emily decided, it might be as close as she'd ever get to paradise.

The mood at the beach was infectious and she soon found herself heading toward the water just to get a better look. Besides the windsurfers there were swimmers, paddling back and forth to a sturdy raft; snorkelers, heads down and flippering away; and further out a number of braver souls shooting across the water on skis. Emily grabbed a nearby lounge chair and sipped her drink contentedly.

'Hey, mind if I join you?' a vaguely familiar voice asked behind her.

Turning around, she saw Nick Marino standing only inches away. 'Not at all,' she said, although, in truth, she was perfectly happy sitting there by herself. 'I was just watching the scene and wondering whether I had enough energy to join in.'

'I know how you feel. When you're not used to this heat it really takes something out of you. But I swore back in Connecticut that I wouldn't complain no matter how hot it got.'

'Me too. We certainly have had some winter, and right now that water looks mighty inviting. I was thinking of trying windsurfing. Ever done it, Nick?'

'Sure have. It's great fun, and not too hard to learn either. I'm a great teacher, if I do say so myself. Come on, let's head over to the beach house and get some equipment.'

'Oh, no, I couldn't impose like that. Annie told me that Hendrick would be able to teach me,' Emily said, hoping to dissuade Nick. Although he seemed pleasant enough, she had always taken a step back from people who came on real strong, and Nick Marino fell into that category. 'In fact, I think she may have signed me up, so I better head over and check. But thanks for the offer.'

'I'll head over with you. Pick up some gear.'

Unfortunately, when Emily reached the beach house, she found out that Hendrick was already out in the water teaching someone else, and she couldn't avoid Nick's second offer. It took only minutes to get the equipment and in no time they were in the water.

Although she'd had some reservations, Emily found that Nick really was a good teacher. He was patient and strong, able to handle the small craft and guide her through the steps at the same time. And he was funny. He had a sharp wit and Emily could see that, as long as you weren't the target, he could be wickedly amusing.

Within the hour Emily was standing, balanced somewhat shakily on the board and skirting across the water. She would catch the wind, feel its pull on the striped sail and lean her body

in not quite graceful counterpoint. At times she dipped precari-
ously, preparing herself for the sharp chill of the water, only to
recoup at the last minute and right the board again. But the
wind was tricky, stalling and surging. Its vagaries were sometimes too much for her and she would topple over. After a while,
she found herself laughing and winded, heading for shore.

'That was fun, Nick, thanks for the lesson.'

'Anytime. I enjoyed it too. How about a drink?'

'I couldn't . . .' Emily started to say and then changed her
mind. She got the sense that Nick wasn't used to women
saying no, and what the heck, she had enjoyed her time with
him *and* she had nothing better to do. 'OK, maybe just one.'
They found two empty lounge chairs and Nick raised the flag
on their umbrella. Within seconds a server came over.

'Two of today's specials,' Nick ordered as Emily settled
herself in the chair. The sun's warmth and the exertion made
her pleasantly drowsy but Nick seemed full of energy. They
talked about their lives back home. Emily shared stories about
her job, but little about her life with Michael, even though
Nick probed. 'Enough about me,' she said, forestalling his
questions. 'How did you end up in the restaurant business,
Nick?'

'A pretty typical immigrant's story, I guess. My grandparents
came over from Italy in the twenties. My grandfather was a
farmer and there were no farms in New York City. But he
knew produce, so he started with a cart and within a few years
he had a small store.'

'And your grandmother?'

'She raised a whole bunch of kids – seven. My father was
the youngest. And she cooked; big hearty meals that she
knew from home. From what I've been told she was an
incredible cook. Anyway, at some point they decided to open
a restaurant. A small place in Little Italy, but pretty soon it
had a great reputation. My father took it over when my
grandfather died, expanded it, made some changes and it
really took off.'

Nick seemed different when he was talking about his family.
More subdued, less flippant. 'So I imagine you sort of grew
up in the business.'

'I sure did. I only have one sister and she had no interest in the place, so I guess it was just assumed that I'd take it over.'

'But your place is in Connecticut?'

'You know New York. About fifteen years ago, Little Italy started to change. My father was older and my mother had died. I think he wanted out of the city. He wanted a little piece of land; he wanted to grow things again. We decided to pull up stakes in the city and ended up in Connecticut. My father got his couple of acres and I handled the restaurant move.'

'That must have been a tough call, I mean with the restaurant's name in New York and all.'

'We were lucky; we had some help.'

Emily watched as Nick talked. His face was amazingly animated, dark eyes moving and flashing, a momentary frown followed by a quick smile. His hands, with their long, tapered fingers, reinforced his every opinion – pointing, gesturing, drawing the listener in. They were almost mesmerizing.

'What an unusual ring, Nick,' Emily said, noticing the large gold band on his left hand. 'What is it?'

'This,' Nick answered, looking down at it and twisting it slightly, 'was my great-grandfather's.' He extended his hand so Emily could get a closer look. Now she could see that its cigar-shaped band had a large, oddly shaped cut crystal bezel. 'It's called a coffin ring.'

Well, that explained the shape, Emily thought. 'It's quite unusual.'

'They're Victorian mourning rings. I was told that my great-grandfather was devastated when my great-grandmother died. She was very young and died in childbirth. Underneath the bezel is a piece of her hair. If you look carefully, you can see writing in the black enameling on the band.'

'What does it say?'

'It's in Italian; it says "Dear Remains". I wear it all the time. It means a great deal to me.' Nick's eyes seemed to darken and, once again, he started twisting the ring.

'I'm sure it must,' Emily said. 'And it's really quite lovely.' Although, she wanted to add, a bit gruesome.

'Time for another,' Nick said, raising the flag on the umbrella.

'Oh, I couldn't. Really, Nick. I'm really feeling wiped. All I want to do is stretch out and take a short snooze right about now.'

Nick seemed a little put off by Emily's refusal – not disappointed, more insulted. 'Well, if you change your mind, I'll be at the beach bar. By the way, I asked Martin to seat us together at dinner, so either way I'll see you later.'

Even though Emily had enjoyed the windsurfing and her conversation with Nick, she was taken aback at his parting remark. She was a little annoyed that he would have asked Martin to seat them together. He hadn't asked if Emily would like to have dinner with him, he had just assumed she would, probably because they were the only two not in a couple on the island. She'd have to make sure she got hold of Martin, and soon.

But for now she could think of nothing but that short nap, so she looked around for a quiet spot where she could conk out for a while.

The only hammock Emily could find was directly in front of the beach bar. For a few minutes she let herself drift lazily back and forth, hoping to fall asleep. But the sounds of cheerful conviviality made napping impossible, so she decided to join in the fun. Couples talked and laughed, sharing stories and advice – the hottest new book, strongest mutual fund, best plastic surgeon or empathetic New York shrink (although it appeared that there were several among the group). What to do with your anxious, but annoying teenager or your wonderful but illegal housekeeper. And how to cook anything from lacquered swordfish to crème brûlée.

Emily enjoyed the banter and met a number of new people, all of whom seemed to know who she was. 'We heard about your disappointment, how awful,' they commiserated, or invited her to join them for dinner . . . or lunch, or sightseeing, or shopping.

She was surprised to see that Jessica was here with Nick at her side.

'Ah, I see you decided to take me up on my offer,' he said somewhat smugly as she strolled over to them. 'Another Strawberry Delight? Good for tired muscles and empty beds.'

'How was the rest of your shopping?' she asked Jessica, pointedly ignoring Nick's remark.

'Great. I see you've been swimming; how was the water?'

'It was wonderful, really. Refreshing, but not cold. And the sun – I haven't felt that warm in months. Nick taught me how to windsurf. It was—'

'Ah, Jessica, you're back,' Martin said, joining the group. 'Listen, I got a phone call from Larry Sampson over at Caribbean Sands. He said that Roger was supposed to meet him this morning to look over the new wing and he never showed up.'

Emily noticed the look of concern that crossed Jessica's face. 'I don't know what to say, Martin. I haven't seen Roger since last night. I'm afraid he walked out of our room in somewhat of a huff and then that Jeep . . . He hasn't been back. His stuff is all there, all his clothes. I just assumed he stayed over wherever he went last night – the Copa or the Sands?'

'Have you called around at all?'

'I haven't, Martin. I probably should have, but . . .'

'Oh, please, Jessica,' Nick interrupted. 'Roger's a big boy and well able to take care of himself. You know what they say: God takes care of babies and—'

'Nick, please,' Martin said, cutting him off. 'Would you like me to make some calls, Jessica? Would that help?'

'Could you, Martin? I hate to impose but . . .'

'It's no imposition. As soon as I get back to the main house I'll call around. Now try some of these wings, they're really spicy but good. Did I ever tell you . . .'

Martin was halfway through his story when they heard raucous laughter coming from the entrance to the patio. Looking over they could see Roger, his shirt rumpled, suit jacket slung over his shoulder, making his way toward them.

'Oh my God,' Jessica muttered softly, her eyes darting from Roger to Nick.

'Well, well, who have we here? Why, Nick Marino. Haven't seen you here in some time. Alone, I see . . . couldn't dig up someone to come along.' Roger laughed. 'Can't say that I'm surprised you . . .'

'Roger, please don't,' Jessica said, her voice quiet and controlled.

'Don't? Don't what? Oh, really, Jessica, Nick and I know a great deal about one another, don't we, Nick?' he sneered as he walked away.

'I'm sorry, Nick. Martin, I . . .'

'Please, Jessica, don't apologize,' Martin soothed. 'You have nothing to apologize for.'

'Martin's right, Jessica,' Nick added. 'Roger's a jerk; it's no reflection on you. But I do think I'll make myself scarce. It doesn't look like Roger's going anywhere. And anyway, I'm overdue a nap. See you all later.'

'Yes, and I have some work to do around here,' Martin said. 'What about you, Jessica? Will you stay or would you rather head back to your room?'

'I'll stay for a little bit, Martin. I'd like to be able to get Roger to come back with me. And Martin . . . thanks so much.'

Emily found herself standing alone as Jessica hovered in Roger's vicinity, keeping a low profile but a keen eye. Relieved that the confrontation was over, she took a few minutes to survey the crowd. This certainly was the place to be in the afternoon.

Martin and Annie both mingled with the guests, offering suggestions for activities, sharing updates on island happenings and checking on how everyone's stay was going. Emily marveled at how skilled they were. Annie stopped to chat for a moment with Nora, who sat at a table by herself while Martin moved from group to group. The two of them seemed to know everything about their guests and used their knowledge to forge friendships between people who might otherwise not have met. Emily enjoyed overhearing it all. It seemed the Mitchells' son was going to med school in the same Midwest city where the Grants' daughter was going to college; Dr Cadwell's most recent article on depression was related to Dr Kurlansky's ongoing clinical trials for sleep disorders; and Nancy Parker's backhand would be the perfect challenge to Allison Strickland's forehand. They seemed to honestly enjoy every minute and never tired of chatting with people. She watched as Annie headed up to the main house with one guest as Martin continued joking and laughing with others.

Emily noticed that the beach was emptier now and decided to try again for her sorely needed nap. Finding an empty hammock some distance away, she was able to keep one eye on the scene while she swayed to the gentle breezes. The words and laughter were muted now and it wasn't long before her mind wandered and her thoughts drifted. Snippets of conversation distinguished themselves from the general hum: 'Had a great time at the Casablanca . . .' 'Indonesian food, very good really . . .' 'Just came by for a swim . . . not much of a lunch crowd . . .' 'My editor thinks I should revamp . . .' 'We really need to talk . . .' 'Meet me . . .' But none of them could penetrate the drowsy haze of Emily's musings.

It took sharper voices to do that, and as soon as Emily heard them she knew whose they were.

'Don't presume to tell me I've had too much to drink,' Roger's voice sneered.

'Roger, please, let's not argue. Why don't we head back? It's so hot and I'd like to take a nap before dinner,' Jessica's voice begged.

'Well, don't let me stop you. You can do what you damn please. Since when did you need me to—'

'Roger, I think Jessica's right. It will be a long night and you look like you could use some sleep,' Emily then heard Martin's patient voice urging.

'How dare you. Who the hell do you think you are?' Roger must have been drunk, as Emily could barely make out his next sentences. 'Telling me . . . you and your second rate . . . think you're such a big deal . . . always sucking up to people . . . pretentious crap. You'll pay for this, Martin, believe me.'

And with that an awkward silence fell. Emily opened her eyes to see Roger's telltale flushed face glaring as he stormed off, heading in the direction of the main house, while the crowd at the bar just stared.

Martin immediately signaled to one of the waiters and within seconds the music of a steel band blared from the speakers. Then, without skipping a beat, he singled out one of the livelier women in the group. 'OK, Maddie, you've escaped me long enough. Now what was that new dance? And John,' he called to the bartender, 'Strawberry Delights all around.'

It took only minutes for the unpleasantness to be forgotten. Like most people on vacation, these folks were out to enjoy themselves and they weren't going to let an unruly guest, no matter who he was, spoil the day. Soon talk and laughter could be heard again.

But Emily's reverie was broken. She gave up on her nap and headed down to the water to take a short swim. It was warm and pleasant, with gentle lapping waves that painted undulating rivulets on the pearly sand. Emily floated, eyes closed, her hair streaming, concentrating only on the water's motion, trying to recreate her hazy peace. But to no avail; brisk strokes and long laps were necessary to drive away a creeping melancholy.

A little bit of exercise was about all she could handle, though, and soon she was heading back up the beach to where Martin and Annie were sitting at a table, alone. Both of them looked anxious as Annie talked quietly to Martin. The crowd had started to dwindle now, most of the guests heading back to their rooms for their afternoon naps. They looked up as Emily approached.

'Why don't you walk back to the office with us, Emily?' Annie said. 'We can see if Penny can get hold of Michael for you.'

'Yes, Emily,' Martin added. 'You head back with Annie. I'll be along in a little while. There are a few things I want to check on before I head over to the dining room.'

'It's getting late, Martin,' Annie said. 'Come back with us. We still have to finish that order.'

'Please, Annie,' Martin said more sharply than he obviously intended. 'I'm sorry, dear, it's just . . . I'll only be a few minutes. Now you head up and ask Penny about that call.'

As they walked along, the veneer of lightheartedness that had gotten Annie through the last hour dropped away.

'Martin's so upset,' she said. 'He's able to hide it from the guests but not from me. This Roger Stirhew thing is a mess. It's bad enough what's happened with Jon but now this . . . the humiliation. It's hard to believe that Roger has the power he does but, then again, few people have seen him like this. Maybe he feels like he can get away with it here. It's so much like a club, you see, that he feels it's safe.'

'I didn't see the whole thing. When it started, I was lying in the hammock,' Emily said. 'But I heard it. And it was pretty awful. Martin was really incredible, Annie. The way he distracted everyone, like it was nothing. He looked so carefree, dancing and joking. But just now, I could see how upset he really was. And sad, somehow.'

'I missed the worst of it too,' Annie said, shaking her head. 'I had gone up to the main house with one of the guests, but believe me I saw what kind of mood Roger was in. While I was up there on the patio, I overheard the most dreadful run-in that he had with Marietta, saying the most awful things and then just storming off. He looked like he was headed for the ocean beach but I couldn't be sure. I was hoping he'd go back to his room. And yes, Emily, Martin is sad, and angry. He's really terribly angry at Roger. At first it was more for Jon but now it's everything. The way he treats Jessica; the way he treats everyone. You heard him last night with Marietta and Nora – the comments, the sneering. It's just repulsive.

'You know,' Annie continued, 'Roger has never been easy to get along with, but at one time he and Martin were something akin to friends. Not when they first met, of course. Then, Roger always had his guard up; he didn't really trust anyone. Oh, he had lots of acquaintances, invitations to parties, was always on the arm of one woman or another. But he had no real friends. Martin actually felt sorry for him. He really went out of his way to make Roger feel comfortable here. And he succeeded.'

'Martin's a good man, Annie,' Emily commented. 'He reminds me of my brother Brian in a way. Sort of innocent in regard to people. Trusting and optimistic. Feeling he can always change things for the better.'

'That's true. He really thought he could change Roger. And he did. Only it didn't change him for the better but the worse. Roger is very comfortable here and I think that's why we see more of the meanness behind the mask. It's left Martin feeling betrayed . . . responsible somehow. I can't wait until he leaves on Sunday. I've had it. And so has everybody else.'

NINE

I t took just a minute for Penny at the front desk to get through to Michael's hotel, only to find that he wasn't there. But he had left a message for Emily saying that he would be in his room at about ten p.m. and he'd try to reach her then. That left Emily only half an hour, so she decided to wait on the patio. She could read her book and there was a cool breeze and the shade of the palm trees.

It was amazing how quiet everything was now. You would almost think the resort was empty. No chatter, no laughter. One almost expected to hear a collective snore. Annie brought Emily a homemade lemonade, tall and cold, perfect for the late afternoon. Emily opened her bestseller to page one for the third time that day.

No matter how hard she tried, though, she could not focus on the book and she found herself looking toward the empty bay beach. As she sat, she was rewarded with the passing of a large catamaran, majestic in its dominance of the water and powerful in its use of the wind. There appeared to be people on deck, probably heading out for one of those sunset sails. An occasional figure, silent and slow, would also periodically walk by. The beach was certainly lovely at this time of day. The sun had lost its intense heat, and royal terns and laughing gulls swooped and perched on the shore.

At one point, Emily thought she saw a familiar figure walking along the shore. Judging by the bent shoulders and pensive demeanor it looked like Jessica. It was hard to imagine how she must feel now after enduring one more scene, once again being the object of Roger's rage. Soon Emily's thoughts were interrupted as Sarah entered the patio.

'You must be the only person still awake here. It's like a ghost town. The beach – and the beach bar – must have been mighty busy this afternoon.'

'They certainly were,' Emily laughed, not wanting to tell Sarah about the scene with Roger. 'I'm just waiting for a call from Michael in London; otherwise, I'd be napping like the rest of them.'

'Have you seen Jon?' Sarah asked. 'He came over earlier, said he wanted to take a swim but there had been two more cancelled reservations for tonight and, well, he just needed a break. I think he really wanted to talk to my father. He loves talking to him about the restaurant and the island – they share so much. Anyway, he hadn't gotten back to Blue Water by the time I left town.'

'I haven't seen him in a while. But I'm almost sure I saw him earlier – in the crowd at the beach bar, I think. Maybe you two crossed paths. Your mother's in the office; maybe she's seen him.'

'Thanks, Emily, I'll check with her. Good luck with your call.'

Not five minutes later, Emily's call came through and she practically flew inside to the phone. 'Hi, hon, how are you? Packing, I hope!'

'Oh, Em. I don't even know how to tell you this. Things are a mess here. The whole deal has fallen through and Harris is on his way over from New York. I'm just trying my best to keep these guys from leaving the negotiating table. There's no way I can leave, Em.'

For a moment, Emily could say nothing, disappointment strangling her words and tears starting to seep from her eyes.

'Michael, you can't mean this. Please. Our whole vacation will be ruined,' she said, anger starting to replace disappointment. 'And what am I supposed to do here? It's all couples and . . . Oh, never mind. Just when do you think this will get settled?'

Michael's voice sounded tired and strained as he responded. 'I can't even tell you, Em. I don't know what to say. Do you want to fly back to New York? Maybe we can get something back on this trip and plan a new one.'

'That would be even worse, coming back to the cold and the snow and the disappointment. And you would still be in London. I couldn't stand it. No, I'll wait it out here.'

'Maybe with Harris coming over we can salvage something,' Michael said. 'There really are only a couple of sticking points,

but things were so botched up by Bixley that these people can't
seem to get beyond it. I've tried to move them along but nothing.
Harris has worked with them for years, though; he should be
able to get things on track. I certainly hope he realizes how hard
I've worked at this. It's an important deal and I don't want to
be seen as the one who screwed it up. You won't believe what
Bixley said, he . . .' As Michael went on Emily tried to stay
focused on what he was saying but found she couldn't. She
didn't really care about Bixley or Harris or the important deal.

'Well, I guess I'll just have to hope for the best, Michael.
There's nothing else I can do. I know it's not your fault; sorry
if I sounded angry. I'm just so damned disappointed. And I
really miss you.'

'I know, Em. I'm disappointed too, and you can't imagine
how much I'm missing you. London's cold and rainy; I haven't
had a decent meal since I got here, and I have to spend all
my time trying to sweet talk these people.'

'This place is beautiful, Michael. You'll just love it when
you get here.' Emily tried to stay positive, not allowing herself
the thought that Michael might not make it at all.

'I know I will, but I'd better get going. I have to meet these
guys for dinner. And I told Bixley not to even bother coming.
I'm better off handling this myself. He'll only say something
to set these guys off. If I can just keep them talking . . . And
Harris will see. He'll realize that . . . Listen, I'll call you in
the morning. Oh, no, I guess it will be afternoon – here, I
mean. Morning there. Maybe I'll even know something by
then. Harris is supposed to be joining the meeting by ten so
maybe I'll have good news. OK? 'Night, Em. Love you.'

'Goodnight, Michael. I . . .' But the phone had already gone
dead. Emily couldn't help the tears that streamed down her
face as she hung up, and it didn't take Annie a minute to
realize what had happened.

'No good, huh?' she said sympathetically.

'Nope. Things are a mess there. One of the partners is
heading over from New York. Maybe that will help. But right
now things don't look good at all.'

'Oh, Emily, you must be so disappointed. I'm sorry. Is there
anything I can do?'

'Nothing, really, Annie. You've been so kind already. And Martin. I don't know what I would have done if I'd been someplace else. No wonder everyone comes back here all the time. It's like a family – a strange family, but . . .'

'How about a walk?' Annie asked, chuckling. 'I have to check around to see if I can find Martin. We just got a call from New York about an order he placed when he was up there. There are some problems with it and they're going to call back in fifteen minutes.'

'What the heck, I might as well. I don't think I'd be able to sleep right now anyway, I'm too keyed up. By the way, did you see Sarah? She was looking for you.'

'I did. She was looking for Jon. I told her I saw him earlier. He came over for a swim and I saw him head down to the beach. But once the stuff with Roger started, I didn't see him again. He must have headed back and she just missed him.'

'I love the beach at this time of day,' Emily said as they walked down to the bay. 'So quiet and peaceful. You must love the peace too, Annie. You certainly don't get much of it.'

'That's true, but Martin and I really love what we do here. We enjoy the socializing and the people. It really is like you said . . . like a family. And, yes, some days it's a very strange family. I can't imagine what Martin is doing. Of course, he's always checking up on the place – the first sign of peeling paint, a sign that's crooked, even the shapes of the bushes – nothing escapes his eye. I think I'll take a look over by the tennis courts; I remember him saying something about cracks on court one. Or maybe I should head over to the ocean beach.'

'Why don't I take a look over that way? I'm going to head back to my room anyway. As nice as this beach is, I just can't shake my mood. Maybe I should try taking that nap again. God knows, I was tired enough before. Did I tell you that Nick Marino ended up teaching me how to windsurf? Hendrick was already teaching someone else and Nick really seemed to want to step in. It was a lot of fun. Nick was a great teacher and he seemed, well, different. But afterward he mentioned that he'd asked Martin to seat him with me at dinner. I know you have enough to do, Annie, but I don't really feel up to . . .'

'Oh, don't worry, Emily. We'll all be seated together.'

'With Roger and Jessica too?'

'No, I don't think we'll risk that tonight. I feel bad for Jessica, but we'll just have to find somewhere else for them to sit. Let me think . . . who's being really annoying this week?'

'I feel bad for Jessica too, but after that scene with Roger this afternoon . . .'

'I know. I know. But I'll tell you, Emily, I don't think people are going to be willing to take Roger's crap much longer. Soon they're going to start giving some of it back to him.'

'You may be right. It certainly seems like Jon's had it, and Marietta. It sounds as though Nick is satisfied being the only one willing to poke fun at Roger. I really think I'd better go take that nap. It looks like I might need it for later.'

'That's probably a good idea. And don't forget, if you do see Martin, tell him to hurry back to the office.'

Emily again took the ocean path; she loved the view of the waves. She was struck by the quiet which surrounded her. No one else was on the path. Even the waves seemed subdued. Just like last night, the whole mood seemed to have changed. It no longer seemed quietly peaceful, but somehow eerie. From the highest point on the cliff, she could catch a glimpse of Cliff House. Martin and Annie had certainly made a wonderful home, quiet and serene here by itself. As she continued walking down the hilly path on the ocean side of the point, the more desolate it seemed. The executive suites here were so quiet they almost seemed vacant – drapes drawn across the windows, no movement on the balconies.

Clouds blocked the sun and muted the usually bright blues of sky and water. The cooling breezes were stilled. The leaves on the palm trees barely moved and their gentle swish was lulled. The terns and gulls no longer flew overhead but perched silently on the pilings. The air seemed heavy, not just with moisture but with melancholy.

The whole stretch of ocean beach was empty except for one distant figure slumped in a chair on the beach in front of the rondovals. At first, Emily didn't realize who it was. Soon, though, she could make out the rumpled suit and telltale red face. Oh, God, she thought, not Roger. He's the last person I want to run into. She considered turning around but knew she couldn't. It would look awkward and rude. There was nothing else to do. She had to walk right past him to reach her hut, so she raised her hand in a half wave.

But Roger didn't respond. At first, as she approached, Emily thought he might be sleeping. But, on second glance, she noticed the drink sitting at his feet and the angle of his head. She knew then that he had passed out.

Hardly surprising, she thought. I hope he gets a good burn. It would serve him right. Emily, like the others, had had it with Roger's nastiness.

But even as she thought those words, she knew she couldn't walk by and leave him there. He could get serious burns on this beach. Even though clouds covered the sun right now, in two minutes it would be out again. And God knows how long he'd been sitting there. From the looks of him, it could have been ever since he left the beach bar.

Emily veered off the path and headed across the sand, hoping to make this as quick as possible. As she walked, she felt as if someone was watching her. She turned her head several times to check behind her. Maybe someone was looking out one of the windows or sitting on a balcony, but she saw no one.

Other than her and Roger, the beach was completely empty. Or was it? Up ahead, up there beyond the rondovals at the edge of the Bluff's property where the shoreline curved – wasn't there someone standing by one of the trees in the small grove, right by the bend? Emily peered into the distance, forcing her eyes to focus, but it was hopeless. There was no one there. This is crazy, she thought. What was wrong with her? She wasn't the type to be easily spooked but something certainly had gotten to her.

Increasingly anxious, Emily called out to Roger, hoping to rouse him, but to no avail. He must really be out of it, she thought. But as she approached the horrific truth became obvious.

Roger was slumped over, his head lying at a crooked angle on his chest. His mouth hung open, slack and misshapen, and his tongue protruded grotesquely between his teeth. His arms dangled ponderously at his sides and his fingers practically touched the pool of blood spreading across the sand.

Emily, unable for a moment to comprehend what she was seeing, reached out her hand as if to shake him. Oh my God, she thought, pulling her hand back in horror . . . this can't be. I thought he was just sleeping . . . Oh, God . . . Help. I have to get help.

Emily could feel the hysteria rising as she looked around. There was no one. She would have to leave him; she had to get help. Turning, she started to run back toward the point. It was then that she saw someone coming from the garden path behind her.

'Martin!' she shrieked. 'Martin, help me. Martin, oh God, I need help . . . He's dead, Martin . . . Roger's dead.'

TEN

It took only moments for a crowd to assemble. Expressions of shock and dismay echoed up and down the beach as word of what had happened spread. Martin, visibly shaken, tried to take charge of the situation, but was surprisingly ineffective in this moment of crisis. He seemed paralyzed by the sight of Roger slumped dead in his chair. And although he kept looking anxiously at the gathering crowd, he said nothing, unable to focus on anything but the sight before him.

Emily, too, was immobilized by what she had discovered. Her heartbeat was rapid, her breathing irregular, and it took several minutes before she even recognized any of the faces in the crowd. Marietta was there, pale and anxious, trying to calm a distraught Nora. Sarah, her face drawn and distressed, was trying to talk to her father, and Nelson, Martin's right-hand man, his long, muscular arms spread out protectively, was trying to move the onlookers back.

It was actually Annie who was able to put some order into the mounting chaos.

'Please, everyone, please stand back!' she cried, her voice strained but obviously in control. 'Nelson, please get the men to bring those portable screens from the dining room. And see if anyone has called the police. Better yet, Martin, maybe you should head back to the office and call them.'

At first, Martin didn't even respond to her suggestion, but when she repeated it he seemed to snap out of his dazed absorption. 'You're right, of course, the police. I must call the police. Everyone, please do as Annie asks. I know how upset you all are but please, stand back.'

Before he could say another word, a disheveled figure could be seen running across the beach toward them.

'Martin . . . Martin!' Jessica screamed as the crowd parted to let her through. 'Is it true? Someone said . . . Oh my God. Oh my God.'

Immediately Jessica turned away, stunned by what she was seeing. Martin grasped her shoulders, trying to support her, but Jessica practically pushed him away and with an ashen face and anguished 'Nooo . . .' abruptly turned and ran from the scene.

Emily, starting to regain her equilibrium, quickly offered to help.

'Should I go after her, Annie? Someone should be with her.'

'If you could, Emily, that would be a big help. Bring her up to Cliff House; she'll at least have some privacy there. Meanwhile, I'll try to manage things here. Oh, thank God, here come the screens.'

As Emily left the beach she was struck by the bizarre scene unfolding there. Resort guests, many dressed in plush pastel-colored, terrycloth robes, milled about as white latticed screens, some still covered in vines and flowers, were placed around the gruesome remains of Roger Stirhew. Annie, composed as always, tried to answer questions and calm the fears of those in the crowd while Nelson directed the workers. Those who knew Roger well clustered together nearby. Anyone walking by would have thought that this was the set-up for some weird beach party, not the trappings of a grisly crime scene.

It took Emily a little while to find Jessica. She sat slumped on a solitary bench behind the tennis courts near the bay beach.

Her eyes were vacant and her hands searched relentlessly in the pockets of her shorts.

'Jessica,' she called softly. 'Jessica, I'm so sorry.'

But Jessica didn't even look at her. 'I can't find my matches. I looked in my pockets. I can't find them,' she said, her voice flat, its cadence staccato-like. 'What'll I do? I can't find my matches,' she said again, looking at the unlit cigarette in her hand.

Emily wasn't sure if Jessica even realized she was there, but she quickly looked around and found Jessica's things scattered on the ground. Reaching down she picked up the cigarette pack and matches, some loose change and an old key.

'Here, let me light that for you,' she said, reaching out with the match and then absently slipping them into her pocket. 'I'm so sorry, Jessica. I don't really know what else to say.'

Jessica seemed to become more aware as she took several deep drags on her cigarette. 'Oh, God, Emily, the scary thing is I don't either. My husband is dead and I don't know what to say . . . I don't even know what to feel. Things had gotten so bad between us. The drinking, the nastiness, the blows. There were times recently when I hated him. I . . . what should . . . how did this happen? All these years . . . Emily . . . what . . .' And then she started to sob.

Emily just held her, as there was nothing else to do. No words were going to make a difference at that point. And then, when Jessica seemed a little calmer, she tried to get her up to the house.

'Annie said we should head up to her house, Jessica. It will be quiet there and you can rest.'

Jessica didn't resist at all. She seemed almost unaware of what Emily had just said and merely nodded as Emily coaxed her off the bench. But as they headed up the rambling path, she started to talk.

'It's funny, Emily – I barely know you, and yet I feel like we're friends. I trust you more than most people here – except the Maitlands, of course.' She paused, as if hesitating or deliberating over her next words. 'You know, I was just seventeen when I first met Roger – seventeen and in trouble. I'd run away from an abusive, alcoholic father and a mother who cared but was sort of, I don't know, helpless. I'd worn out my welcome at the homes of friends and I was down to my last twenty bucks. So I hitched a ride to Atlantic City and tried to get a waitressing job at one of the casinos. Oh, I was smart enough and people said I was pretty, in a tough sort of way. Made up, I looked older than seventeen, so I thought some place would hire me. But by the end of my second day I was beginning to give up. I was sitting on the boardwalk and, finally, just started to cry when I felt a pat on my shoulder. And this middle-aged guy says, "Can I help?" I'd always had a pretty smart mouth so I just looked at him and said, "Not unless you're in the market for an inexperienced, underage waitress who can't even afford a room in a fleabag hotel or a decent meal." I was too tired and disheartened to even hide my desperation.

'He was actually kind, Emily. "You're too young and too pretty to be so discouraged," he'd said, and then smiled. "A waitress? Hmm . . . I may be able to help. Here, take my card. Go see Tommy Leone over at the Sandpiper, tell him Roger sent you. I'm sure he'll be able to find a spot for you."

'At first I was amazed, but then the cynicism born of a hundred beatings kicked in. "Wait a minute," I said to him. "What's the catch? I may be hard up, but I'm not so desperate that I'm willing to pay your price."

'He said something about someone so hard boiled having such a sweet exterior. And then, "There's no price . . . but suit yourself. You have my card – use it if you like, and perhaps I'll see you next time I'm in town."

'I had no choice. If his card could get me a job, I'd use it. But, you know, Emily, I never did understand that whole thing. Roger's kindness that day, wanting nothing in return.

'It was almost a year before I saw him again. By then I was settled and safe, making pretty decent money and even better tips. I was waitressing in the lounge of the Sandpiper, and I'll tell you, I was a lot nicer when he showed up at the bar one quiet Tuesday night. I even apologized to him, but he just waved it aside and said he was happy I was doing OK.'

All the way up the steep hill, Jessica talked and Emily listened. She barely even paused when they got to the house.

She was living in the past. Gone was the polish of recent years. Jessica had become the scared teenager that she had been when she first met Roger. The change was striking. She sat hunched on the living-room couch, her eyes downcast one minute then darting back and forth. Her words were hesitant and her voice trembled.

'He wanted me to have a drink with him but I told him that Tommy, the bartender, was my boyfriend, and he didn't like me drinking with the customers. But he just said, "Don't worry about Tommy. He won't mind. He's got a vested interest in keeping me happy."

'I didn't know what he meant, but I knew I owed him a lot more than a few minutes at the bar and I had learned to be a lot less proud in the past few months. The last thing I needed was trouble on the job. So we had a drink.'

'It was really surprising, Emily. He was friendly and interesting to talk to. I didn't learn too much about him, but he obviously had some bucks and at least he didn't proposition me like most of the other jerks I met there.

'He was right, too. Tommy didn't mind my spending the time with Roger, even though he usually kept a close watch whenever I even looked at another guy. At first, I figured he thought Roger was just too old to be much competition.' Jessica paused for a moment, rubbing her eyes and brushing her hair back from her face.

'Over the next year it would just sort of go like that. He'd show up, usually on slow nights, sometimes for just a few minutes but sometimes for a couple of hours or more. Once or twice he'd had a few too many, but I still didn't mind being with him. I'd listen to him talk about his life, his job, his divorce. He seemed kind of like a father, you know?

'Then, one Thursday night, things changed. Roger stopped by for a few minutes but only to ask me to have dinner with him on the Saturday night. Right away, I hesitated. I could tell this would be different. I tried to think of a nice way to refuse. By this time I was really crazy about Tommy and we were spending more and more time together.'

Jessica's voice reflected the depth of her emotions: soft one moment, wry the next. Even her way of speaking changed. Gone was the polished, clipped Connecticut accent. 'Shows ya how little I knew. When I told Tommy about it, I was sure he would say no way, but he didn't. "What, are you crazy, Jessica? Roger Stirhew is a very big guy in the bar world. He knows a lot of people, people who could be real helpful – to both of us."

'I stupidly said, "But what about us, Tommy? What about our relationship?"

'And he just put his arm around me and said, "Oh, baby, this has nothing to do with us. You know that. You're just gonna have dinner with the guy; you're not gonna sleep with him. You're just gonna spend some time with him. Let's just take this nice'n slow. OK? Let's see where it goes."

'And that was it. I started seeing Roger and everything seemed OK for a while, but then Roger started to change. He became more demanding, wanting me to spend more time with him, wanting to know about my friends and always asking about Tommy. When I'd balk he'd become distant and sullen, and I started to get real uncomfortable with what was happening.

'But Tommy was still perfectly OK with it all. We still spent a lot of time together and sometimes . . .' Jessica laughed softly at the memory, '. . . Tommy would be practically walking out of the apartment as Roger was walking in. And whenever I'd tell Tommy how uncomfortable this was making me feel, he'd brush it aside.

'"Hey, look," he'd say. "The guy's lonely and you spend a little time with him. He doesn't give ya a hard time, takes ya great places and never puts a hand on ya. What's the big deal?"

'But then I realized I was pregnant with Tommy's child.' Once again, Jessica paused and tears started to run down her cheeks.

'Oh, I knew at first that Tommy would be unhappy, but I was actually relieved. This would put an end to the problem of Roger, I thought. Tommy and I would settle down and get married. I'd have to find a different job; I wouldn't be able to stay on at the lounge and we could never live off Tommy's salary. But that was OK. I'd never minded hard work, and now I really had something to work for – the baby.

'But boy, was I stupid . . . Tommy was more than unhappy when I told him. He wanted nothing to do with any baby and he made no bones about it. "It's me or the baby, that's it. Either get rid of it or I'm outta here," he said. "Simple as that."

'Then the penny dropped. It wasn't that he saw Roger as competition – he just didn't care. I had been a fool, not for the first time in my life, but I was determined, for the last.

'"Get out, Tommy," I told him. "And don't bother makin' any threats. I should have realized you wouldn't want the kid. Well, guess what? I wouldn't get rid of this baby for you or anybody else. This baby is mine – for once in my life, something that's all mine. And don't worry, I won't ask for anything from you. As a matter of fact, I don't want you to have anything to do with us. This baby isn't going to spend his life surrounded by losers like I did."

'For a few hours I felt really good, until the fear and confusion set in. I had nowhere to turn. No close friends. I'd kept in touch with my mother but, if anything, things had gotten worse at home. My father's drinking bouts had gotten more frequent and his fuse had gotten shorter. There was no way I'd expose my baby to that. Oh, God, what could I do?'

Emily could actually feel the fear that Jessica was describing: stomach wrenching, nauseating fear.

'And then Roger called. I knew I could ask him for help. A new job; perhaps he'd loan me some money. Just to get by till the baby was born. And afterwards I could find day care, whatever.

'Roger was more than willing to help . . . but this time there *was* a price. Marriage. Roger wanted to marry me and Emily, I swear, to this day I still don't know why. Maybe he wanted his own family to show off. For Roger, the baby was a big deal. His first wife had never gotten pregnant and they'd never found out why. He thought he'd like to have a child, someone to raise and groom; someone to carry on his name. Of course, he insisted that everyone believe that Jason was his. We'd been seen out together for over a year, but Roger obviously moved in completely different circles to Tommy – no one I met through Roger knew I already had a boyfriend. He thought everyone would be impressed at his standing by me – you know, doing the right thing.

'But I didn't have much choice. Roger was the only one

who could help me and if the price was marriage then that was it. Funny, I didn't even mind really. Roger seemed kind enough, although there had been moments . . . But I quickly pushed those out of my mind. The baby was the most important thing and Roger would be able to give him the best in life.

'From the beginning, Roger was obsessed with how Jason would be raised, talking about buying a new house in just the right community and making the right contacts. Appearances were everything. And it wasn't long before Roger was demanding that I change mine. Tone down my hair color, go natural, wear less make-up, lengthen my skirts and loosen my pants. Oh, I guess I shouldn't complain – he had great taste. It was his intensity that was sometimes frightening, and the occasional cruelty. That first year after Jason was born, if he thought I was wearing too much lipstick or eye make-up, he wouldn't say anything, just walk up to me and smear it over my face. Or if my skirt was too tight, he would rip it, almost tearing it off me. Sometimes he'd ridicule the way I spoke or the words I used. It was as if I didn't matter anymore. Maybe I never did. I existed only as Jason's mother and I was required to be the mother that Roger wanted. I rarely challenged him and when I did he was quick to imply that Jason would be the one to suffer.

'I remember he once said to me, "You're no longer a cheap waitress in Atlantic City, my dear. Children in Westport don't have mothers who dress like sluts."'

She paused for a moment and looked at Emily. 'I know it seems hard to imagine, but there were lots of things I loved about my new life. After all, I'd never known that kind of financial security. And when I was unsure of something, there were a slew of people to help me out – the English nanny for Jason, a decorator for the Westport house, a personal shopper at Bloomingdale's and Neiman's, a trainer at the gym and a tennis instructor at the club. I had it all.

'I was lonely, though, Emily. I pretty much kept to myself. It was self-protection mostly, coming more from insecurity than anything else. And Roger's drinking was increasing. By this time there was little to our relationship except my required presence at business events. So I decided it was time to do something for me. I had always been a smart kid and I loved school when I wasn't hungry or tired, so I decided to enroll on a college course. At first I kept it a secret from Roger, afraid of what he'd say, but when I told him he was OK about it. I think he sensed my increasing restlessness and knew I'd only get more and more unhappy if I didn't do something. And even though I don't think he felt any obligation to make me happy, he didn't dare risk my becoming too unhappy. You see, there was Jason to consider. I was just a convenient addition, but Jason was his life. If I'd left with him . . . Oh, God, Emily, why is life always so difficult? So you see, I can't say that I ever really loved Roger, but he meant the world to Jason. This is too horrible. Who could have done this?'

'I don't know, Jessica. The beach was empty when I found him.'

'You found him?'

'Yes, it was awful. I was just walking back from the main house. I'd gone there to call Michael. By the time I'd finished talking the beach was empty and I was heading back to my room for a nap. I was kind of surprised to see Roger out there in the sun but then I thought he had passed out. You know . . .'

'Oh, I know. He had a lot to drink at the beach bar this afternoon. I tried to dissuade him. I'm sure you know what happened.'

'Yes; I heard it. I was lying in the hammock and heard the yelling. I saw Roger storm off.'

'After he left the bar, I went for a long walk on the beach and then headed back to the room. I actually saw Roger sitting out there in the sun. I even tried to wave to him. Sometimes he cools down pretty quickly after one of these outbursts, but not this time. I could see he was still drinking so I just went in to lie down. I was by myself.'

Emily thought it was best for Jessica to keep talking, so she listened quietly.

'It was the commotion on the beach that woke me up. At first I couldn't figure out what had happened. I thought maybe there had been an accident. But then I heard someone saying something about someone being dead and then Roger's name.

I ran as quickly as I could. I don't know why. I guess it didn't matter at that point. You just sort of think you can do something. Change things. Bring something back. I don't know.'

For a few moments Jessica just stared, her eyes vacant, her lips silently trembling.

'Isn't life strange,' she mused as if to herself. 'I remember when I was young and poor, trying to fend off an abusive father who couldn't get his head out of a bottle. I used to dream of being rich, of having all the clothes and things I wanted, taking trips, going out to fancy restaurants. I thought that if I had all those things I'd be the happiest person in the world. And then I had them and I was no happier. And I was still fending off an abusive alcoholic.'

Suddenly she looked intensely at Emily. 'Oh, I shouldn't say I was no happier. Given the choice between rich and poor I'd choose rich any day. And of course there's Jason; nothing's more important than him. Oh, God! Jason. How will I tell him this? He loved his father, you know, and I never heard Roger say a harsh word to him. No matter how nasty Roger was to me, he adored Jason. What should I do, Emily?' Jessica asked sadly. 'How will I tell Jason? Maybe I should head back home? Yes, that would be . . .'

'You need some time to think, Jessica,' Emily said, realizing for the first time that Jessica would not be free to return to Connecticut. With the circumstances surrounding Roger's death obviously criminal, there'd be a lot of questions needing answers before anyone would be going anywhere. 'Talk to Annie and Martin. Think about what might be best. You have time to decide all those things.'

Jessica stopped talking and retreated inward, her eyes once again taking on that vacant stare. Emily guided her, as she would a child, upstairs to lie down. Although the temperature was still in the seventies, Jessica immediately wrapped herself in a light cotton blanket that lay at the end of the bed. Not much of a shield, Emily thought. Oh, Jessica, I'm afraid that by the end of this, you'll need something a lot stronger than that.

ELEVEN

Cliff House, Martin and Annie's home, sat high on the bluff with commanding views of both the ocean and bay beaches. As soon as Jessica was settled, Emily hurried out to the veranda to see what was happening on the beaches below. To her it seemed like only seconds had passed but she soon realized how wrong she was. Dusk was already gathering and the ocean beach was swarming with police. Revolving red and blue lights were intersected by the piercing white flashes of a detective's camera. The screens had been partly removed and Roger's body was once again visible as the police examined the murder scene. Not surprisingly, there were still a number of hotel guests milling about. At first, she couldn't see Annie or Martin, but then she was able to pick them out, off to the side talking with the man who seemed to be in charge.

She had been watching for only a few minutes when she saw an ambulance move up along the sand and park next to Roger's body. The medical examiner had obviously completed his examination and they were removing the body to the morgue in Oranjestad. Emily shivered as she watched. Her job had exposed her to some pretty unpleasant sights, but body bags had not been one of them. Somehow it seemed almost disrespectful to watch and Emily turned her eyes away until it was done. As the ambulance drove off, Annie and Martin, arm in arm with their heads bowed, began walking toward the house, followed by a contingent of police.

Emily knew the police would want to talk to her fairly soon and she was anxious to get it over with. Recounting the story of discovering Roger's body would not be pleasant and she imagined that the questioning would be pretty thorough. From what she had heard, there was little crime on the island, particularly major crimes like murder. She was sure the police investigation would be intense. Aruba's biggest industry was tourism and a murder didn't just kill the victim; it put trade at risk too.

'Oh, my dear, how are you?' Martin asked solicitously as they entered the open veranda. 'I'm afraid I wasn't a great deal of help out there. Such a shock, really. I was so stunned.'

'Thank God you came along when you did, Martin. You could see what kind of state I was in. Just your being there helped. I guess there wasn't much any of us could do. Not for Roger, anyway.'

'No, but I'm glad you were there for Jessica. Is she inside?' Annie asked.

'Sorry to interrupt, Annie, but is this Emily Harrington?' inquired a tall man in a dark suit standing directly behind Annie.

'Oh, sorry, Thomas. Yes, this is Emily,' Annie answered. 'Emily, this is Inspector Moller from the Aruba police. He's heading up the investigation.'

'Nice to meet you.' Emily realized that her words sounded pretty foolish under the circumstances but didn't know what else to say.

'Martin, where will we be working from?' Inspector Moller asked.

'I think it would be best if you worked out of our house here rather than the main house. This is all so disturbing. I'd like to try to keep some distance between the guests and the investigation, if we can. There's a large study on this floor. It has a desk and a small conference table. We often use it for meetings. There's also a phone and fax in there, so you should have most of what you need.'

'That sounds fine, Martin, but I must caution you. From my preliminary investigation it would seem that a number of your guests have information that's pertinent and I'll have to pursue that. I'll try my best to be discreet. But you know how these things are. People talk. There's always a weird fascination with something like this. Hopefully we can keep the press out of it . . . for a little while, anyway.'

'Of course, of course, Thomas. I know you'll do your best,' Martin answered, his brow furrowed. 'And I also know it's only your desire to be polite that keeps you from mentioning that we're all suspects until this is solved. Now let me show you to the study.'

'If you give me a few minutes to get set up then Ms Harrington, I'd like to speak with you first,' Inspector Moller said, turning back to Emily as Martin showed him out of the room.

'Come, Emily,' Annie said. 'Let's see how Jessica's doing, and you look like you could use something to calm your nerves.'

'You're not kidding, Annie. Seeing Inspector Moller makes this all too real. My God, a murder investigation! It's hard to believe.'

'It certainly is. Roger's death, all of us as suspects, the effect on the Bluffs . . . Isn't it ironic that Roger's death could actually make his threat a reality. You know his last words to Martin this afternoon were "You'll pay for this." I'm sure he never imagined how, but this murder could certainly hurt this place way more than any of Roger's catty reviews. My God, Emily, who could have done this?' she said, rubbing her hands back and forth over her eyes before continuing. 'I mean, I know there are enough people here who were angry with Roger. Strange, after our chat before . . . but angry enough to . . . I wonder how much anger one needs to do that? What finally makes us lose all control, and then . . . Oh, I just can't start thinking like this. Somehow, we'll get through it. Let me get you some brandy, Emily. I'll have a glass too.'

Time was beginning to have less and less meaning for Emily. It seemed like hours had passed since she had spoken to Michael, and she was amazed when Annie mentioned that it was only six o'clock. The brandy helped to calm her nerves but a mind-numbing fatigue was starting to set in. She and Annie went upstairs to check on Jessica and, although she wasn't asleep, she didn't seem to be awake either. Still in a trancelike state, she lay on the bed in the guest room and stared with vacant eyes at the slowly rotating ceiling fan.

'Jessica,' Annie asked, 'can I get you anything? Something to eat, a drink? Emily's with me. We thought you could use some company.'

Jessica turned her head but it was hard to tell if she'd heard what Annie had said. There was no response; she just stared quietly for a moment and then shut her eyes. Although they stayed for a few minutes, she didn't open them again.

'We'll head back downstairs, Jessica,' Annie said, smoothing the cotton blanket around her. 'I'll stop by again in a little while, and Martin called Doctor Biemans. He said he'd come over; he should be here shortly. Try to get some sleep. You must be totally drained.'

By the time Emily and Annie got back downstairs, Inspector Moller was waiting for Emily. Although she could understand why he wanted to talk to her first, she was dreading the interview. She was exhausted and was actually trying to block unwanted images of Roger from her mind. The thought of answering endless questions that would dredge up every nuance of the afternoon was overwhelming. But she knew she had no choice.

As she entered the study, Moller stood. 'Ms Harrington, please sit,' he said, his voice kind and his manner solicitous. 'You must be drained by all of this. I'll try not to take too long but . . .'

'I understand,' Emily responded quickly. 'And please, call me Emily.'

'Emily, then . . . Let me take a minute to review what we know.' As Moller went over a brief timeline of what had happened, Emily watched him. He was tall – taller than Michael – and trim. Like many of the people on the island, he was tan and muscular, a sailor perhaps in his spare time. He was attractive – in his mid-thirties, Emily thought. His eyes were a startling blue when he stared at her, and his sandy hair was cut short with an unruly part on one side.

'Now, Ms . . .'

'Emily, please.'

'Yes, Emily, perhaps you could tell me what you saw. Try to be as complete as you can. Even small details could be important.'

As Emily recounted the events of the afternoon, Moller listened intently. Emily could see he was a skilled investigator, detailed and precise, first taking Emily through the occurrences step by step and then asking random, seemingly unrelated questions. When Emily became confused or upset he was patient and reassuring, but persistent in digging for details. He seemed particularly interested in whether Emily had seen anyone else on her way to her rondoval. At first she had answered no but, with his probing, she remembered her feelings of discomfort on the path, and then even more so as she crossed the beach to Roger.

'Look, I know it sounds ridiculous,' she said with a self-dismissive wave of her hand. 'But I could have sworn someone was watching me. I looked around a couple of times but I didn't see anyone.'

'Did you notice if anyone might have been looking out one of the windows?' he asked.

'I think I looked up at the windows; I'm almost sure I did. You know, I just couldn't shake that feeling, so I checked. As far as I could tell, there was no one there.'

'So you saw no one in the vicinity, not near the ocean path or at a window, or behind you, back by the point?' he persisted.

'Wait a minute,' Emily said, suddenly remembering. 'How stupid of me. I'm not sure, but at one point I did think I saw someone – not on the path but off in the distance. Down there at the end of the Bluffs' property where the shoreline curves, standing by a tree there. When I looked a second time the image was gone. Or maybe it was never really there – at least that's what I thought then. I was beginning to think I was seeing things, but now I'm not so sure.'

'There's not much light left, but I'd like for the two of us to take a walk down the ocean path. I want you to point out exactly where it was you thought you saw someone and where you were standing. Then we can try to figure out exactly what you saw. I know this is difficult Ms . . . Emily, but I'm sure you realize now just how important this could be.'

'I do. I just hope I'm not leading you on a wild goose chase. It may have been no one at all. And even if it was, I can't remember anything about them.'

'Don't even try to do that at this point. We can try to help you recall whatever impressions you might have. Let's just go take a look first,' Inspector Moller said as he ushered Emily out of the room.

'Martin, Emily and I are going to take a walk out on the

ocean path to see if she can refresh her memory about some details. We should be back shortly, and then I think Emily could use a break. We have a pretty extensive search going on out there. I'm hoping we'll find something that will give us an idea who did this. I've asked my men to be as discreet as possible.'

'Have you figured out what the murder weapon was, Thomas?' Martin asked, a look of distaste coming over his face.

'A small-caliber handgun. We're almost positive it was a .22. The wound was small, but certainly fatal. Shot in the heart from close range, too. Whoever did this wanted Roger to know just what was happening, I think.' Thomas paused, momentarily distracted by his own thoughts, before continuing, 'We've drawn up a preliminary list of people who we'd like to interview this evening. Could you arrange to have them available? And any chance you'd have another room we could use, Martin? A small one would be fine, so we can do more than one interview at a time. It would just make things go faster.'

'Certainly. We have a small den down this hall – you can use that. It's actually right near the study so it should work out well,' Martin offered.

'Oh, and how is Mrs Stirhew doing?' Inspector Moller asked.

'She's been sedated. Doctor Biemans came out from the hospital. He just gave her something mild to help her rest.'

'I'd like to be able to talk to her, just for a few minutes. I know how upset she must be, but . . . Let me know as soon as she wakes up. I really need to see her.'

As Emily and Inspector Moller walked along the path that stretched from Cliff House to the main house, it was obvious that although things had quieted down it was far from a normal evening at the Bluffs. It was dusk, a time when most guests would be in their rooms just starting to get ready for dinner, but the restaurant terraces were actually crowded. No one was dressed for dinner, and it looked as if many of the guests had just headed over there after the excitement on the beach. Emily could see Nelson, obviously covering for Annie and Martin, moving among the guests still trying to settle everyone down. As they approached the main house, Inspector Moller stopped her.

'Where exactly did you start from, Emily?' he asked. 'Was it the main house?'

'Yes, it was there on the patio just off Reception. I had just spoken to my fiancé on the phone and—'

'Where did you say your fiancé was?'

'London. He had to go there on business,' Emily started to explain. 'And then the deal got screwed up. He was supposed to meet me here today.' Emily was startled to feel tears trickling down her face. 'I'm sorry,' she said quickly, wiping them away. 'But now he doesn't know when he'll get here. I wish he wasn't so far away.'

'So you're here by yourself then?' Inspector Moller continued, leading Emily toward the terraces. 'You took the call in the office?'

'Yes, Annie was there. And Penny. She had put the call through for me,' Emily answered, unsure why she felt the need to explain, and feeling increasingly uncomfortable as she and the inspector walked down the steps to one of the terraces.

Suddenly, all conversation stopped as everyone on the terrace turned to stare.

'OK, now, Emily,' Inspector Moller began, seemingly oblivious to the crowd. 'You finished your phone call and left the main house. Which way did you go? By the way, was there anyone else on the patio when you left?'

'No, as I said, it was very quiet. Everyone must have been napping. The only other person I saw was Sarah, but that was before my phone call came through. And I actually left the main house with Annie. I was going to go for a walk with her. She was looking for Martin to finish an order in the office. I went a little way with her, over by the bay beach. But I wasn't in any mood for a walk, so I headed back to my rondoval.' She pointed to the winding path. 'I followed the ocean path there, around the point, to where my rondoval is.'

'And when did you first see Roger?'

'I could see that there was someone on the beach as soon as I rounded the point. Right about here. I couldn't tell who it was, though; I was too far away.'

'And you didn't see anyone else on this path? So when did you sense that someone was watching you?'

'It wasn't until I was walking across the beach, in front of these.' She pointed to the buildings that housed the executive rooms and suites. White, two story with small, charming balconies. 'I looked up, thinking maybe there was someone sitting out on one of the balconies or looking out of one of the windows. I've noticed people sitting out on the balconies before. I remember thinking how beautiful the flowers were. That splash of color. And there's a beautiful breeze off the water. I'm sorry; I guess you're really not interested in the breezes. There was no one on any of the balconies.'

'Are you sure you checked the windows?'

'I looked, I'm almost sure I did, but they all seemed shuttered. Or most of them. Maybe one, toward the end, was slightly ajar.'

'OK, now, you're coming along this path. At what point did you realize that it was Roger down there?'

'Just moments after that. I guess it was right about here. It all happened so quickly it's really hard to say exactly when.'

'By the way,' Inspector Moller asked, 'where is your room, Emily?'

'Ours is the last rondoval, all the way at the end.'

'And the Stirhew's – theirs is right next to yours?'

'Theirs is actually two away.'

'And who's in between?'

'I don't really know them. I don't think Roger and Jessica did either. I just met them this afternoon. The Phillips. They're from Ohio; he's a doctor – an orthopedist, I think.'

'So you realize that it's Roger, then what?'

'Well, I wasn't too happy about seeing Roger. I don't know how much you've heard about him but he was pretty mean when he was drinking, and not much better when he wasn't, actually. He had been drinking this afternoon at the beach bar. There was a real scene there. He had a fight with Jessica, she was upset and wanted him to go back to their room, and then Martin tried to intervene. Roger was furious, started screaming at Martin and then just stormed off.'

'How long have Martin and Roger known each other?'

'Years, I think. That's what Annie said, anyway.' Emily suddenly realized that Inspector Moller was asking about a lot more than how Emily found the body. 'Anyway, I could see that it was Roger and, as I got closer, I could see that he was sort of slumped in his chair. At first I thought he was sleeping, then I figured he had passed out. I was tempted to just leave him there, but I couldn't. So I started to walk—'

'Wait now, Emily, was it at this point that you thought you saw someone up ahead?'

'Yes, right about now. I was looking up there where the beach takes a turn.' Emily pointed to the distant spot. 'It's impossible to see at all now – there's not enough light. But that must be the end of the Bluffs' property. There are trees and bushes there. And for a minute it looked like there was someone standing right next to the trunk of that middle tree. I'm kind of embarrassed to admit this, it's really not like me, but for some reason I was really spooked by then. I just wanted to wake Roger and get back to my rondoval. But, of course, you know that as soon as I got really close, I realized what . . . and I just started screaming for help. And then I saw Martin . . .'

'Coming from behind you?'

'Yes, coming from the garden path, over there, the one that leads to the rondovals here on the right and the suites that line the lower part of the bluff on the left.'

'OK, Emily, I think that's enough for now. I'd like to go over this again in the morning. Maybe we can walk out here again when it's light.'

'Sure, I'm pretty tired right now. I can't even think straight.'

Dusk had turned to darkness as Emily and Inspector Moller started back. The path was quiet and empty. Most of the rooms were darkened, their residents seeking the solace of company and cocktails on the terraces. Distracted and pensive, each mulled over their own thoughts. Emily's were confused and circuitous. They spoke little, stuck in their own heads, and Emily was relieved when the lights of Cliff House came into view.

TWELVE

The house was much busier when Emily and Inspector Moller got back to it. Lights blazed in every room downstairs, there was a police crew putting in some kind of phone line and half-a-dozen people were seated around the living room.

'Glad you're back, Thomas,' Martin said as they came in. 'There are some questions about how you want to do this. Most of the people on your list are here. Those staying at the Bluffs, anyway. We reached Sarah in town. She was going to pick up Jon. They should be here soon.'

'Thank you, Martin. I know how difficult this must be. I can see the resort is full. Who's taking care of the guests?'

'Nelson and Penny are both over there. You know, between the two of them, they can probably run the place as well as I can.'

'Well, maybe for a short while . . . I see my men are here.'

'Yes, they've been setting things up inside. I've ordered some food from the kitchen. Most of these folks haven't eaten anything and even though no one feels particularly hungry, I think it's best. What about your men, Thomas?'

'No, no, don't worry about us. It's a good idea for the others, though. Actually, I'd like to take a few minutes to meet with my men. Perhaps in the large study. Oh, and did Mrs Stirhew . . . what's her first name again . . . Jessica? Did she wake up?'

'A few minutes ago. She still seems pretty shaken, though. She's upstairs with Annie. We wanted to give her as much privacy as we could. Just let me know when you want to talk to her.'

'OK. Why don't you see to those people getting something to eat and by then we should be ready to start.'

There was a buffet set out in the dining room and Martin encouraged everyone to take a plate. Although they all protested at first, the smell of the food soon lured them. Emily took a small plate and, wanting to be alone, she headed out to the patio where she sat quietly in the shadows. But her privacy was short-lived as she saw Marietta and Nora heading for a small table nearby.

Marietta seemed to be holding up well but Nora still looked distraught; her face drawn and pale, her eyes red and swollen. Emily could sense Marietta's intensity as she overheard her speaking as they walked. 'We always knew someone could find out, Nora. It was a risk we were willing to take. I was lost before you came along. You know that, Nora. Parties every other night, "doing lunch" as they say, cocktails before dinner – they all added up to fodder for my column and disaster for my liver. I was headed down the same road as Roger if it hadn't been for you.'

'Oh, Marietta, I was nothing, you had everything,' Nora practically moaned. 'So witty and smart, entry into the best homes, invitations to the most elegant parties.'

'Nora, you know those invitations weren't for me, not really; they were for what I offered. If it weren't for my column I wouldn't get any of those fancy invitations, in spite of the St. John name. A poor relation, that's all I was. A poor relation whose father gambled away a fortune, the black sheep of a very white herd. All I had was my wit and my entrée. I knew I had to make them work for me. The society column was my answer.'

'And you've worked so hard at it all these years. And now this. We've been so careful, always playing our roles, watching our words, our every gesture . . .'

'I don't regret our relationship, not for a minute. And, don't you see, Nora? Now there's no reason why any of this should come out. Roger's gone . . .'

Emily could keep her presence secret no longer and she coughed loudly as they came closer. 'Marietta, Nora, I guess you two had the same idea. It's so busy inside, I needed a little peace and quiet.'

Although Marietta looked disconcerted for a moment, she was gracious as always. 'Of course, Emily, you must be incredibly drained. Nora and I were just saying how shocking this whole thing is.'

But none of them actually talked about the afternoon's events, although there was little else on their minds. Emily recounted her phone conversation with Michael, just to distract them really, and Marietta was appropriately, if perfunctorily, sympathetic. After only a few minutes, Annie joined them.

'Nora, Inspector Moller wondered if he might talk with you now. And Marietta, Officer Vogt is waiting for you in the small study,' she said, trying to make the summons seem more like an invitation.

Both Nora and Marietta visibly paled as they stood. Marietta squeezed Nora's hand and smiled slightly. 'Don't look so upset, Nora,' she said. 'We know little enough about any of this.'

'I know, Marietta, but it's just . . . What if . . . Does he . . . What if he . . .'

'Just tell the truth, Nora,' she said, cutting Nora off in mid-sentence, although Emily was not sure if it was deliberate or not. 'You certainly have nothing to fear or to hide.'

Martin was quickly at Annie's side. 'Come, you two,' he said, an unconvincing lightness in his voice. 'The den and the study are back this way; I'll show you. Annie, please get a plate and have something to eat. You haven't had anything.'

'Maybe I will. Actually, more than anything, I'd like to sit down for a few minutes.'

'Good. You sit there with Emily and I'll bring you a plate as soon as I show Marietta and Nora to the study.'

'Thanks, Martin,' she said as she sat down on the wicker lounge, her legs stretched out before her and her head thrown back. 'I'm exhausted. You must be too, Emily.'

'I am, but actually Martin was right – the food helps. Poor Nora,' she said, watching as the two of them left the patio with Martin. 'She's so terribly upset. It's funny, she seemed so competent when I first saw her . . . My God, was that just yesterday? And now she seems so frail, somehow.'

'She seems very frightened, doesn't she? You know, I remember when she first started coming here with Marietta. She was much younger then . . . weren't we all? But when she first came, she seemed very timid. Not secure and compe-tent, the way she's been these last few years. Marietta has certainly been a wonderful influence on her, and now this. It's like she's back where she was then, frightened and insecure.'

'Do you have any idea why?' Emily asked, treading cautiously.

'Oh, Emily, lives are often more complicated than they appear on the surface. Marietta and I have been close for years and there are some things . . .'

'It's OK, Annie. I didn't want to say anything – I'm almost embarrassed but I overheard Marietta and Nora talking . . .'

'Then you know. What you probably don't know is that Roger . . . remember that row I mentioned earlier,' Annie said. 'Just this afternoon, right after Roger left the bar. Well, Marietta had just left Reception and was heading back down to the beach bar. They met on the path. He was horrible, nastier and more threatening than I've heard him before. He threatened to expose Marietta and Nora. And, to top it off, he said some pretty awful things about Nora. Stuff about her being involved with the police. It sounded like it was a long time ago, but it would still be awful for her if it became common knowledge. The whole thing was horrible. Marietta was devastated. She was so upset she was beyond caring. I brought her back to the main house and we sat for a while. She just talked and talked. She kept saying, "It seems hard to imagine" and something about after all these years, something carefully planned and guarded. It was as if she was talking to herself. Calling herself arrogant for having taken on Roger in her column. But she had had it with his nastiness and, at the time, thought her comments might change him somehow.

'Emily, it's been so awful,' she continued, wringing her hands as she talked. 'It seems the feud had started weeks ago, at a party in New York. Roger was drinking, as he was doing more and more, and he started on Jessica. Marietta had seen him do this before but never so meanly. She just couldn't stand it. Too reminiscent of her own father, she said. So the next day, in her column, she made a comment. It was veiled, of course, but anyone who was at that party knew what she meant. And, you know, word gets around. Roger was furious but she figured he'd get over it.

'He didn't, of course, and so the threats started. So much hatred, where do you think it came from, Emily? I could see if he had had a terrible childhood, brutal and numbing, but he didn't. From what I hear he was adored by his parents, pampered and indulged. They were simple people, too kind to see what their indulgence had wrought. Roger was truly unable to see or feel others' pain. His own egocentricity made him unable to empathize with anyone.'

'What was Marietta going to do?' Emily asked.

'I don't know, and now . . .' Annie said. 'She was so upset. Talking about how hard she had worked, so very hard. Her early years; years of not so benign neglect. She had a disillusioned mother, ineffective in response to her own neediness, and a gambler for a father. He lost a fortune, mostly on the horses; but, I hear, he was also a welcome guest in the best casinos until the money ran out. By then his family wanted nothing to do with him. His deals and schemes bought him some time but he was playing with other people's money and eventually he got caught. Two days after the indictment came down he put a gun to his head and shot himself. Six months later Marietta's mother was in a mental hospital.'

'What happened to Marietta?'

'Her Uncle Andrew took her in. By the time she was sixteen, she was considered a part of his family, the constant companion to her cousin, Andrea. Anyone who dared to inquire about her background was treated to one of the infamous St. John looks and was immediately silenced.

'Marietta was actually a lifesaver for her cousin. Andrea was very pretty and very sweet, but incredibly shy. Those cruel enough used to say pathologically shy, but she wasn't really. She was just one of those fragile creatures who needed to be nurtured and protected like tender blossoms. Marietta was much stronger. Life and loss had helped her form a hard shell, one that was quite big; big enough for the two of them, actually. And she was quite willing to use it to protect Andrea. It made her feel strong and good.

'But then Andrea fell in love with Hamilton Graham and it was Marietta who felt lost. She said how strange it was, because she was so outgoing and social people would say to her, "You must feel wonderful now that you can have a life of your own." But she didn't, of course. When she was with Andrea she had to take on a different persona, one that would protect

Andrea. She had to be witty and bright so that Andrea could feel safe in her shadow. If she talked, Andrea didn't have to. If she met new people, Andrea met them too. If everyone laughed, Andrea laughed too. With Andrea gone, Marietta wasn't sure who she was; all she knew was the role she had been playing. But she knew that role well. So that role, and a little help from her Uncle Andrew, were what she used to make a new life for herself. Marietta St. John, socialite, became Marietta St. John, recorder of everyone else's social lives.'

'How did she meet Nora?'

'Well, for a while Marietta enjoyed her new life. It was fun and exciting. There were always things to do – parties, events. Nothing happened that she wasn't invited to. And it wasn't long before she had a certain amount of power – heady stuff for someone who had so often felt powerless. But she desperately missed the intimacy of a relationship. For her, those feelings left with Andrea and she didn't find them again until she found Nora.'

'Has she known Nora for long?'

'Oh, years and years. Nora actually started out as Marietta's companion – let's see, it must be almost twenty years ago. Marietta had fallen, a stupid accident skiing, I think. It cost her a broken leg and she couldn't manage on her own. Nora was perfect. Sweet and caring, and a good worker. Marietta says that right away she reminded her of Andrea. The same shyness and fragility. Not physically. Nora could do any kind of work. But emotionally.'

Annie looked around, checking to see if anyone was close by. 'Before long their relationship had become one of mutual caring. Nora looked to Marietta for the love that would fill a desperate emptiness, and Marietta once again had someone who needed her. And then their relationship became a loving one, her presence veiled for all the world in the guise of live-in companion. Oh, Emily, if you could have seen Marietta this afternoon. At first she seemed thoroughly beaten. Her eyes were dull and reddened, and streaks of blue and black mascara, like rivers, ran down her cheeks. There was nothing regal left of her, no high drama, just a withered old woman trying to deal with the cruelty and fear. It was awful. But then, as she talked, the anger seemed to fester, growing deeper and more virulent until she couldn't contain it anymore and it just spewed forth.'

'She and Nora have worked so hard at keeping their secret,' Emily said. 'Roger's threats must have been devastating for her. No wonder she and Nora are so upset – and on Inspector Moller's suspect list.'

'I certainly can't blame them but . . . Oh, thank God. There's Sarah and Jon.'

THIRTEEN

A s Annie got up to kiss Sarah, Emily couldn't help but notice how glum she and Jon looked.

'How are things going, Mom? Do the police know anything yet?'

'Nothing. They've just started to interview people, really. Except for Emily. She was the first one; she found Roger's body.'

'That must have been awful for you,' Sarah said sympathetically, turning to Emily.

'And then to have to go over and over it with Tommy. That's even worse,' Jon added.

'Inspector Moller and Jon went to school together,' Sarah explained.

'I remember when we were in high school, Tommy would argue about almost anything. We loved it, of course. Not only did we have the best debating team in the Caribbean, but he could sidetrack any teacher in the school. Once we were supposed to have a history test, but we'd had a basketball game the night before so none of us had studied. Tommy got into a discussion with Mr Howland about the role of the Caribbean in World War II. We didn't have the slightest idea what he was talking about, but he managed to use up half the period and the test had to be postponed. It was really great . . . Is he inside, Annie?'

'He is, but he's talking with Marietta's friend Nora right now.'

'Oh, boy, poor Nora. I bet he had a ton of questions, Emily.'

'He did. Not that I was surprised, but really there was so little I could tell him.'

'Well, he certainly can be relentless. But he's damn good at what he does. There was a series of fires in town. I guess it was about a year ago . . . small ones, so not too much damage, but dangerous all the same. Something like that's pretty rare around here. And at first it seemed like there was nothing to go on, no clues, no witnesses. But it only took Tommy about two weeks to figure it out. He never stopped – questions, questions and more questions.'

'You know, you're right, Jon. Not only is he relentless but he has this way of sort of zeroing in on the smallest detail and just not letting go. Like me thinking someone was watching me or there was someone down at the end of the beach. I felt so foolish, but he—'

'You saw someone?' Sarah said, surprise in her voice.

'I didn't know you saw someone,' Annie added.

'That's just it, Annie, I'm not sure I did. It was just a feeling. That's why we walked back out on the path, retraced every movement, but nothing. I know the inspector won't let it go, though. He wants to do it again tomorrow.'

'What's this?' Martin said, joining the group.

'Emily saw someone,' Jon explained, turning to Martin.

'It's nothing. Oh, now I feel so ridiculous. I thought I saw . . . Let's just forget it, really. It turned out to be nothing.' Emily suddenly felt wary.

Martin handed the plate of food to Annie and turned to Emily. 'Have you told Thomas about this?' he asked.

'Yes, yes, I have, Martin. But nothing came of it. I remember so little. It was just something . . . I don't know . . . in the distance.'

'Well, don't be troubling yourself, my dear. I'm sure Thomas will figure this out. I have great confidence in him. Now, Sarah, Jon, there's some food in the dining room. Thomas and Officer Vogt are still talking to Marietta and Nora, so why don't you two get something to eat while you can.'

'I'm really not hungry,' Sarah said. 'This whole thing is just so awful. Do they know anything yet, Dad?'

'Not much, I'm afraid. They believe Roger was shot in the heart with a .22 caliber handgun.'

'Could someone have tried to rob Roger?' Emily asked. 'After all, sitting out there all alone, he was a perfect target. Did he have anything valuable on him, money or . . .?'

'We haven't really had any problems like that here on the island,' Martin answered. 'Not like this, in broad daylight, and here. Thomas told me and Emily that he was shot from very close range. No, he seems to think that this was very personal. That whoever did it wanted Roger to know just what was happening.'

'How horrible,' Annie said.

'It is horrible,' Jon said, 'but you've got to admit Roger had become a pretty horrible person. Not that I would have wished this on him, but I can't say I'm surprised. And to be brutally honest, I can't say I'm going to miss him either.'

'Oh, I know what you're saying, Jon. It's just that . . . Oh, I don't know. I think I'd better go check on Jessica.' Annie turned to leave the terrace. 'Please, Sarah and Jon, get something to eat.'

'Speaking of something to eat,' Martin said, indicating the plate he had brought for Annie.

'I just can't eat, not now, Martin. Maybe after I've checked on Jessica. Sarah, you take my plate. I'll be back down shortly.'

Martin handed Sarah the plate. 'Jon, I wonder if you could give me a hand with something. It'll just take a minute, sorry, but . . .'

Sarah sat with Emily as Jon and her father walked off, the two of them deep in conversation. 'Jon is so upset, even though he doesn't let on,' Sarah murmured. 'He didn't like Roger, and he was pretty open about it. I think he feels badly now . . . and worried too. You know when you've said things . . . But who hasn't said things about Roger?'

'I know how he feels,' Emily sympathized. 'It's kind of like speaking ill of the dead, only reversed. But he won't be the only one feeling that way. I bet most of the people here are thinking back on the things they said about Roger over the last few days.'

'It's just that he had become so difficult to get along with, and then that review of the restaurant . . . Jon was really shocked. Oh, let's talk about something else. Jon's coming back and . . . it's just been so difficult for him.'

Emily was also anxious to talk about something else, so she drew Jon back to the pleasanter moments of the night before. 'I loved your tag sale story, Jon. I've been to more than a few of those myself. How long did you live in New York?'

'About six years. For two of those I trained at the CIA, not the Langley CIA, mind you, although the training was probably just as tough, but the culinary CIA. It was actually outside the city, more upstate. Ever heard of Hyde Park?'

'Actually, I've been there. My father was a real history buff and he'd pack us kids up and haul us to some historic site or other at the drop of a hat. Franklin Roosevelt was born there.'

'That's right. It was a great little town, I thought the training was tops and they actually placed me in my first job. That's where I met Sarah.'

'Oh, I didn't realize you met in New York. I assumed you met here on the island.'

'No,' said a visibly relieved Sarah, joining the conversation. 'I had come to New York to study fashion design. I was just twenty at the time. I had started college here on the island but it really wasn't what I wanted. Alex convinced me to try New York; take some classes at FIT see how I liked it. I loved creating new things out of old ones and I used to haunt the East side thrift shops looking for finds. I'd look for quality pieces that I could give new life to – a Chanel jacket, a Judith Leiber bag. And fabrics. I had a passion for old fabric.'

'So one day she stops in at this thrift shop down the street from the restaurant where I'm working . . .' Jon continued.

'And I find these hats. They were the most wonderful hats, really. Fine straw and covered with softly faded silk flowers. They must have been from a wedding party; they couldn't possibly have been worn more than once. How could I leave them behind? And they gave them to me really cheap. After all, who would want four identical hats?'

'But as soon as she came out of the store carrying these hats loose in her arms—'

'No bags big enough, of course.'

'—it starts pouring with rain. The next thing you know, in she comes to the restaurant, in the middle of the lunch crowd, and walks right into the kitchen. Well, Emily, I don't know how well you know New York, but maybe you've heard of Andre Montand. He was the chef at the time. Probably one of the best in the world, but certifiably crazy . . . He was rumored to have physically ejected a delivery boy who happened to walk into the kitchen after four o'clock one freezing January afternoon. He had a rule about when people could come in. So out the kid goes, falling and bruising his elbow, and three days later the lawyer's letter arrives . . . Naturally everyone in the kitchen froze when Sarah walked in.'

'Oh, he wasn't like that at all,' Sarah said, coming to Montand's defense. 'I think people make those stories up. He was actually a dear, insisting that I have some hot soup and dry off a little, and then giving me four huge plastic bags to cover my hats.'

'Not only that,' Jon said incredulously, 'he insisted I walk Sarah out and find her a cab so she, and her hats, wouldn't get wet. It was amazing, although I must say Sarah did make an arresting sight, sopping wet and weeping for a quartet of soggy silk flower hats . . . It wasn't just Andre Montand who was taken with her.'

'That was it, really,' Sarah said, placing her hand over Jon's. 'From then on Jon and I were pretty much inseparable. It was the only thing that kept me in New York those couple of years. I was so homesick.' Sarah's voice took on a note of sadness, whether at the memory or the realization that their reminiscence was coming to an end, Emily couldn't be sure. 'By the time I finished school and it was time to head home, we had already decided that we wanted to come back to the island for good. Jon got a job at the new Hilton and I joined a local crafts cooperative in Oranjestad.'

'Jon,' Martin called, motioning from the doorway. 'There's a call for you. You can take it in here.'

'Thanks, Martin,' he said, heading out to the kitchen. 'I was expecting that.'

It would be hours before Emily realized she hadn't heard the phone ring.

Annie came back down the stairs with a subdued Jessica by her side. 'Jessica is going to sit with you while I get her some food. She's promised to try to eat something. I'll be right back.'

'How are you feeling?' Emily asked, unsure of what to say.

'I'm so sorry, Jessica,' Sarah began. 'I wish there was something I could say that would help, but . . .'

'Thank you, Sarah, I know,' Jessica said. 'It's just such a shock . . . I haven't done anything about telling Jason yet. Tomorrow . . . maybe I should ask my mother to fly down here with him. Then I could tell him when he gets here. I can't have anyone else tell him. Annie said the police wanted to talk to me. Have they talked to the two of you yet?'

'I've spoken to them. An Inspector Moller. He's very nice, Jessica, and he seems very competent. I'm sure he'll find whoever did this,' Emily said, unable to even voice the words 'murdered Roger' to her. 'He's talking to Nora right now but he should be finished pretty soon. I guess you're anxious to get this over with.'

'I am, Emily. I'm so tired. I'd just like to go back to my room and lie down. Tell me, have they found out anything? Who else are they talking to?'

'A number of people, I think. Marietta, of course. And Sarah and Jon, and I suppose Annie and Martin.'

'Martin and Annie must be so upset. Are they talking to any of the other guests?'

'Not that I know of. But I only know of the ones here at the house. I don't know if they're talking to other people at the main house. I'm sure they will at some point.'

'Oh, Annie, thank you,' Jessica said as Annie arrived with some food. 'But you really shouldn't have. I don't think I can eat anything. I guess they'll be ready for me soon. I'm so tired.'

'As soon as you've talked to Thomas you can go back up and lie down. Some of that's the sedative, although the shock must have been . . . Martin and I thought it would be best for you to stay here in the house with us. There's plenty of room and it's much more private.'

'I'd like that, Annie. Actually, I don't think I could face going back to that room.'

'What about you, Emily? The Phillips' have asked to have their room changed. They're uncomfortable down at that end of the beach. I'm sure we could find another room for you too.'

'No, that's OK. I guess I hadn't even thought about going back down there. But I'll be fine; you have enough to do without having to look for a different room for me.'

'Oh, God, I guess he'll be after me now,' Jessica said as she saw Inspector Moller walking down the hall with Nora.

'Mrs Stirhew – please, don't stand. Let me say how terribly sorry I am about this awful tragedy. I know how difficult this must be . . . There's no rush . . . Please, finish eating. I can wait.'

'There's no sense waiting. I can't eat and I'd like to get this over with,' Jessica answered.

'I understand. I'll only take a few minutes, I promise.'

With that Jessica and the inspector left the room and a silence settled over the group. Nora sat back down on the couch, looking considerably more relaxed than a few minutes ago.

'He really seemed to be a very nice man,' she said. 'Is Marietta still in with that other policeman?'

'She is,' Annie replied. 'I'm sure she'll be out in a few minutes.'

But Marietta wasn't out in a few minutes. Jessica was finished talking to Inspector Moller and had gone back upstairs, and still there was no sign of her.

'Inspector Moller, where is Marietta?' Nora asked as Moller came into the living room to get Jon Peterson. 'What's taking so long?'

'I'm sure she'll be finished very soon, Ms Richmond,' he answered. 'Officer Vogt is just very thorough, that's all.'

'Well, I certainly hope she is finished soon. Marietta is not very strong, you know. She shouldn't be upset like this.' Nora was now bold in Marietta's defense. 'I don't even know if she took her medication. Annie, do you know if Marietta took her pills? This is ridiculous; I've lost track of everything.'

'I'm sure she did, Nora. Relax. Why don't you have some coffee?'

'I can't relax, Annie, and I can't sit and have coffee. How about if I pick up some of these dishes and things?'

'No need to do that, Nora. One of the staff will come up later.'

'No, please, it will give me something to do,' Nora said, signs of her earlier discomfort returning.

'Well, in that case, that'd be great. I guess we would be more comfortable with all this stuff out of the way.'

'Maybe I'll give Nora a hand,' Sarah said. 'This sitting around is getting to me too. I could use something to occupy me.'

But just as Sarah got up, Officer Vogt headed into the living room with a disturbed-looking Marietta in tow.

'I'm sure Inspector Moller will also want to talk to you, Ms St. John, but I'm not sure when,' he was saying. 'And now I'd like to speak with Sarah Maitland, if I could? Are you Ms Maitland?' he said, looking at Sarah.

'Yes, I'm Sarah Maitland . . . Mother, would you make sure that Jon gets something to eat when he gets out? He hasn't had anything and he must be exhausted. Now, what is it you'd like to know, Officer Vogt?' she said with surprising command as they left the room.

The course of the interviews carried on for another hour. Everyone continued to sit around in the living room, saying little and wondering when it might be over. Emily found herself yawning and anxious to head back to her room. Martin and Annie were the last to be interviewed and finally, a little after ten, Inspector Moller asked to speak to the group.

'I'd like to thank all of you for your assistance here this evening. I know how difficult this has been and I'm sure everyone is upset and exhausted. Officer Vogt and I will be meeting to review what we know at this point. We'll also meet with those officers who have been speaking with the other guests and those who have been conducting the search. I'm sorry to say we will probably have some follow-up questions for you in the morning. But, for tonight, I think everyone should head back to their rooms to get some sleep.'

'Oh, and Emily, I do need to talk with you again now,' Inspector Moller said. Emily felt her heart sink. 'I promise you it will just be for a minute.'

And so, as everyone bid quiet goodnights, Emily headed back to the den with Inspector Moller.

'I'm sorry, really. And I just have one question. I know you've said you recall little about the figure you saw at the end of the ocean beach . . .'

'I'm not even sure there *was* a figure,' Emily corrected him. 'I told you when I looked the second time there was no one there. The more I think about it, the more I think the whole thing was just my imagination.'

'I'm sorry, Emily,' Inspector Moller said, more solicitous now than before, 'but I don't think the whole thing was your imagination at all. I think there was, most definitely, someone out there . . . And I think that someone may have been Roger Stirhew's murderer.'

Emily was visibly shaken by the thought that she could possibly have seen the murderer. 'That's not possible. I didn't see or hear anything.'

'As far as we can tell at this point, and we'll know better tomorrow, but right now it seems that the time of death was just about the time you discovered Roger's body. I think that distant figure had just fled the scene as you approached and was watching from the tree. I need to ask you to think very hard about this, and forget about the second time you looked – think only about your first glance down the beach. This is very important, Emily. Would you say the figure was a man or a woman?'

Emily was still stunned to think that she might actually have seen Roger's killer. Her thoughts were racing. Almost as if he could sense what was going on in her head, Inspector Moller said, 'Please, try your best to focus on that moment. Think carefully; try to picture it in your mind. Was that distant figure a man or a woman?'

As much as Emily tried, shutting out all other thoughts and picturing only that moment in her mind, she just couldn't do it. 'I'm sorry,' she said. 'No matter how hard I try to think about it, I just can't tell. It was such a short look. I'm really sorry, but I honestly don't know which it was.'

'It's OK, I know how hard you're trying. Maybe after a good night's sleep you'll be able to recall more. We'll talk again in the morning. And Emily, just one more thing. Please, until then . . . be careful.'

FOURTEEN

The full impact of what Inspector Moller had said didn't hit Emily until she was walking back to her room. Careful? she thought. Why did she have to be careful? And then, of course, it hit her. If she really did see somebody at the end of the beach, then that 'somebody' certainly saw her. And if, as Inspector Moller believed, that 'somebody' could be the murderer then . . . then what? Surely whoever was there must realize how far away she was; how difficult it was to see anything. Besides, wouldn't they be long gone by now?

And although she tried to shake off these thoughts, Emily was very conscious of how quiet it was as she approached her hut. There were only eight rondovals on the ocean beach and now only five of the others were occupied. In fact, when she checked as she was walking by, there were lights on in only two of them. And those two were much closer to the point. There seemed to be almost no one down near her end.

Emily was amazed at how a number of the features that she had loved about the Bluffs, just this morning, were now cause for concern. The ocean beach was so empty. The rondovals were pretty spread out and there were only a few other rooms, further back in the small two-story building right by the point. The room doors had no locks; no need for them, Martin had said. And although the main house was wired like a modern office, individual guest rooms had only intercoms, not phones.

Emily had relished the isolation when she first arrived, picturing herself and Michael spending solitary hours wrapped in each other's arms with no interruptions, human or otherwise. But now, as she passed the spot where Roger's body had been, that same isolation made her feel not so much scared, but vulnerable.

She couldn't help stopping, needing to peer down the beach at the small grove of trees once again. It was very dark now, no light except the crescent moon, and she figured she wouldn't be able to see anything. But for a moment, she thought she'd spotted the outline of someone moving behind the trunk of the nearest tree. Oh, that's impossible, she thought. I have got to stop this. Maybe she should have asked Annie to change her room after all. She could still do that, actually. Just walk back to the house. Annie had said it wouldn't be too much of an inconvenience.

But she was here now, so what was the point? She was so exhausted that she would have no trouble falling asleep. She could always buzz the main house if there was a problem and, actually, the path back looked pretty uninviting right now.

When she entered her hut, Emily turned on all the lights, and although she felt foolish she checked the bathroom and the closet. Reassured that she was alone, she relaxed a bit. A tray with a small bottle of chardonnay and some cheese and fresh fruit sat on the coffee table in front of the couch, a sweet gesture from Annie and Martin.

At first, she thought about taking a long, relaxing bath. She was sure she had seen some bath oil in the shell, but the thought of the unlocked room door made her feel too exposed. She was too tired, anyway. She would change and get into her bed with her book and a glass of wine. That was just about all she could manage. And so for the fourth (or was it the fifth?) time she tried to get beyond page five.

Within minutes, though, she had fallen into a deep sleep. She was oblivious to the noises of the night, the swish of the elegant palms, the rolling of the steady surf, the eerie caw of a single bird and, beneath them all, the soft footsteps of a silent figure slowly making its way along the garden path to her lonely rondoval. She was peacefully unaware of the peering eyes that watched her through the rear window. She settled herself in the bed, bunching her pillow under her head, turning on her side and stretching her arm out on top of the pure white sheets. She did not see the hand that reached out to test the window, pulling carefully to see if it would open. And just as it started to, the lights of a passing car illuminated the scene, forcing her night visitor to flee.

Emily was awakened by the sound of the car on the service road that ran behind the rondovals. She was amazed that she had fallen asleep so quickly, her reading glasses still on and her book in her lap. The sound of a car at the Bluffs, particularly at night, was unusual and she was reminded of last night's incident with the Jeep. She got up to investigate and wasn't surprised to see a police cruiser slowly making the rounds of the grounds. Obviously Thomas Moller wasn't going to take any chances, Emily realized. What she didn't realize was that that police cruiser might just have saved her life.

The rest of the night passed fitfully. Emily slept poorly in spite of knowing that there was increased security. In fact, the police presence made her unable to stop her mind going back to the scene on the beach, retracing her steps, hearing Jessica scream at the sight of Roger. She would dose off, sometimes for an hour but often just for a few minutes, and then wake with a start, at first uncertain where she was and then disturbed when she remembered. More and more, Inspector Moller's words echoed in her mind: '*Be careful.*'

When she awoke in the morning she felt drained and on edge. She had few expectations for the day. Hoping to find some peace, she thought she might order coffee and a newspaper from room service and sit on the small patio outside her room. The newspapers were actually those from the day before, flown in overnight, but that mattered little to Emily. They would serve more as a distraction than anything else.

Stepping outside, she could see that the beach was spectacular this morning. The sky was a clear deep blue with only a few white puffy clouds. They must be just for decoration, Emily thought. The sun shone brightly, causing the water to sparkle frenetically, almost blinding to her early morning eyes. The air was warm, with gentle breezes, and the ever-present surf rolled lazily to the shore. The sand, white and clean, was pristine, except for the patch surrounded by yellow police tape, an instant reminder of yesterday's violence. Seeing this, Emily abandoned any thoughts of having breakfast on the patio, and anyway, she hoped that Michael would be calling and couldn't wait to hear the sound of his voice.

As soon as she reached the terrace of the main house she met Martin busily overseeing breakfast.

'Emily, my dear, how did you sleep?' he asked solicitously.

'Unfortunately not well, Martin, even though I was so tired. I just couldn't get all of this out of my mind. I fell into a deep sleep at first but then I heard a car. I looked out and saw the police car on the grounds, and strangely it made things worse. I don't know if I mentioned this, but last night Inspector Moller cautioned me to be careful. It kind of spooked me. I just never thought that I might be in any danger. Maybe he's just exaggerating. What do you think, Martin? Do you think I could be in danger?'

'I would certainly hope not. Thomas knows his business, although I do think at times he overreacts. Still, if he thinks you might be at risk, perhaps you should stay up at the house too. There's plenty of room, and it might even help Jessica. She seems comfortable with you and I think she's making arrangements to bring Jason down tomorrow. Her mother is coming with him but I know it will be a very difficult day for her. I'm sure she could use the support.'

'You know, Martin, last night when I left your house I wasn't concerned about staying in my own room. But by the time I got there, I was sorry I hadn't taken Annie up on her offer. I guess I didn't realize how lonely and vulnerable I would feel. I think you're right. Although I truly love the rondoval, I think I might feel better staying at the house until Michael arrives. How is everything this morning? Do the police know anything more?'

'No, not really. Thomas has been here since seven. If he ever went home, that is. He's certainly tireless. Anyway, when I spoke with him earlier he said there wasn't anything really new but there were some things they were pursuing. As you can imagine, Emily, it's awkward for both of us. Technically I'm a suspect, albeit along with many others, but Annie and I have been friends with Thomas's parents for years and I know that makes it difficult for him.'

'I didn't realize. That must be difficult for you too. Is Annie inside?'

'No, she's back at the house with Jessica.'

'How's Jessica doing? Is she feeling any better this morning?'

'She does seem somewhat better. I think making some plans helped. Her mother and Jason should be here at about two tomorrow. She won't tell him until he gets here and hopefully by then Thomas will know more. Now, shall I get you a table?'

'In a minute, Martin, but first I was wondering if Penny was around. I want to try to reach Michael and she placed the call for me yesterday.'

'Penny's not in yet. She and Nelson were here pretty late last night. I told both of them to take some time off this morning. It wasn't easy trying to calm all these people and from what I hear they did a wonderful job. Actually, even though everyone is certainly still talking about it this morning, I think people are a little more relaxed; they seem to have gained a little distance . . . but come into the office, I can certainly place that call for you. Or better yet, why don't you sit and I'll get you when it goes through. Now, let me see if I can find somewhere quiet.'

'I'd appreciate that, Martin,' Emily said. 'A quiet breakfast would be perfect.'

As they entered the dining room, Emily was conscious of the number of pointed glances and whispered comments that followed her as she made her way to her table. A few people smiled and nodded, understanding in their eyes.

I guess everyone must know, she thought. With her luck this was probably her fifteen minutes of fame, and she had been hoping it would have been as a lottery winner. Oh, well, nothing like a hearty breakfast to start the day off right.

It was only minutes before Martin came in to get her. 'Your call has gone through – Michael's on the line. Why don't you take it in the office?'

'Oh, that's great, Martin. Could you cancel my breakfast order?'

'I'll have them hold it until you're finished. You just hurry along. Oh, and Emily, I didn't mention anything to Michael about Roger's murder. I didn't know if you wanted to or not. Is he a worrier?'

Martin's comments gave Emily pause. She had planned to tell Michael all about the murder and her part in the discovery of the body, but Martin was right. Michael would just worry and what would be the point of that? There was nothing he could do from London. She'd wait till he arrived to tell him. By that time maybe everything would be resolved.

'Michael? Michael? Are you there?' Emily asked, hearing static on the line.

'I'm here, Em, good news!'

'Oh, thank God. What's happening?'

'It looks like we're almost finished here. It didn't take Harris more than a few hours to get things straightened out. I sure can see why he's a partner. And the good thing is that he realized it was Bixley that screwed things up. I told you I was a little afraid that this would be dropped on my doorstep, but I was right, Harris is pretty perceptive. He could see . . . Oh, I guess you don't want to hear all this.'

'Well, I do want to hear it,' Emily said, laughing at Michael's exuberance, 'but maybe not right now. When will you be leaving there?'

'I'm not quite sure yet. It should be soon, though. Right now I have someone checking on flights for me. The timing isn't great so I may have to take a crazy route to get there. But I'm determined to make it today. And Em, get this, Harris wants me to have lunch with him. I'm heading out now, then hopefully off to the airport. I can't wait to see you, Em.'

'Me, too. I have so much to tell you, you won't believe . . .' Emily said, forgetting for a moment her resolve not to say anything. 'It's wonderful here, Michael. I know I keep saying this, but you'll love it.'

'I'll love anyplace with you, Em. I'd better run if I want to meet Harris – don't want to make a bad impression. I'll be in touch again soon. Love ya.'

Emily practically danced back to the dining room, the gloom of yesterday's events forgotten for the moment. 'He'll be here sometime today, Martin. Isn't that wonderful?'

'I'm so glad for you, my dear. Hopefully he'll make it in time for the barbecue this evening. It really is a lot of fun. We had thought of canceling it, but that would be unfair to the guests. Although they all feel terrible about what happened, most of them didn't really know Roger. They knew his name, of course, but not him. Anyway, it's their vacation and we have an obligation.'

'Of course,' Emily agreed. 'I was talking to a couple yesterday – the Phillips. He's a doctor, an orthopedist. They were in the rondoval next to me. These two weeks are the only real vacation he takes all year. You just have to make the best of it.'

Martin and Emily's conversation was interrupted by a deep voice from behind. 'Well, you've certainly been busy since I last saw you.'

Emily turned to see Nick Marino heading toward her. 'Sorry, didn't mean to sound so glib. It must have been an awful shock for you,' he continued. 'Couldn't believe it when I heard. Couldn't believe I slept through the whole thing either. Police and everything. How's Jessica doing, Martin?'

'As well as can be expected, I'd have to say,' Martin answered. 'Dreading telling her son, of course. That, I think, will be the hardest part.'

'I don't think I ever met their son. I'm sure it will be awful for him, and her. Please tell Jessica I'm thinking about her. I was no fan of Roger's but this must be just devastating. Can I join you for breakfast, Emily?' Nick asked.

'Gee, Nick.' Emily paused for a moment. He seemed genuinely sorry for Jessica, but after his opening comment she couldn't figure him out. Who was he? The helpful, friendly guy who taught her windsurfing; the sentimental grandson of Italian immigrants carrying on the family's business; or the callow, self-centered playboy, immune to everyone but himself? She was just too tired to deal with it this morning.

'After yesterday, I promised myself a nice, quiet morning. It really did take an awful lot out of me. I'd be terrible company,' Emily answered, not wanting to have to talk about yesterday's events. Already she had felt her mood darken further as Nick spoke about Jessica's loss. 'A quiet breakfast and a long walk is about all I'm up for.'

'Emily's fiancé is expected to arrive from London sometime today. I'm sure it will be a busy day for her,' Martin added, somewhat pointedly.

'Uh oh, so I guess my sailing partner is gone. Great for you, though, Emily. What time is he expected?'

'I'm not really sure yet; he's supposed to call later.'

'Well, in that case, I'm just going to have to steal Annie, Martin,' Nick responded. 'And now a table for one . . . Maybe I'll see you later, Emily.'

'Hope you didn't mind my adding that, Emily,' Martin said as Nick headed for a corner table. 'I like Nick, but sometimes he seems a little forward to me, especially around women, and he was right to apologize about that remark. I know he couldn't care less about Roger, but whether he liked him or not, the man is dead.'

'Not at all, Martin. Actually, I'd like to thank you. I feel the same way you do about Nick. I mean, he seems nice enough, but he's a little full of himself . . . Anyway, I meant what I said about a quiet breakfast, and I feel like taking a long walk. It's really the best way for me to get my head together. At home I would run for miles around the city. There's nothing better.'

'Well, there certainly are plenty of places for long walks here, and some beautiful scenery, too.'

'I figured there must be. What do you suggest?'

'Since you went toward Oranjestad yesterday, how about going in the other direction? It's beautiful and very different. I think you would appreciate it, though. You'll have to pass the spot where Roger was killed but—'

'I know. I guess there's no avoiding it. It's so hard to get that image out of my mind. Maybe my walk will cure that. I think I'd like to get a better look at that small grove of trees too . . . Oh, no, I just remembered . . . Did Inspector Moller mention anything about wanting to talk to me again?'

'Not to me he didn't, but I know he had a couple of

interviews scheduled. I'm sure he'll be here for most of the day. Go have your walk. If Thomas is looking for you I'll tell him where you are. And I'm sure he's not going anywhere in a hurry. From the sounds of it we'll all be spending some more time with him today, so you can talk to him later rather than sooner. And the walk will help.'

'I guess you're right. Now let me grab a quick breakfast and get out of here before anything else happens.'

'I have a better idea. How about a breakfast to go? I'll have the kitchen pack one for you. It will only take a minute and there are some lovely cliffs and dunes to picnic on. It certainly would be peaceful.'

'That would be perfect, Martin. What a wonderful idea.'

And within minutes, Emily was off.

FIFTEEN

As she walked along the ocean beach, Emily steeled herself to pass by the area cordoned off by the yellow police tape. She could still see the chair's outline in the sand and the dark, reddish brown trail of blood under it. She didn't have to close her eyes to imagine the scene; it was incredibly fresh in her mind. And she couldn't stop herself from staring up ahead at the small grove of trees at the end of the Bluffs' property, trying to recapture the image she had seen yesterday. But it was no use. No matter how long or how hard she stared, she couldn't recall anything.

Once she reached the spot she couldn't resist stopping. The grove was dense with vegetation and sand blown up from the beach covered the ground. Emily pushed aside the branches and ventured beyond the bordering brush. Here it was cooler, sheltered from the sun by the tree limbs overhead, and yet still open to the ocean breezes.

Although not deep, the grove offered what seemed like perfect shelter and Emily searched for anything that might help her remember what she had seen yesterday. Finding nothing, she turned to look back at the ocean beach and was shaken to realize that there was such a clear view of the spot where Roger had been killed. Anyone standing here would have seen her finding the body. And if they had seen her peering intently toward the grove, they couldn't help but think she had seen them.

All of a sudden Emily felt very vulnerable. Anyone watching from the executive suites would have seen what she was doing – watching from there was almost like sitting alongside the path around the bluff. Her pulse started to quicken as she emerged from the trees and, without pausing, headed quickly onward. Worried, she looked back once or twice, but her natural sense of composure returned quickly as her feet and her mind gained some distance.

In spite of her earlier disquiet, Emily was able to appreciate the beauty of the morning. As usual, clear skies and a bright sun heralded the day, and although there was a cool breeze coming off the ocean Emily could tell it was going to be a hot afternoon. As she walked further away from the resort the landscape changed dramatically. This was the uncultivated part of the island, barren and forlorn, the only vegetation the twisted, wind-bent divi-divi tree.

Within minutes, the terrain became more and more desolate, harboring small hills and sand dunes, interspersed with towering rock formations. And although empty, it was majestic in its solitude. Emily was reminded of those grainy gray photographs of the moon's surface which had fascinated her as a child. Of course, here the land's monotony was counterbalanced by the sea's majesty. Roaring, roiling waves driven by the *passaat*, the fierce winds from the east, pounded the shore, inexorably reducing solid rock to gritty sand.

After going about a mile or so, Emily looked for a spot to have her breakfast. One particular cliff, high and rocky, offered a commanding view of the sea. Here she sat, among the crabgrass and the brush, watching the antics of a small blue-green lizard scurrying among the rocks while she hungrily devoured the strong coffee and flaky croissant which Martin had thoughtfully provided. She imagined that in the distance she could see the coast of Venezuela only fifteen miles away.

She would have to bring Michael here, she thought. It was so different from the other side of the island, almost like another country. Unfortunately, the excitement of Michael's call was fading, and she found herself once again reliving yesterday's events.

She thought about Martin, who seemed to be holding up pretty well but must be under a terrible strain. Between watching out for Jessica, taking care of the guests and, worst of all, being a suspect himself, he must be exhausted. But he certainly didn't show it.

Emily wondered how everyone else was faring this morning. It was hard to imagine that they were all suspects. Roger had never managed to upset Nick, but Nora and Marietta, Sarah and Jon, and Martin and Annie – they all had reason to be angry at Roger – and were. But kill him? Emily just couldn't imagine that. Annie? Never. And Sarah? It just couldn't be. Jon and Martin were both off the radar at the time, but surely not . . . Someone had done it, though, and it must have been someone whose anger at Roger had gotten out of control. Emily hated to admit it, but it could have been any one of them.

And then there was Jessica. Certainly after what Emily had observed in the last two days, Jessica had many reasons to be angry at Roger. He was demeaning and abusive and Jessica gave every indication of an abused wife, despite trying to hide it. Was it possible that it had just become too much for her? Roger had been drunk and nasty when he left the beach bar; had Jessica gone after him? Emily couldn't remember. She recalled seeing Jessica later after the incident – at least she thought it was her. She was walking on the beach and looked so dispirited. Jessica said she had taken a walk on the beach, so it must have been her, but how long after the incident was that? Could they have had more words . . . or blows? Maybe Jessica just exploded, left Roger and went into her hut. A small handgun is easy to hide. She certainly wouldn't be the first abused woman to do that.

Feeling her mood growing even darker, Emily consciously put those thoughts out of her mind and decided to resume her exploration. This time she looked for a sturdier path, wanting to walk a little faster, hoping the exercise would help to lift her mood. She stretched her legs and swung her arms, lifting her face to the sun and feeling the breeze blow her hair.

She took a closer look at the divi-divi trees, and could see how their awkward shapes were caused by the almost constant easterly winds, mild now but powerful at full blast. Their trunks were skinny and their branches were thickly woven and bent, helter-skelter, toward the milder southwestern shore, like nature's compass. Looking carefully, she could see the small yellow and white blossoms that gave off a fragrant scent. Martin had told her that the tree's odd name came from the shape of its seed pods. The seed pods are high in tannin and a black dye, and some of the locals use the pods to clean their shoes. There was little else to see, just some prickly pear and barrel cactus. But the lack of vegetation meant less distraction and actually helped Emily keep up her pace, so she went several miles in no time.

From here the path turned into a rugged dirt road, rougher on the feet because the land was rock hard. Off in the distance she saw three wild donkeys standing still in a group. They seemed to be staring straight at her. In some spots there were narrow side paths which led to a series of intricately connected caves. Only a few towering rock formations and some barren hills broke up the landscape.

Emily approached the highest of these and immediately noticed a strange sight. The path was lined with scattered white crosses and small coffins. Primitive palettes bore sad, simple paintings of the stations of the cross. And interspersed among these were hand lettered signs, haunting and evocative, 'Pray for us sinners', 'At the hour of our death', and 'Pray, pray' they intoned.

Emily felt chilled, but she still approached the small mustard-colored chapel that stood at the end of the path. Surrounded by hulking boulders and huge candle cactus, the chapel seemed a forlorn way station on a sorrowful journey. So different, Emily thought, from the one she had visited yesterday with Annie. The heavy wooden door heaved and creaked, as if in protest, when she opened it. The interior provided no warmth or comfort. It was simple and stark, and its low light and thick walls seemed to reinforce its sense of loneliness and isolation.

As she started toward the stone altar, Emily was distracted

by a scraping noise outside the far window. Frightened at first, she chided herself for behaving foolishly. But a couple more steps and she heard the sound again.

'Who's there?' she called, her voice trembling slightly. But the only answer was the low moaning of the wind. She backed up slowly, inching toward the side wall and listening intently. Nothing. Emily didn't know what to do. She was afraid of what might be outside but she had no desire to remain in this barren spot. She would have to chance it. She couldn't just stand there. She wanted to get out of here and, God, she was so far from the Bluffs.

As she crept quietly toward the back door she was startled by the sharp crash of a wooden shutter followed by the high-pitched whizzing that fired past her ear and smashed into the far wall. A bullet. Without thinking, Emily ran, scrambled for the ledge and threw herself out the small window.

She landed harshly on the ground and tore down the path, this time too concerned with her own mortality to even notice the morbid signs. She could hear pounding footsteps behind her and was tempted to turn around. But a second bullet crashing into a nearby boulder convinced her that her only chance lay in a quick escape. She knew she was in good physical shape and if she could just make it to the abandoned caves she might be able to hide.

Her heart raced to the beat of the blood pounding in her ears as she ran. She felt a mounting sense of hysteria as she realized yet again how vulnerable she was. Her fear started to cripple her and she knew that she would be dead if she did not conquer it. Determined, she forced herself to focus only on the path ahead and was relieved to see the outline of the first cave. The opening was painfully small and she scraped her arms and legs as she dived in.

It was murky and silent inside, cool – almost cold – and close. She could no longer hear the sounds of her pursuer but that didn't mean she was safe. She didn't know if she had been seen entering the cave so, much as she wanted to, she couldn't stay near the opening. She crawled deeper into the blackness, hugging the wall as a guide and a support. Somehow it grounded her, the sense of touch and smell compensating for her reduced vision.

She had only gone a few feet when she heard noises at the mouth of the cave. For a moment, she faltered. A debilitating sense of futility came over her and she sought her own body for comfort, wrapping her long arms around herself to quiet the sobs that started to spill forth. Lying rolled in a fetal position, she tried to regroup. You must stop this, she told herself. You cannot just lie here waiting to be found. Enough, you must move. Now. You must move now. And from some untapped well of strength, she did.

Slowly and carefully, she crawled along, ignoring sharp pokes and stinging scrapes until she came to the opening of a deeper cave. She had no choice but to go on; there was nothing but danger behind her.

It was a well of blackness inside. Like a tomb, Emily thought . . . my tomb. No, there must be a way out of here. I must see if I can stand. But as she did a few coins spilled out of her pocket, making a series of sharp pings on the rock.

Emily never knew if it was the noise or the movement, but suddenly a mass of bats was swarming out from the recesses of the cave. They swooped and swirled, squealing and squeaking. Thousands of small wings flapped, tiny claws caught on Emily's clothes and tangled themselves in her hair. She could feel them scratching her face and tried desperately to brush them away. She waved her hands frantically, slapping at their wings, but there were too many of them. She couldn't keep them off her. It was then that she started screaming, high-pitched wails, no words, no thoughts even. Just sound. And mercifully, then silence, as Emily passed out on the dank, dark cave floor.

SIXTEEN

Emily had no idea how long she lay there, but when she came to it was still and quiet except for the distant hum of a motor somewhere outside the cave. At first, she was afraid to move, terrified that she would unleash another swarm of bats. The thought made her skin crawl and her stomach turn. Anything was better than that. She would just have to face whatever was waiting for her outside. And besides, since she was still alive, it seemed likely that her pursuer had left.

And so she began the slow crawl to the mouth of the cave. It was easier in this direction. The opening, although small, provided enough light that she had something to aim for. And that was all she needed. Within minutes she was there, peering out, trying to adjust her eyes to the harsh light. She could see no one, although the boulders provided enough cover if someone wanted to hide. She would take her chances – she couldn't stay here.

She started down the dirt road and on to the path, tentatively at first. She was alert to every sound and kept a constant watch over her shoulder. The day had gotten much warmer and the sun made her skin bristle after a while. She knew it was too hot to run so she tried to walk quickly, anxious to get back to the refuge of the Bluffs.

Tears welled in her eyes, whether from fear or relief she could not tell, and she tried to keep her mind blank, resisting the urge to ruminate on the events of the morning. But the closer she got to the point, the angrier she became.

She was not going to let someone do this to her. Obviously, whoever killed Roger believed she could identify them and was willing to kill her to stop that. This was not the action of a person losing control and acting in a rage, something she could almost understand. This was cold and calculated. But how could she fight back?

The last mile was tortuous. Emily's feet ached and her bangs and scrapes were taking on a fiery cast. She was tired and thirsty and longed to just lie down. From the sun's position in the sky she figured it was only late morning. Incredible as it seemed, she had left the Bluffs less than two hours ago.

Once again she passed the small grove of trees but this time she didn't stop, walking quickly by, relieved to be back on the Bluffs' property. The lushness of the grounds almost overwhelmed her. It symbolized everything cool and soothing and safe. And the sight of Jon Peterson's Jeep on the service road that ran behind the rondovals brought fresh tears.

'Jon! Jon!' she called, waving her arms. Suddenly she felt

as if she couldn't take one more step, and as he pulled the
Jeep next to her she knew what a sight she must be.

'My God, what happened to you? Here, let me help you,'
Jon said, jumping down from the driver's seat. 'You're all
scraped and bruised. Where were you? Did you go out to
the cliffs? Did you fall? My God, Emily, what happened?'

'Oh, Jon, just help me get in, please. I think it looks worse
than it is. I did go out to the cliffs, and then out beyond the
dunes. I found a small, deserted chapel . . .' Emily said, stopping suddenly. She couldn't even talk about it.

'You went all the way to Alto Vista? That's a distance, but
what happened out there?'

'It's a long story, Jon, but I think I . . . Oh, could you maybe
just drop me up at the main house? That would be a big help.'

'Of course,' Jon answered, but then he paused. 'I'm sorry
that you've gotten caught up in this. Martin says Tommy thinks
you might be at risk. It's OK if you don't want to tell me what
happened, but I'm sure it had something to do with Roger's
death. It seems so unfair.'

'It's just that . . . I don't think I can get out of it at this
point. And I do feel some sort of an obligation. I can't help
it. Finding Roger like that I . . .'

'Obligation? Obligation to what? To a man who used his
power like a goddamned sword, ready to cut down anyone
who wouldn't bow down to him? Who threatened to destroy
anyone who crossed him? Who brutalized his wife for daring
to try to protect him from his own drunken moods? What do
you care what happened to Roger?'

Emily was taken aback by the ferocity of his response. She
had seen traces of his anger at Roger before, but nothing like
this. This sudden outburst spoke to something much deeper
and perhaps more deadly. Was it pure coincidence that she'd
bumped into him first after her ordeal in the cave?

'I know. I know, Jon,' she said, her voice measured, almost
soothing, trying her best to calm him down and not show any
fear. 'It's not really an obligation to Roger. It's to the others,
to Jessica and Martin – and to you. Everyone's a suspect at
this point. And I can see how angry you are. Sarah told me
how hard you worked to get where you are . . .'

'Hard? Do you have any idea what it was like for me? My father was a Swiss banker working on Grand Cayman. I was just six when we arrived here, but it was always understood that this was only temporary and some day we would all go back. My parents would talk about how I would attend university in Switzerland, get some experience and eventually take over from my father. Years of trips. Every summer, every school vacation we would go back, just so that we would maintain our connection with our homeland. I hated it. The cold weather, the sober reserve of the people. I would spend the whole vacation longing for the warmth of the sun and a Reggae beat. My father never understood. He was very good to us but he was a very serious man. I used to joke that he was the kind of man that never retired for the night without putting his shoe trees in his shoes. He could never accept that the islands had become my home.

'And then when he heard I wanted to become a chef . . . Well, if it hadn't been for Martin I don't think he ever would have accepted it. And he barely did at that. They're back in Switzerland now. Oh, we keep in touch but . . . That's why the restaurant was so important – I had achieved something my father could understand. I was going to be a success.'

'But Jon, surely you'll recoup. Sarah said it would just take a little time . . .'

'Oh, Emily, don't you see? Sarah doesn't know how bad it is. She's so innocent in many ways. I risked everything, and now I may lose everything. And why? Why did he do it? There was no reason . . . it was so . . . No, Emily, I don't understand your sense of obligation . . . not where Roger Stirhew is concerned. As far as I'm concerned, whoever killed Roger . . . well . . . never mind. Let me get you back to the main house. You look awful. And Emily, I think Tommy's right – you are in danger.'

When Emily got to the main house, mulling over the last few hours, Annie was at the front desk talking to a striking-looking young woman whose voluptuous body, slick with oil, was concealed only slightly by a neon-green bikini and her long flowing blonde hair. Her petulant expression and pouty lips seemed to glower as she tapped two perfectly manicured red fingernails on the front desk. 'Maybe you didn't hear me right,' she said, tossing her head back. 'I have to have a separate room. I'm not gonna listen to his snoring all night.' Her voice was sultry and querulous. Was she from the island? Emily wondered. 'He knows that's the deal. You can ask him yourself when he gets here tonight.'

'I'm sorry, Ms Turner, but I just explained to you. This reservation was made very late and I don't have another room for tonight . . . or tomorrow night. We will have something on Sunday evening but that's the best I can do.'

'Look, I know one of those huts is empty – why can't I have that? That would be perfect. Acks Tony.'

Ah, one of the grammatically challenged, Emily thought, amused at the conversation.

'I'm not really sure if those units are available. I'm sure you're unaware but we've had . . .'

'I know, I know, I heard all about it. I don't care if the guy caught it on the doorstep, I gotta have my own room. And if that one's empty, I don't see any reason why I shouldn't get it.'

'Well, I'll have to check on that. I'll let you know later. Now, I certainly can arrange for a car into town this afternoon. What time would be good?'

'I don't know. I still hafta make a hair appointment and I gotta have a pedicure. I got this great new pink polish. You know, for my pink suit. You can make those for me, can't you?'

'Of course,' Annie answered, maintaining her calm. 'But better yet, here comes Penny. She's an expert at this.'

'Oh, thank God someone here can help . . . She wasn't able to do much for me, maybe you can,' the spoiled Ms Turner could be heard saying as Emily and Annie headed for the office.

'We won't be accepting their reservation again,' Annie said, her face grimacing at the aftertaste. 'But, my God, Emily, what happened to you?' Her concern was mounting as she noticed the cuts and bruises crisscrossing Emily's skin.

'Martin, send for the doctor!' she continued as Martin entered the office.

'No, no. I don't need the doctor, really. It's just scrapes. I went walking. You know, Martin, out beyond the bend . . .' Suddenly Emily stopped. 'It looks worse than it is, really.'

'Well, let me at least get the nurse,' Martin said, heading toward the fitness center. 'She can clean and dress those scrapes.'

'Now, Emily, what happened?' Annie said.

Emily actually felt more comfortable with Martin gone. What is happening to me? she thought. I feel like I can't trust anyone. Martin, of all people, this is ridiculous. But it was Martin who suggested that she go walking beyond the ocean beach, out to the dunes. No, it wasn't possible . . . it just couldn't be.

And even though Emily felt as if she was overreacting, she couldn't help it. 'Annie, I'm getting scared. I didn't realize how much danger I could be in. Inspector Moller mentioned it, but I never thought he meant . . . Oh, God, I went for a long walk, out by the dunes to a place – Jon called it Alto Vista. It was beautiful, but desolate.'

'It certainly is lonely. You should have told someone where you were going. We could have arranged a car or at least had someone check on you when you didn't get back.'

'I . . .' Emily barely stopped herself from mentioning that Martin had suggested she walk in that direction. 'That's just it; I wanted to be by myself. I wanted to go walking. I needed to get away and I thought a long walk would help clear my head. Clear my head – I almost lost it. Someone tried to kill me, Annie. Out there in the chapel. I got away. I ran and hid in the caves. It was horrible, these bats, thousands of them . . .' Emily stopped, suddenly unable to go on. Her skin was crawling and her palms sweating from the very thought of the bats. 'Ugh, I can't even talk about it. That's how I got all scraped. Running and crawling in the caves.'

'Emily! We have to call Thomas. Sit down; you must have been terrified.'

'You know, Annie, I know it sounds crazy but I was more scared of the bats than anything else. I've always hated them, just the idea. And there must have been thousands.'

'Did you see anyone? Any idea of who was in the chapel?'

'No one. I didn't see anyone and once I started running I didn't dare stop. I tried to look back but the trail was so rocky, I was afraid I might fall, and then I never would've gotten away. What should I do, Annie?' she asked, even though she knew she needed to speak to Inspector Moller. My God, I'm actually testing her, Emily thought. Even Annie.

'Do? Why there's only one thing to do. I'm going to call Thomas right now. You can't take chances with this, Emily; this is really serious. Whoever is responsible for this is a madman.'

'Emily, this is Debbie Parsons, she's our nurse,' Martin said, returning. 'She'll clean up all those scrapes. Now what happened?'

'I can't possibly go through the story again, Martin,' she said, reluctant to say anything.

'Someone tried to kill her out at the chapel at Alto Vista. This is insane, Martin. Maybe we need to close the resort for a few days. I know the disruption it would cause for the guests and all our regulars, but this can't go on. It's amazing she was able to get away. She hid in the caves. You need to find Thomas. I think Emily should talk to him right away.'

'I'm not sure where he is, but I know he's on the grounds. Let me take a look around. Meanwhile, Emily, you should lie down for a bit.'

By the time Emily's wounds had been treated, Martin was calling on the office phone. 'Thomas is up here at Cliff House, Emily. He'd like you to come up, as soon as you're finished there. If you're feeling up to it, that is.'

'I'm just about finished now. I'll head right up. I'm really anxious to talk to him.'

'I'll walk over with you,' Annie offered. 'Not that I think anything would happen here, but I'd just feel better. I want to see how Jessica's doing anyway. Why don't you join us for lunch after you've spoken to Thomas?'

'I'd like that,' Emily answered as they headed down the terrace steps. 'I was thinking about Jessica earlier. It must be so hard to be in her position. I mean, it was obvious what a sham her marriage had become, but still, he was her husband. And there's Jason to consider . . .'

'It's even worse than that, Emily. She's certainly a prime

suspect in his murder. Thomas has talked to her twice already this morning. I know he's trying to be sensitive to her position, but the issue of where she was when this happened has come up several times. Jessica herself has talked to me about it. Even though she feels she has nothing to hide, the questioning is taking its toll.'

'It must be awful for her,' Emily said, 'and from talking to her yesterday, I know she doesn't have much of an alibi. Annie, you don't think it's possible . . .'

'I don't want to believe that Jessica could have done this but, think about it, she took so much abuse from him it's not beyond the realm of possibility. You know she's pretty young, even though she looks so sophisticated. I don't think she's even thirty yet, and she's had a hard life.'

'Does Inspector Moller think she's guilty?'

'Maybe . . . I don't know. He's spoken to several people more than once. Martin. Jon. Marietta. I don't even want to think about it, Emily. Obviously some of them are people I love very much. And as much as I don't want to think it was Jessica, I guess I'd be lying if I didn't say I'd prefer . . . Oh, let's not talk about it anymore.'

'Whoa,' Nick Marino said, almost colliding with Emily and Annie on the path. 'You too must be busy solving the world's problems – you're hardly even aware of where you're going. Ouch, Emily, what happened to you? Hope the other guy looks worse.'

'It's nothing, Nick,' Emily said, not wanting to go into the story. 'Just a small accident. How are you doing?'

'OK. Doing my bit to boost the morale here, although things seem to be picking up even without my help. And speaking of picking up . . . tell me, Annie, that Mrs Sutherland, the very pretty, very young brunette – is that a look of total boredom I see on her face when she's with the very mature Mr Sutherland?' Nick chuckled at his own wit. 'I just stopped up at the house to see how Jessica was doing. She seems a little better. She said she got out for a bit this morning. I think it helped. She's less nervous. She's in with that police inspector now . . . What's the latest scoop on the investigation? Any real suspects yet?'

'Inspector Moller pretty much keeps his own counsel, Nick,

and from what I hear,' Annie answered, a trace of annoyance in her voice, 'the Sutherlands are very much in love.'

'Oh, well, can't blame a guy for trying. Now that Emily's fiancé is on his way, I'm getting desperate. When is he arriving, Emily?'

'I'm not sure yet, although I imagine it won't be until sometime this evening.'

'Hey, so it sounds like you'll be free for a while. How about lunch?'

'I can't now, Nick,' Emily answered, amazed at his insensitivity. 'I need to head up to the house; Inspector Moller is waiting for me.'

'Again? You're certainly getting a lot of his attention. I hope he realizes he's cutting in on my time. Well, maybe a swim later. I'll buzz your room.'

Emily and Annie resumed their walk up the path and, as soon as Nick was out of earshot Emily turned to Annie with a smile. 'You know, Annie, I think maybe Nick would enjoy sharing a table with that poor little Ms Turner this evening. She seemed to be at a loose end.'

'Perfect idea, Emily. A match made in heaven, I think.'

Inspector Moller was waiting for them when they arrived at the house. His eyes were darkened with concern and he reached his hand out as if to touch the scratches on her face.

'Emily, my God, you look awful. I must say I was worried about something like this happening. Martin didn't know what had gone on exactly, so please come and join me in the study. I'd like to go over this in some detail.'

'OK, but first I'd kill for a . . . bad choice of words. Sorry. I'd really love a cup of coffee.'

'You head in with Thomas,' Annie said. 'And I'll get you both some.'

Emily spent over an hour with Thomas Moller, who wasn't kidding when he said 'in some detail'. And although his main focus was on anything that would help them figure out who had done this, he was considerate and kind in his questioning. Over and over he asked, 'Are you sure you didn't see anyone? Maybe in the distance as you walked? In the chapel? As you turned to run?'

And over and over Emily would answer, 'No, no one. I was just interested in getting away at that point.'

'OK, you didn't actually see anyone.' Then, relentlessly, 'But what was your sense? Sometimes we pick up sensations without even realizing it. Was it a man or a woman? Tall or short? Old or young? Try to think, Emily, please.'

'I just don't know,' Emily answered at first, but then with his gentle prodding she thought she had come up with something. 'You know, it certainly couldn't have been someone who was a good shot, because I don't think they were that far away from me and they missed. And whoever it was wasn't able to catch me running down the path. I mean, I was able to make it to the caves and hide.'

'I hate to tell you this, Emily, but I think whoever did this intended to miss. To scare you off. They want you out of here. They're afraid you know something and think you're going to tell. And it seems to me they know a good bit about this investigation too . . .'

'But how could that . . .'

'They know you haven't yet given us the information we need. They may or may not know why. Either way, they're trying to scare you off before you do. No, Emily, they weren't even really trying. Believe me, if they had wanted it, you'd be dead now.'

Emily was stunned by Moller's words. Get rid of her? To what lengths would they be willing to go? This was insane. Maybe she should leave the island. It would be different if she had the information Inspector Moller needed, if she could at least help find Roger's murderer, but she couldn't even do that. Maybe she should try again. Maybe this time she'd remember.

'I want to try again, Thomas,' she said emphatically. 'I've got to try. There must be something I know. If this person is willing to go to such lengths to get rid of me there's got to be a good reason. And I've got to believe it was something I saw on the beach yesterday.'

'Good. I was certainly going to push you to try again, but I wanted to give you some time. I'm sorry this is happening to you and I'm worried. But I think your attitude is all important.

Even though you still can't recall it, like I've said, I'm also sure you saw something. If you believe you can remember it, I think you have a better shot. Now why don't we take a break and then head outside again. One of these times you'll pass that spot and it will hit you, I'm sure of it.'

Annie was waiting in the living room when they came out. 'Well, that took a long time. Emily, how are you feeling? Maybe you should lie down for a while. Thomas, this is getting more and more serious, isn't it? Any ideas?'

'Nothing concrete yet, I'm afraid. But we'll get there, Annie. I know we will. Meanwhile, you're right that this is serious. Until it's over we'd better keep a closer eye on Emily. From now on she's staying up here at the house. I don't want her in that room by herself.'

'Well, thank God we don't have to worry about that anymore,' Annie responded. 'Emily's fiancé is supposed to be arriving sometime today. And Thomas, Martin and I were talking earlier. Maybe we should close, just for a few days, so . . .'

'Absolutely not, Annie,' Thomas responded, his voice firm. 'I want these people just where they are. All of them. And I don't want any of the guests attempting to leave. I can force them to stay, but I'd rather not. No, I want them to choose to stay, to go on with their vacations.'

'We are trying, Thomas, but the stress . . . It's hard on me but it's Martin I'm thinking of. It's just too much.'

'You can't shut down, Annie. I know how difficult this is for you and Martin but for the next several days I want life at the Bluffs to be normal – or as close to normal as it can be.'

'Normal,' Annie said, lost in thought for a moment. Then she turned to Thomas and Emily. 'You two must be starving. How about some lunch?'

'Not for me, thanks. I've got a couple of people I need to talk to, but I'm sure you could use something to eat, Emily. Then after lunch we can take another walk over to the ocean beach.'

'That sounds fine to me,' said Emily. 'I could use something to eat and some time to relax. I guess the exertion of the morning is starting to hit me.'

Lunch was a quiet affair. Jessica was even more subdued and distracted. She talked a little about Jason and her mom coming but seemed increasingly dispirited. At first Emily thought it must be the tranquilizers that the doctor had given her, but when Annie asked if they were helping, Jessica said she hadn't taken them.

'They make me feel dull and distant, almost like I'm not part of what's going on. And even though there's a part of me that finds that a relief, I can't afford to act that way.'

'Jessica, Jason doesn't arrive until tomorrow. It's all right to give yourself a little time,' Emily said, trying to reassure her.

'It's not Jason's arrival that I'm worried about, Emily. It's Inspector Moller. Annie will tell you. How many times has he interviewed me now – three? Four? I can feel his eyes following me,' she said, the anxiety mounting in her voice. 'I know what he's thinking. I have no alibi. Roger and I had been arguing, and not for the first time. He's thinking I did this, isn't he, Annie?'

'Oh, Jessica, I don't think that's true. Not that you're not a suspect, like most of us here. You are. But I don't think Thomas thinks you did it. If you ask me he seems kind of at a loss at this point, counting more on Emily than anyone else.'

Jessica turned to Emily. 'Someone said something about that. Something about your having seen someone?'

'Inspector Moller thinks I saw the person who did this. Over there, by the small grove of trees. When I was walking down the beach, I thought I saw someone but I wasn't sure. Inspector Moller thinks it was the killer as Roger was murdered just before I got there, but I haven't been able to recall any details. It was far away and the person, if it was a person, was close to the trunk of the tree, I think. Partially hidden by it; maybe even standing behind it. I just don't know.'

'And unfortunately Thomas isn't the only one who thinks Emily might have seen someone,' Annie added. 'You're too distracted to have even noticed the scrapes on Emily's legs and face . . .'

'Oh, God, Emily, I'm sorry. What happened to you?' Jessica said, looking aghast at the scrapes and bruises.

'I went for a walk this morning, down past the grove of trees and round the bend where the shoreline curves, along the ocean side. I went on beyond the dunes. Someone followed me, I guess. Actually took a shot at me.'

'A shot? But why . . . I . . . Oh, I see, if you saw someone then they . . . God, you must have been terrified.'

'It was pretty scary. I got these trying to get away. I really thought I was finished. I hid in some caves and I guess whoever it was couldn't find me. Although, Inspector Moller thinks they weren't even looking. He thinks they got what they wanted – to scare me off.'

'That's incredible,' Jessica said, seemingly shocked. 'Well, you must have seen something this morning. Something that will help them find whoever did this.'

'I'm afraid not. I was too busy trying to get away.'

'What are you going to do? You're in danger here. Maybe you should leave. If you can't remember anything, what's the point? Just get out,' Jessica said, her voice rising. 'If you should think of something, you could always call the police. I would feel awful if anything happened to you, Emily, almost as if it were my fault.' Her eyes darted from Annie to Emily. She bit her lower lip and for a moment her face looked pinched, almost haunted.

'That's foolish, Jessica. None of this is your fault. No, I'll stay, for a while anyway. Michael is arriving sometime today, and that will go a long way toward helping me feel safer . . . I have to keep trying. If I know something that will help, I have to try again.'

'In fact, I think I hear Thomas now,' Annie said. 'Sorry, Emily, but I'm sure he's come back for you.'

SEVENTEEN

Emily wasn't overjoyed to see Inspector Moller again, but she did want to get this over with. The pressure was getting to her. Not pressure from this morning's incident; that wasn't pressure, it was pure fear. No, this was a subtler feeling, subtle but familiar – the feeling that it was her responsibility to solve this thing. She knew that was crazy, but ever since her mother's death Emily had felt an over-whelming sense of duty – at first to her sisters and brother and later, when their lives seemed settled, to her job. She sometimes, like now, wished that she could let go a little, but she also knew that there were a lot of people whose lives would be a whole lot simpler if she could just remember what she saw on that beach. Of course, there was one person . . .

But she wasn't going to let herself think about that. She couldn't or it would paralyze her. She would focus only on the task ahead.

'Ready, Emily? We should get started. The bay beach has gotten pretty busy and I'm afraid some of the guests will head over to the ocean beach. I'd rather it be empty when we do this, like it was yesterday.'

'No problem. I'm ready,' she answered, heading for the front door. As much as she dreaded doing this, she realized that Thomas' presence was reassuring.

'We'll be back shortly, Annie. This shouldn't take too long,' Inspector Moller said. 'Actually, I may want to talk to you and Emily together when we get back.'

They walked slowly down the garden path, Inspector Moller trying to recreate a little of the previous day's setting for Emily. In fact, he insisted that they go as far as the bay beach to the point where her walk with Annie had ended and she had headed back to her room.

Emily recounted her steps, recapturing some of yesterday's mood, her disappointment about Michael and her fatigue from the sailing lessons. Today the air was clear and the sun bright, but yesterday afternoon had been completely different. The early sun had been covered by passing clouds, the air heavy and muggy. And the beach had been completely empty . . . except for Roger.

As she walked toward the ocean beach today, she saw that there were a few people there, quietly reading or dozing in lounge chairs. When she passed them, they would look up, surmising, she supposed, what was going on. The yellow tape was gone, so it was hard to see the exact spot where Roger had been, but as she got closer she could still see the traces of blood in the sand.

'Now, Emily,' Inspector Moller said as they walked along. 'Try as best you can to let your mind go back. I know it's a little more difficult with people around . . . maybe I should have told Martin to close this beach. Anyway, it's too late now. Try to focus on just the spot where Roger was and the grove of trees. And let's talk this through. You arrived at this spot and you thought, what?'

'At this point, I saw the glass on the sand, and I had seen him drinking at the beach bar earlier and heard the argument. So I figured he had just had too much to drink and with the sun and all had just passed out.'

'The argument at the beach bar . . . what exactly happened? I've gotten a couple of versions. Everyone remembers things differently, of course. What do you remember?' Inspector Moller asked.

'Well, it all happened pretty quickly from what I heard. I was in the hammock, so I didn't even look over till the yelling started. It was Roger, of course, and he was obviously drunk or close to it. I guess Jessica was trying to stop him from drinking and he got angry; started being really nasty to her. For a minute, I thought it was going to come to blows. I guess Martin did too and that's why he stepped in. Roger went into a rage and started screaming at Martin.'

'What was he saying?'

'All I remember is something like, "You'll pay for this, Martin, believe me." I don't know if Martin even took him seriously, but the next thing you know, Roger had stomped off.'

'And did anyone go after him?'

'I'm trying to remember, but I don't think so.'

'Not Martin or Jessica?'

'No, no, not Martin. He had his hands full trying to distract everyone, kind of get the party going again. I don't know what happened to Jessica. I didn't really see her leave, but I think I saw her later, when I was trying to call Michael. I was sitting on the patio off Reception, just sort of killing time waiting to call him. I thought I saw her in the distance walking on the beach.'

'Who else was at the beach bar, that you recall?'

'Well, Martin was there, of course, and Annie, for a little while anyway, until she left to go up to Reception. Nora was sitting at a table by herself. I don't remember seeing Marietta. Then more and more people came off the beach. The sun had gotten quite hot and the air was a little heavy, so I think the drinks and the music were a big draw.'

'Did you see anyone else – Sarah or Jon Peterson, perhaps?'

'I did see Jon briefly, in the crowd at the beach bar. But then Annie said she saw him going down to the beach for a swim before the argument with Roger, and didn't see him again.'

'So it's unlikely he heard the arguments and the threats?'

'I'm not sure where he was exactly at the time. It's possible he heard them – it was pretty loud. But he didn't come up to the bar again, so I can't be positive. Sarah wasn't there at all. She came to the main house a little later; I was still waiting for my phone call. She was looking for Jon, as a matter of fact.'

'Did Sarah seem OK, calm? Anxious?'

'She seemed fine really. That was just about all she said – had I seen Jon – and then she went in to check with her mother.'

'Was she surprised that she couldn't find Jon?'

'I don't remember, really,' Emily answered, becoming increasingly uncomfortable again with the probing nature of the questions. 'She mentioned something about the restaurant, but I honestly can't remember what it was.'

Inspector Moller, sensing Emily's growing discomfort, quickly changed the subject back to trying to recreate what Emily had seen. 'OK, so what were you feeling as you stood looking at Roger?'

'That was when I started to feel uncomfortable, like someone was watching me, but I couldn't see anyone. I started to walk across the sand and for some reason got distracted. My eye was drawn to the small grove of trees down there.'

'OK, Emily, now think. What was it that drew your eye? Was it someone moving, maybe?'

'I don't think so, not that I can recall. But it was something . . . I know, it was something shiny. By then the sun had started to move from behind the cloud and it must have been, I don't know, something that glinted in the sun. A watch maybe or a piece of jewelry. I just don't know. I'm sure I didn't see what it was but now that you mention it, there must have been some movement. That means that there must have been someone there! Why can't I remember?'

'Don't try to rush it Emily. It'll come. Each little piece is important. I think you're right – something did glint in the sun, but I don't think it was jewelry or a watch. I think it was a gun. I think whoever killed Roger saw you coming down the path and purposely hid in that grove of trees. And I think whoever did this might have considered killing you too. It may have been your screams that saved you. They were probably afraid someone was nearby and would come right away, so they just took off. But they're certainly worried that you know more than you've said. That's why they followed you this morning and that's why they're trying to scare you off.'

'Sooner or later this person is going to be successful and then whatever I know or don't know won't really matter,' Emily said, aware now of the grave danger she was in. 'I mean, after what happened this morning . . . how do I protect myself? What should I do? Maybe I should just head out of here and go home.'

But Emily knew, even as she said the words, that no one was allowed to leave the resort, and the look on Inspector Moller's face confirmed it. 'Sorry, Emily, but I'm afraid that's one option you don't have. But don't you worry about that; from now on you'll have plenty of protection. Not that you'll notice it. That's the idea. In fact, some of it's already in place. But let's get back to what you saw . . . OK, so something shiny attracted your eye – what else?'

'Well, let's see. I looked hard and certainly my first impression was that there was someone there.'

'Why, what was it that made you think that there was someone? Think, Emily. *Think.*'

'Color, it was color. There was something that jarred with all the greens and browns up there and it's not there now . . . red, it was something red. I'm almost sure of it. I don't see any red up there now, do you?'

'No, Emily, I don't. That's good, that's very good. Now, could you tell what it was?'

'Oh, God, I'm trying, I'm trying. Give me a minute. Maybe it was just a bird or a flower. No, nothing, nothing at all.' Emily shook her head back and forth, frustrated and angry at herself. 'Why can't I see it?'

'It's all right, Emily. Take it easy. We're certainly a little better off than we were before. Would it help, do you think, if I had someone stand there? Perhaps actually seeing someone would help.'

'I don't know. I'm afraid it would just confuse me. Replace the image I'm trying to retrieve. Maybe I should keep trying a little longer.'

'All right, but not now. Enough for now.' Thomas's voice was gentle as he placed a hand on Emily's shoulder. There was warmth in his touch and Emily felt somehow comforted. 'You take a break. Go to the beach. Relax. And Emily, whatever you do, don't go around telling people what's happened here. For your own sake.'

Neither Emily nor Inspector Moller noticed the rustling of the bushes at the end of the path. It wasn't much of an opening, almost imperceptible really, but it was enough. Enough for someone to see all that had gone on . . . enough to hear the words spoken with growing intensity . . . enough to know that Emily was starting to remember.

EIGHTEEN

Emily decided to take Inspector Moller's advice but first headed back to her room. She buzzed the office and asked them to let Annie know she wouldn't be coming back up to the house. She desperately wanted to shower and change.

The water smarted as it beat down on her scrapes, but it was refreshing to wash off the layers of dust and grime, the grim reminders of her morning's adventures. She stood there, running her hands through her hair, allowing herself to revel in the rushing stream, unthinking and relaxed. And as she stepped out of the shower, her first thought was Michael. Michael was coming!

By this evening he would be here and they could finally start the vacation they had dreamed of. She would tell Inspector Moller that she would give it one more try and, OK, if he wanted to try with a person standing there she would try that too. But that was it. She had to stop thinking that this was her responsibility, and if she couldn't remember after two more tries then she just couldn't remember. He'd have to solve the crime some other way. She had waited a long time for this vacation and she deserved it, not to mention that she and Michael desperately needed some time alone to discuss their relationship.

That decision out of the way, she put on her bathing suit, packed her sunglasses and suntan lotion, but not the book this time – she had given up on it – and headed for the beach.

It was crowded on the bay beach: swimmers and snorkelers paddled by just offshore; windsurfers, colorful sails unfurled, sped by at a jaunty clip; and sun-worshippers lazed in hammocks and loungers. The mood was light and airy, and Emily could see that for many of these people Roger's death was a thing of the past, tragic but fading.

She found an empty lounge chair and set her bag down. As she walked over to pick up one of the fluffy white towels from the counter of the equipment shed, she decided to check on the availability of snorkeling gear. Hendrick was there ready to fit her and give her a quick lesson if she liked.

'Sounds good,' Emily said. 'I've never gone snorkeling but my fiancé has. This way I can surprise him when he arrives later.'

They spent about twenty minutes in the water and Emily quickly got used to the mask and snorkel. She kept her head down and her body prone, only occasionally forgetting and trying to put her feet down. She was amazed by the quiet and sense of solitude which descended almost immediately as she swam, and she became transfixed by the sound of her own breathing, steady and rhythmic.

Hendrick went on to teach someone else and Emily slowly paddled down the beach, soothed by the warm, tranquil waters. She lost all track of time and place as she wound her way around the undulating mounds of staghorn coral, basket sponges and sea fans. Colorful fish, neon yellow and blue, some striped and spotted, seemed to play tag with her as she swam. She thought of nothing, allowing both her mind and her body to drift, unaware that there was another swimmer nearby, one not so interested in either the coral gardens or the fish, but only in Emily, carefully watching her every move.

Soon Emily could feel her body getting tired and as she lifted her head out of the water she realized that she had reached the small cove at the end of the bay beach. Its solitude was complete and she couldn't resist spending a few tranquil minutes stretched out on a flat rock warmed by the sun. She closed her eyes and allowed her mind to drift along with the soft lapping of the bay.

Emily was so relaxed that she actually fell asleep. When she awoke, cooled momentarily by the sun's disappearance behind a dark cloud, she had no idea whether she had been lying there for a few minutes or a few hours. She sat up and gazed out at the placid water. Seeing that the sun was still high in the sky, she realized that her deep sense of renewal had resulted from only a few minutes' sleep.

It was when she turned to gather her gear that she realized that she had not been totally alone. There, protruding from her snorkel mask, right where her eyes had been, was a short-handled knife. That was it – no dire warnings, no threatening words, but a clear message, chillingly simple and daringly delivered.

Emily quickly looked around her, more from instinct than anything else. She knew she would find no one. Whoever had delivered this message had done so quietly and quickly. They had not needed to wait around to see her reaction; they'd know soon enough if she'd heeded their warning.

But whoever had delivered this message had seriously misjudged Emily. At that moment, she might as well have been back on the streets of the Bronx arguing that she wasn't too small to play first base. Anger flooded her veins and her resolve strengthened. All thoughts of giving up left her and she once again became determined to see this thing through.

Being as careful as she could, she walked along the edge of the beach, carrying the snorkel back to where she had left her stuff. She wrapped it in her towel and put it in her bag for Inspector Moller. No sense dwelling on it. Thomas would be back soon, and until then she'd have to make the best of it. Hmm, she thought, just when had she started thinking of him as Thomas?

As she headed over to the beach bar she passed Marietta, resplendent once again in her white-feathered cap and cat's-eye sunglasses. Emily could not help but be reminded of a bird. A crane, she thought, the kind with the white-feathered comb on its head, whose lean frame would mirror Marietta's own.

'Marietta, it's good to see you looking so much better,' Emily said graciously as she passed. 'You looked so worn last night.'

'It was wearing, but I am feeling much better today,' she said and then, without taking a breath, prattled on. 'And although I feel terrible saying it, and I would not have wished it to happen, not me . . . I've never had a mean bone in my body, you know, and it certainly is awful for Jessica, although perhaps not. What do you think, my dear? Well, anyway, as I was saying, there is a certain relief in not having to deal with Roger's unpleasantness anymore.'

'I can certainly understand why you're feeling that way. How is Nora feeling today?'

'Much better. You can see the relief in her face. She's taking a swim. She loves the water and she's quite a good swimmer. Although she sometimes appears delicate, she's really very strong. She runs the marathon every year. I hear you're a runner, Emily. Have you ever run the marathon? My God, I could never imagine doing something like that, all that sweat . . . but the water is lovely. Although, I just like to splash myself with it, just to cool off, really.'

Emily could picture just what she meant. When she was a kid, her parents would pile all of them into the old station wagon and head out to the beach – Orchard Beach or Rockaway – where they would swim and play well into the evening. There she would see these small groups of older 'ladies,' perhaps four or five in a line, bathing caps fastened securely to their heads (although Emily could never understand why), who would wade carefully into the water until it lapped their knobby knees. Then, squatting slightly, they would splash the water up on their arms and torsos. They would laugh and shriek at the chill, goose bumps rising on their arms and legs, the summer heat vanquished for the moment. They would never think of going for a 'swim'. Emily imagined they didn't even know how. But that image of those ladies all in a row was one which she would never forget.

'Well, I'm glad you're feeling better, Marietta.'

'Oh, I am, I am, and aren't you a dear to be concerned. I'm really feeling much better, in spite of that inspector with all his questions. And don't think I don't know what he was up to. "Hadn't you quarreled with Roger? Over what?" He must have asked me that ten times. As if he didn't know all about it. But really, if everyone who had words with Roger had killed him, why, my dear, he would have been dead years ago. No, no, this whole thing is no concern of mine. I've even started writing my column for next week. I always try to do one from here. It's great for the place, and no one deserves it more than Martin. My readers seem to like the change from New York society. And there's almost always one or two people here that I can scoop. Of course, Roger's death will have to be the subject of this one. Everyone will expect it. I'm trying to get a focus right now on how to present it in the proper light. You know, it's not the usual subject for my column, but being here and him being who he is . . . ugh . . . *was*, I just can't ignore it. I don't suppose there's any more news?'

'Not that I've heard,' Emily said.

'I saw you with Inspector Moller a little while ago. Why on earth is that man bothering you, of all people? You didn't even know Roger. But I did hear someone say that he was hoping you could help him. Whatever is that all about?'

'Well, unfortunately, he didn't get any help from me. But I'm sure he must have lots of leads to track down.'

'I don't think so, Emily. In fact, people seem to be talking about you quite a bit – some sort of clue, they're saying. You must let me know if you come up with something. You must promise me! It would be so exciting, a real scoop for my column. And you would be famous! Ah, here comes Nora now.'

'Hello, Emily. I saw you out there snorkeling. The cove is beautiful, isn't it? But those scratches, what happened to you?'

'Oh, it's nothing, Nora, just a mishap out by Alto Vista.'

'Oh, my dear,' Marietta said. 'How awful, you're all scraped up. And here I am going on and on, not even noticing. Did you go to the chapel there? Isn't it beautiful? Forlorn, of course, but beautiful. Martin drove us out that way yesterday. Then we went on to a local artist's gallery. I bought the most wonderful watercolor. It's so important to support these local artists, don't you think? The painting is quite delightful. Where do you think we should hang it, Nora? Perhaps in the music room. No, I don't think so. The dining room? No. Oh, dear, I don't really see it anywhere. Never mind. Now, you were saying, my dear, you went to Alto Vista. Isn't it beautiful?'

'It was,' Emily said, amazed at the transformation in Marietta. 'Perhaps I'll go back there with Michael. Right now, though, I'm on the lookout for a lonely hammock and a piña colada. I'm going to enjoy the sun.'

'Oh, that's right, your young man is arriving. I hope we'll see the two of you at the barbecue tonight. Will he be here by then? That will be the best thing for you. I'm sure you can't wait. And then that Inspector Moller will stop bothering you. After all, it's your vacation and all. What time do you expect him?'

'I'm not sure, but I certainly hope he'll make it for the barbecue. I hear it's one of the most enjoyable events at the Bluffs.'

'It certainly is. So even if Michael hasn't arrived make sure you get there. You know, there'll always be room at our table. There's usually a big group of us and without . . .' Marietta paused. 'Anyway, I hope we'll see you later. Enjoy your afternoon, Emily.'

Emily couldn't help but wonder as she set off for the beach bar. Marietta certainly was a character, so talkative today, relaxed yet so in control. But there was something about the conversation that bothered her, and for the life of her she couldn't put her finger on what it was. Something that was said, she was almost sure of it . . . what was it? She tried to think back over their conversation, but as she neared the beach bar all thoughts of it disappeared.

It seemed that Emily wasn't the only one with a thirst; there was already a lively crowd assembled.

'Emily, how are you?' asked Catherine Phillips pointedly. 'We heard it was you who found Roger. How awful for you. I looked for you yesterday evening but you weren't at dinner. Of course, how could you possibly eat after that? We couldn't even stay in our rondoval. Not right there, in front of where . . . you know . . . Roger . . . you know. Anyway, someone said you stayed in yours. I don't know how you could do that after what happened.'

'Perhaps I shouldn't have, but it was fine really. I was so exhausted nothing could've kept me awake.'

Carter Phillips, carrying a tall, cool drink for Catherine, joined them. 'Well, Emily, you've become famous – unfortunately so, I'm afraid,' he said loudly before turning to his wife. 'Here, my dear, perhaps this will help . . .' He turned back to Emily. 'I'm afraid Catherine still hasn't completely gotten over what happened. Tell me, is it true what I hear? That you saw the killer?'

'No, no, that's not what happened at all,' said Emily, becoming alarmed that this was being spoken about so openly around the island and knowing the safest option was to stay cautious. 'I thought I might have seen something, not necessarily some*one*, down at the end of the beach by the small grove of trees. That's all.'

'That's all!' said Catherine, becoming agitated just at the thought. 'Well, I would just die if I thought I had seen the . . . you know . . . killer. Can you imagine that, Carter? Actually seeing a . . . *killer*. Have you talked to the police? What do they say?'

'I've spoken to the police but really there's nothing much

to talk about,' Emily said, trying to play down the whole thing. She noticed that the Phillips weren't the only ones interested in this conversation. A number of people nearby were staring at her and listening closely to what was being said. 'I don't even know for sure if there was someone down there, so I haven't been much of a help.'

'Well, if I know people, that Inspector Moller will keep at this,' Carter continued. 'Tenacious, I'd say. Just doesn't let go. I saw him questioning that guy over there a while ago, and the guy was looking really angry. But the inspector kept on at him.'

It was impossible for Emily to tell who he was talking about as there were so many men standing in the direction of Carter's nod. Maybe I should take a walk over there, she thought. She was curious as to who was getting so angry being questioned by Thomas – someone who had something to hide, perhaps?

'Well, Mandy Thompson said he was bothering her just before,' Catherine began before Emily could excuse herself. 'Something about someone in a red shirt. Really, what are we supposed to do, remember what everyone wears? Just because Mandy said she thought some guy was wearing a red shirt at the bar yesterday afternoon. It was just ridiculous. It's a good thing he hasn't been asking me any questions, apart from that first evening. Well, he certainly knew then that I had nothing to tell him. But even so, it was distressing. And I told Martin that. Why, I barely slept all night.'

'Now, now, Catherine. I know this is upsetting but, as I told you, you did sleep. I heard you. I'm not saying you weren't a little restless but really there's nothing poor Martin can do about this.'

'I suppose you're right. Still and all, this is our vacation.'

'That's right. Now let's put all this behind us and start enjoying ourselves. Tonight's the barbecue, and you know how much you love that,' Carter said. And then, turning to Emily, he added, 'Each year we dress up in costume for the barbecue. You can if you want. It's great fun really.'

'Oh, it is,' Catherine said, all remnants of petulance leaving her voice. 'Do come, Emily. We're going as pirates. We won't be the only pirates there, not by a long shot. But I'll bet we'll be the best. I spent months looking for these costumes and then altering them, adding small touches to make them more authentic. Carter is wearing an eye patch. I do hope we win this year. Last year we took third place but I think we'll do better this year. What do you think, Carter? Do you think we'll win?'

'For your sake I hope so, my dear,' Carter said with the slightest roll of his eyes. 'I know how hard you've worked. Now, Emily, can I get you something to drink?'

'No, thank you, Carter,' Emily said quickly, seeing her chance to make a quick getaway. Although she loved parties, she was having a hard time empathizing with Mrs Phillips' anxiety over her pirate costumes. 'I'm actually looking for someone and I thought I saw them over there. But thanks for the tip about the barbecue. And I'll be rooting for you tonight.'

Emily made her way to the other side of the bar to check out the crowd. She recognized a few people but still had no idea who Carter Phillips was talking about. She did see Mandy Thompson in an animated conversation with Nick Marino, who had his arm around the sexy Ms Turner, who was now wearing a neon-pink bikini and, of course, had matching pink nails. Hmm, thought Emily, something about water finding its own level . . .

They barely acknowledged her as she approached, both women obviously enthralled with whatever Nick was saying. In fact, it was Nick who finally turned to her. 'Oh, Emily,' he said somewhat sheepishly. 'Let me introduce Mandy Thompson and Tammy Turner. Tammy just arrived this morning and, like you, she's at loose ends for the day.'

Her ends are a lot looser than mine, Emily thought. Then, turning to Tammy, she said, 'Although we didn't meet, I did see you earlier at the front desk. Something about a room?'

'I thought I'd never get that stuff straightened out,' Tammy said, her indignation rising. 'Of all things. Can you imagine? I couldn't get my own room. Me . . . I always get my own room. Tony, my partner, understands that . . . and that Annie woman, who is she anyway? Nothing like Penny – she's so sweet and helpful. She fixed the whole thing. I mean, what gives? There's this great room standing empty, just because some guy got himself killed on the beach nearby? It's not like it happened in the room, jeez . . . And even then, I might've been willing to take that room. It's a beaut.'

Emily groaned inwardly. The thought of having the petulant Ms Turner as one of her near neighbors was an unsettling one. She'd have to take great pains to avoid her. 'Well, I'm glad to hear it worked out for you,' she said, purposely avoiding any mention that they would be neighbors.

'Well, Nick, what do you say? Wanna be my Blackbeard for tonight?' Ms Turner said seductively, returning to the obvious object of her desires. 'Tony's not gonna be here till tomorrow and I got a great costume. Wait till you see it. I'll bet I win that contest. Can you imagine, some of these old dames think they're gonna win? The only way they'd win is if—'

'Speaking of seeing things, Emily,' Nick said, cutting Tammy off in mid-sentence. 'Rumor has it that you may have seen the killer.'

'That's a rumor, Nick,' Emily said, trying to dispel everyone's interest. 'I just thought I might have seen someone, up ahead by the trees at the end of the beach. I don't know why everyone's making such a big deal out of this. It could have been a branch of a tree or a bird, for all I could tell.'

'Are you going to the barbecue?' Tammy asked Emily, seemingly oblivious to the conversation around her. 'Everyone goes in costume. It's a lot of fun. But don't count on winning. I got a great costume. As I was saying, I got that contest won hands down.'

'Well, I bet that Inspector Moller has been all over you,' Mandy said to Emily, ignoring Tammy and obviously trying to draw Nick's attention.

'I saw you out with him earlier, Emily,' Nick said. 'You two seem to be spending an awful lot of time together, and he doesn't seem like the type who wastes his time . . . although I can't imagine how any time spent with you could be called wasted.'

'I've just tried to be helpful, but I can't tell him what I can't remember, although . . .' Emily quickly stopped herself, remembering Inspector Moller's warning. But it probably didn't matter. Emily could see that was already turning his attention back to the sultry Ms Turner. 'Actually, I think I've done all I can but I guess we all have to keep trying. Well, time to get myself a drink and head out for that empty hammock. See you later, Nick.'

'So what about it, Nick?' she could hear Ms Turner saying as she walked off. A perfect pair, just as she had thought.

As she headed for the bar, Emily saw Martin chatting with several guests.

'Emily, over here,' he called. 'Come and meet the Parkers. Mark is a friend of Jon's and Nancy went to school with Alex in New York. She actually introduced the two of you, if I'm not mistaken, Nancy.'

'She sure did. You know Alex. She insisted that I come down to the island when my parents were away one Christmas vacation. She had decided months before that Mark and I would make a perfect match and that we had to meet.'

'She had actually tried to fix us up a few months before but it fell through,' Mark added. 'But Alex was undaunted. She wouldn't give up. She was sure that Nancy and I were perfect for each other.'

'And she was right,' Nancy declared, contentedly.

'Mark and Nancy just arrived today. They're living in New York right now. I think somewhere near you, Emily.'

'Michael and I live on East 43rd, close to the United Nations. I'd introduce you to him but unfortunately he got stuck in London on business. He should be here this evening.'

'Oh, we know that situation all too well. Mark has been with Fitch, Sturgis for a while but he's starting a new job next week right on 53rd. We're on East 48th so it's perfect, a great location, and there's a small park right down the street, so when the baby's born . . .'

Emily hadn't even noticed that Nancy was pregnant, although it wasn't all that obvious. 'Oh, how wonderful. When are you expecting?'

'In June. We're really excited,' Nancy said.

'And maybe a little nervous,' Mark added.

Emily felt immediately drawn to Mark and Nancy, chatting comfortably about jobs, neighborhoods and families. Nancy was a legal aid lawyer who worked with family court, so she and Emily had a lot in common. And Fitch, Sturgis was one of the firms that Michael had been considering before he started at Michner, Dawkins, Harris & Smith.

'Michael interviewed with Fitch, Sturgis. How did you like it, Mark?'

'Oh, it's a great firm, but you know the demands, and now with the baby coming . . . Nancy and I talked about it. It's tough. The money's great, but in the end we decided it wasn't really working for us.'

'I love my job, Emily,' Nancy added. 'So after the baby comes I'll stay on part time. With Mark's new job he'll have a lot more time, so we'll be able to work it out. We could never do that if he was still at Fitch.'

Emily was amazed at the similarities in their situations; although, it seemed that Mark and Nancy were a little further along in resolving the settling down issues than she and Michael were. She couldn't wait for Michael to meet them; maybe it would help. A different perspective, but was it one that Michael could appreciate? Martin and Mark wandered off briefly and by the time they got back Emily and Nancy were fast friends, making plans to meet at the barbecue that evening.

'I'm almost sure that Michael will be here by then. Wouldn't you think so, Martin?' Emily asked.

'I would imagine, although it depends on where he's coming in from. But it certainly can't be much later than that.'

'Maybe Sarah and Jon can join us,' Nancy added. 'Although I guess that would be difficult for Jon.'

'I thought so too, but I'm way ahead of you,' Mark said. 'I just spoke to him. The barbecue doesn't start till seven-thirty, and Jon says the restaurant won't be busy so he can easily get away.'

'Sounds great,' Nancy said. 'And now it's time for me to head back to our room for a nap or I won't be going anywhere this evening. We'll see you later, Emily. Why don't we meet on the terrace before the barbecue?'

'Great,' she said, feeling more and more distant from the

horror of Roger's murder. 'I'm really looking forward to it. See you then.'

Emily was quite content to settle herself comfortably on the wide white hammock, a soft pillow under her head and a gentle breeze in the air. She would have her nap here, she thought, allowing her mind to wander.

It was as if Inspector Moller and the investigation were eons away but, of course, it was only a few minutes before reality rudely interrupted.

'Well, Emily,' he said, appearing by her hammock. 'Shall we give it one more try?'

NINETEEN

Oh, damn, she thought, he is beyond relentless. What was it Nick had said? "He doesn't seem like the type who wastes his time." Her earlier resolve had already waned, melting in the midday sun. She resented the intrusion, and why did he keep asking the same questions over and over? She was a witness – the first on the scene – and yet she probably knew more about the investigation than any of the other guests thanks to the discussions she had had with Inspector Moller. An uncomfortable thought suddenly struck her. Could it be that Thomas suspected her? He might seem to be confiding in her, but was he trying to trip her up? Could she have misjudged him so much? His support, his concern? No . . . surely that was ridiculous. And anyway, there could be no reason for Thomas to be suspicious of her. Even though, like many people involved, she had no alibi, she also had no motive. She hardly even knew Roger. But maybe she should be a bit more wary of where this was going. She'd give anything to forget all that had happened, but she knew that she couldn't run away from this.

'Sorry, Emily, I can see from your face that you'd rather I wasn't here, but this can't wait.'

'I know, Thomas,' she said, reluctantly pulling herself out of the hammock. 'It's just so strange, that's all. Some of the people here hardly even knew Roger and they're quickly forgetting what happened; others weren't even here yesterday so the whole thing barely exists for them. And I seem to be caught right in the middle of it. I end up being the one to discover Roger and I pretty much know everyone who's a suspect. I can't even safely go for a walk and now . . . I have something to show you.'

Emily reached into her bag and drew out the towel-wrapped knife. 'Another message . . . I was lying over in the cove, stretched out on a rock. I guess I fell asleep and when I woke up, I found this.'

Thomas's face darkened. 'Hmmm . . . it seems our killer is getting more daring, or more desperate. Did you touch this?'

'I was pretty careful. I tried to keep it just as I found it, pretty much like that.'

'Well, we'll check it for prints, and maybe we can track down this knife. But I have to tell you, I'm not hopeful. It's a fisherman's knife, pretty common here on the island. But we'll see what we can do.'

'Michael's coming this evening. We've been waiting for this vacation for so long. I want to be like everyone else here. I just want to . . . I just want to remember and for this whole thing to be over.'

'I know how difficult this must be for you, and I know how schizophrenic the mood here seems. A lot of people want to forget all about what's happened and it's Martin's and Annie's job to try to help them. This place is their livelihood and most of those guests have nothing to do with this. They paid a lot of money to stay here and they deserve to enjoy it. But don't let that surface gaiety fool you,' he continued. 'This is serious business. Just because Roger wasn't the best-loved person in the world doesn't mean we're not going to pursue this till we find his killer. Martin and Annie may seem to be trying to put this behind them, but it's just appearances. Remember, a lot of these people are still suspects.'

'And I want to help, really I do,' Emily said in earnest. 'But I'm tired of it. I keep going over and over it in my mind.

Again and again. It's no use. I can't remember. Maybe I should just give up.'

'You can't give up, Emily. Not just because we need your help, but because you're in too deep. Remember there's a murderer out there who's afraid you know too much. Even if we let you leave here immediately, you couldn't feel sure that you wouldn't be followed.' Thomas seemed genuinely concerned for her welfare, which helped to dispel her earlier thoughts. 'Remembering what you saw on that beach has become as important to your safety as it is to my investigation.'

'I guess so,' Emily answered. 'I . . . I need to ask you . . . When I was talking with Jessica at lunch . . . she thinks that you . . . Do you think she did it?'

'Look, I'm not going to lie to you. Jessica's a pretty strong suspect right now. She has no alibi and from what I hear Roger was—'

'Oh, I know what Roger was. And I have to tell you, I don't know if I'd even blame Jessica . . . but I just don't believe she did it. I've talked to her; she really confided in me. She was so upset . . . but she was honest too. I mean, about Roger . . . their marriage. No, no one could put on that good a show. Jessica couldn't have done it.'

'Believe me, I'd like that to be true but so far . . .'

'All right, one more try, let's go,' Emily said, realizing the truth of what Thomas was saying. She had no choice.

'Let's do exactly what you did yesterday,' the inspector said. 'We'll start at the point where you left Annie. I think the ocean beach should be fairly quiet now; most of the crowd seems to be at the beach bar. But it may not be completely empty. You'll have to block out whoever is there and just try to focus on the grove of trees. OK?'

'OK,' Emily answered, trying to psych herself up. The more time she spent with Thomas, the more she wanted to be successful. She was beginning to realize how difficult this inquiry must be for him. His friendship with Martin and Annie, and Jon being one of his oldest friends must make this whole investigation so much more complicated. Yet she could see his resolve; his determination to find the truth.

Once again she relived rounding the point and seeing Roger

slumped in his beach chair. She recounted her concern that his face would get burned out there in the sun, and her belief that he had obviously passed out. And then, she came to the spot where she had become distracted by something, something flashing in the sun down by the grove of trees. When she had looked she had seen nothing, and then she had remembered, that flicker of something red, moving . . . moving as if behind the trees.

'OK, Emily. Let's focus on that flicker of red. Can you remember anything more? Anything, the smallest impression. You don't have to be positive, just an impression.'

'I guess the best I can do is point out where I saw that flash of red. Would that help?'

'It might; I'll take anything at this point. We really have nothing else, except a lot of suspects, most of them with very strong motives and very weak alibis. Why don't we walk down there and you can show me.'

The beach was perfectly empty now, not like earlier, but as Emily walked along she started to get that feeling of being watched again. She felt foolish mentioning it – Inspector Moller would begin to think she was crazy – but she couldn't shake it. By the time she reached the grove of trees she couldn't resist turning around to see if there was anyone watching them, maybe sitting on the low beach wall or on one of the balconies.

'What's the matter, Emily?' Inspector Moller said, sensing her mood.

'It's that feeling again, like someone is watching me. You must think I'm crazy. I'm beginning to think I'm crazy. I know there's no one there but I just can't shake it.'

'I don't think you're crazy. Just because we can't see someone watching us doesn't mean that there's no one there. There are plenty of spots where someone who doesn't want to be seen could hide and still have a pretty clear view of what's going on here. And I have no doubt that there's someone watching your every move. Someone who's mighty interested in what's happening. But let's just try to focus on the trees for now. And remember, there are some good guys out there too.'

'OK. For what it's worth, that flash of red was just about here,' she said, indicating a spot about chest high, and then remembered what Catherine Phillips had said about Thomas bothering Mandy Thompson. 'A shirt, Thomas. It must have been someone's shirt. I only saw it for a second, so I know whoever it was must have tried to hide themselves in among the trees.'

'Did you see a lot of red or just a little? That might help us decide if the person was heavy or thin.'

'I don't know, just sort of average, I guess, but average doesn't really tell you a hell of a lot, does it?'

'Nope, it doesn't. Anything else you can think of?'

'Nothing, absolutely nothing. This has been less than helpful. Sorry, I just can't seem to remember, no matter how hard I try.'

'Why don't we walk on a little further. This is the route you took this morning, isn't it?'

'Yes, straight around the bend and along the path that follows the ocean.'

Once again, Emily found herself among the dunes on this wild and desolate coast where the landscape resembled the moon more than the earth. Daunting waves crashed along the shore and hulking rocks and boulders sat on its edge like ramparts. The trade winds, stronger this afternoon than earlier, sprayed water and sand in the air around them.

'Let's walk back this way!' Inspector Moller cried, having to raise his voice to be heard above the gusts. 'It will be calmer back here and we'll be able to talk.'

The landscape mirrored Emily's mood, all thought of Michael and the barbecue long gone. It was hopeless. She couldn't remember anything else, no murky shape or vague outline. Nothing that would even help narrow down the suspects, let alone find the killer. There had to be something, some way to reach what was locked inside her brain.

'I know this is unusual,' she said, 'but how about trying a hypnotist? I saw it used once back home. It was in a missing person's case and it actually worked.'

'And it's really not as unusual as you might think,' Thomas said thoughtfully. 'We've tried it in the past but not with a great deal of success. Particularly with cases like yours, where you're not even sure of what you saw, or how much you saw. We've been more successful in cases where the person was fairly sure that they had actually seen the image but had blocked it for some reason. I don't know, Emily, maybe a flash of red was all you saw and maybe you didn't even see that.'

'You sound even more discouraged than I am. But I have to admit that I feel like I'm becoming less sure of what I saw by those trees. You would think, after all these tries, that if I'd seen anything more it would have come back to me by now.'

'The mind is a strange thing, Emily. We had a case a couple of years ago where a woman witnessed the murder of a neighbor, knew she had clearly seen the killer, but couldn't recall anything about him – not the color of his hair, his eyes or even his skin. It wasn't until two years later, during an argument with her husband, that the image came back to her. It was him. He was the man she had seen running from the neighbor's house. He had never talked about it, convinced that she hadn't realized it was him or had chosen to cover up for him. She turned him in, of course. He had been abusive for years; the shrink was convinced that her fear of him had totally blocked the image.'

'Why did she finally remember?'

'Who knows? The theory was that the fear that he was going to kill her overcame the fear that he was going to beat her, and that finally unlocked the image. There is another way though,' Inspector Moller continued. 'A way I had hoped to avoid, but it may be the only way at this point.'

'Look, I'm willing to try almost anything. I want this thing over with, not just for myself but for Martin and Annie . . . and Jessica, of course. There's got to be some resolution for everyone.'

'OK. Now, I wouldn't even take the chance of trying this if your fiancé wasn't coming today, because you have to know that this could be dangerous. But with him here I feel a little better. You see, it's not really all that necessary for you to remember what you saw, it's only necessary that the killer think that you're on the verge of remembering. And then . . .'

'Then, I would be the bait.'

'That's right. I'm convinced that whoever murdered Roger is already coming after you. They've tried warning you. If they think that you're not only still cooperating with the police, but close to remembering something significant . . . well, they have no choice. They have to try to shut you up. And this time it'll be permanently.'

'How would you do it? I mean, what would you say?' Emily asked, her voice awash with concern and curiosity.

'Well, I believe whoever the murderer is, he or she has been observing us pretty closely. So we would have to start the charade now, on our way back to the main house. When you come to the spot where you looked over toward the grove of trees, I would ask you to actually pretend like you were seeing something. Just a shape – something vague – since we don't really know what you're supposed to be seeing. And don't say much. Just that you think you remember, the flash of red, a shape . . . that's all.'

'And will that be enough, do you think? I mean, it's not really much more than I've already said.'

'It'll be enough to give someone the impression that the image is coming back to you. Remember, this person is not far from the edge as it is. Then, when we get back to the main house, I'm going to talk about a breakthrough, loudly enough to be overheard. And ask to arrange for you to meet with Salena Cartera. She's a noted hypnotist on the island. Of course, we won't be able to arrange it until tomorrow . . .'

'And then what?'

'And then, the hard part . . . then we wait.'

'Where would I go? What would I do? Who would be around to offer protection?'

'You'd have to go on about your business as if nothing had happened. By the time we get back and set this in motion, it will be fairly late. I guess that you and Michael are planning to go to the barbecue this evening?'

'Well, yes, I had made plans to meet another couple on the terrace at seven-thirty and head over together. That is, if Michael is here by then. He thought he would be, but you never know.'

'I would hate to have to do this with him not here, but I'm afraid that's a risk we'll have to take. Once we set this in motion there's no turning back. But there'd be plenty of protection out there for you, Emily, as I've said. We'd be very careful. You wouldn't know who, of course, but you can rest assured that you wouldn't be alone. And I have my officers patrolling too, of course.'

'Well, I guess I'll have to trust you on that one. You know, the more I think about it, I don't really have any choice, do I? It's kind of like damned if you do and . . . Oh, well, what the hell. It's worth a try. It's certainly better than doing nothing and just waiting for . . .'

'We'll protect you, Emily. You have my word on that. So, are you ready for that Academy Award performance? Shall we head back?'

TWENTY

Emily and Inspector Moller were talking animatedly as they rounded the bend back to the small grove of trees. Emily stopped and walked back and forth, looking carefully and finally gesturing to the spot where she had 'seen' the flash of red. She motioned to several spots, openly gesturing with her arm, pointing and moving it back and forth, up and down.

She again felt as if she was being watched, but this time she could feel venom in the eyes. Was it real or just the power of suggestion?

'It's eerie, I already feel like the killer is watching me,' she whispered to Thomas. 'But I'm not sure if it's real or just because I know I'm putting on an act for someone.'

'Oh, it's real all right,' he said quietly. 'In my business you develop a sixth sense about that. If you don't, you're not in the business for long. Someone's watching us all right . . . But don't look around. Remember, we don't want them to suspect. You're doing great. From this point on, we both have to play our parts. Now walk down the beach to the spot where Roger was and then turn back to face the grove of trees. Then point.'

Emily did as she was told, walking purposefully now, as if to complete something she had started. When she got to the right spot she turned and pointed to the trees.

'I think I'm remembering something,' she said, not loudly but with some animation in her voice as she walked back to him. 'It's not clear but that red flash . . . I think it was a shirt, and the person was moving.'

'Good, Emily,' Inspector Moller said, his voice matching her own in tone and mood. 'Can you remember anything else? Try, but remember what I said – easy, don't force it.'

'I'm trying,' she said, some of the animation leaving her voice. 'It's so fleeting . . . why is it so fleeting?'

'I know how difficult it is, Emily. But it's getting better. Can't you feel that?'

'I do think it's getting better, but it's taking so long and I've remembered so little.'

Inspector Moller turned to her as if proposing his idea for the first time. 'What if someone could help you remember?' he said. 'Would you be willing to try it?'

'How?' Emily asked, her voice purposely showing some curiosity. 'How could someone help?'

'We've tried this with a few cases and we've had some success with it. A hypnotist. A woman in Oranjestad. She's worked with us before. Would you be willing to try it?'

'I guess so,' Emily said, making sure she sounded uncertain at first. 'Yes, yes, I'd be willing to try it . . . anything to put an end to this.'

'Good,' Inspector Moller said, as if excited now. 'Let's head back to the main house.'

The two of them walked back as if a weight had been lifted from their shoulders, as if the success of the hypnotist was not merely a possibility but a certainty. If only this were true, Emily thought as she walked. It was a much more comforting prospect than what was really awaiting her.

The young officer who met them as they entered the main house seemed taken aback at Inspector Moller's demeanor.

Usually serious and quiet, the inspector had a reputation for keeping his thoughts and plans close to the chest. So when he loudly directed the officer to contact the hypnotist, Salena Cartera, and do it immediately, the young man just stared.

'Oh, never mind, I'll do it myself. Emily, why don't you have a seat on the terrace. Ah, Martin, I think we're making some progress. Maybe Emily would like something cool to drink, it's very warm out in that sun . . . I need to make an important call. We're bringing in Salena Cartera. May I use the office phone?'

'Of course, of course. Salena Cartera, what an intriguing idea. Emily, what can I get you? It sounds like you've earned it. Tell me, what's been going on?'

Emily hesitated before answering Martin. When Inspector Moller had talked about spreading the idea that Emily was remembering stuff, it had sounded OK. But telling it to Martin seemed like just plain old lying. And what about the others? She thought of them as her friends. She was really uncomfortable with it and couldn't bring herself to do it.

'I'd love a lemonade, Martin. Tall and cold. I'm hot and tired, and just want to relax for a couple of minutes.' She knew that Martin was much too polite to ask the question again and this gave her a few minutes to think of what to say.

As he came back to the table, she immediately asked, 'Anything from Michael? I guess he hasn't arrived or you would have mentioned it. Any calls?'

'Nothing yet. It should be soon, though. If he's coming through San Juan he should be here within the hour. Venezuela would be a little later. Now, it sounds like you're making progress.'

'She certainly is, Martin,' said Inspector Moller as he exited the office. 'It's starting to come back. I think we're getting somewhere. And with Salena's help, I think we might just sew this up. Unfortunately, she's not on the island. But she'll be back in the morning and is very willing to help. Excited, actually. She said she would come out here. Is that all right with you, Martin?'

'Fine, fine, of course. I know how good Salena is, Thomas. I think it's a great idea.'

The guests sitting on the terrace couldn't help but overhear the conversation, and although there were only a few of them, Emily knew that the news would be all over the place in a very short time. After all, the use of a hypnotist to help retrieve crucial evidence from a key witness in a murder investigation was the type of thing that movies were made of. In fact, even as they sat there, Emily could see the voluptuous Ms Turner put down her drink and leave the terrace. She could barely maintain her usual saunter as she headed toward a group of sun-worshippers still sitting on the beach. It was quite obvious from her haste that she couldn't wait to tell them what she had just heard.

'As I mentioned earlier, there were a couple of pictures up at the house that I wanted to show you,' Inspector Moller said to a bewildered Emily. 'Like we discussed, it's important for you to explore every avenue. I'd like to do that now, if we could?'

'Oh, sure, I forgot,' Emily said, not having the slightest idea of what he was talking about.

'Is Annie up at the house, Martin?' Inspector Moller asked. 'Would it be all right if Emily and I headed up there?'

'Yes, Annie's there, and Jessica, poor thing. Jason is scheduled to arrive around noon tomorrow. She's still unsure what to tell him. It's the whole murder thing. Such a harsh thing for a child to hear, especially when he loved his father so much. But of course she can't keep it from him much longer. He's bound to hear it. I understand it's hit all the New York papers.'

'We tried to keep it quiet as long as we could,' Inspector Moller said. 'Do you think the publicity will hurt, Martin?'

'It certainly could,' Martin answered, obviously concerned. 'But you know, Thomas, a lot depends on who did this and why . . . and more importantly, how the reporters are treated when they arrive,' he continued somewhat wryly.

'Oh, Martin,' Emily sympathized. 'You and Annie must be worried.'

'Well, I won't say I'm not, but you truly never know how these things will go. Remember several years ago, Thomas, when Carlotta Devine was killed by her husband at Coral Reefs? He, of course, was in a jealous rage because Carlotta was there with her European lover. She had told him she was going to an East Coast health spa to get "retooled." But, as fate would have it, she was inadvertently photographed at the airport here with another man by a news reporter doing a story about the boost in tourism since the closing of the oil refinery. Her husband just happened to see the clip. Usually he didn't even watch the news, but with Carlotta away he had a lot of time on his hands. Incredible.

'Anyway,' he continued, 'the reporters spent more time writing about the place than they did about the murder. "Romantic hideaway." "Luxurious surroundings." The fact that Charlie Stemple spent most of his time that week offering them free drinks and the more than occasional meal, well . . . his business jumped twenty per cent the following year.'

Emily laughed in spite of the underlying gruesomeness of the story.

'So if you're looking for me in the next couple of days you'll find me trying to get a handle on the newspaper reporters . . . in the bar. All joking aside,' Martin added seriously, 'I hope the place won't suffer, Emily. It's everything to us. It's not just our business, you know, it's our lives. Now, I better get back to my work or we won't have any business. Tonight's a big night here. You and Michael are coming to the barbecue, I take it?'

'I certainly hope "we" will be coming. We're planning to meet Mark and Nancy beforehand. As long as Michael gets here on time, that is. Either way, you'll certainly see me there.'

'We should be heading up to the house,' Inspector Moller urged.

'I hope this won't take long,' Emily said as they headed out the door. 'It's been such a long day. I'd really love to take a nap before the barbecue.'

When they were out of Martin's earshot, Emily felt she had to let Thomas know how uncomfortable the thought of lying to Martin had made her feel. 'I didn't realize that this would mean lying to people I care about. I know I should have but . . . I think you'd better be ready in case Annie asks any questions. It was difficult enough with Martin; it will be impossible with Annie.'

'I know it's difficult, but there are people here who are still suspects.'

'I know, but Martin? I'm sorry, I just have such a hard time believing that. I know, I know what you're going to say . . . the path this morning, Martin's anger over the review, the fact he went missing at the time of the murder. And at times I've wondered. But then I just have to spend a few minutes with him and . . . it's just so hard to imagine.'

'Look, it's hard for me to imagine too, but I can't take any chances. Remember, Emily, this is no game. It's your life we're gambling with here. Anyone who's a suspect, even if it was my own mother . . . OK, maybe not my mother, but absolutely anyone else, gets the same story. And that includes Jessica, too.'

'Just don't ask me to be the one to tell it. I've never been a very good liar. I'm a pretty good actress but a bad liar. With most people this is like playing a role but with Martin and Annie . . . maybe we could just not say anything to Annie?'

'The whole idea of this is to spread the word, Emily,' Inspector Moller reminded her.

'OK, but remember, I'm counting on you to do this . . . and what pictures are you talking about?'

'That was just an excuse to get up to the house.'

'Why? Why not just let Martin tell Annie and Jessica? He's bound to, and that way I wouldn't have anything to do with it.'

'I need to see Jessica's reaction when she hears you're starting to remember.'

'No . . .'

'Look, Jessica's a suspect – the prime suspect. I know you see her as the grieving wife, but she's had a hard life. I've done some background work on her. Her father was abusive and an alcoholic. The guy she was living with before she married Roger was no bargain and Roger had become increasingly abusive over the years. At one time, I guess Jessica was willing to put up with all that stuff but in recent years . . .'

'You know how I feel about this . . . if she did it I wouldn't blame her . . .'

'A lot of people wouldn't. More and more juries are

responding to the battered wife defense. And Jessica certainly comes close to fitting that picture. Was the fight the other afternoon the last straw? Who knows? But it certainly is more than just a possibility.'

Annie and Jessica were sitting on the balcony when Emily and Inspector Moller reached the house. Jessica looked better, less drawn, but still, her eyes were red and her expression sad. Annie looked tired and worn; not at all the way she appeared when mingling with the guests. It was now obvious what a toll this was taking on her.

'Thomas, Emily . . . Martin called to say you were heading up,' Annie said as they neared. 'He said something about pictures.'

Emily wondered how much Martin had said, and if Inspector Moller had lost his opportunity to observe Jessica's reaction.

'Yes, there are some pictures that I wanted Emily to look at.'

'How's it going, Thomas? Anything?' Annie asked, concern marking her face.

'Well, nothing definite, Annie. But both of you will be happy to hear,' he began, shifting his gaze to Jessica, 'that Emily is making some progress. Not a lot, not yet. But enough so that we think it might be an idea to call in Salena Cartera. Salena is a very talented local hypnotist,' he said, as if explaining to Jessica. 'She's helped us before and we think she might be able to help us here.'

Emily wasn't sure what she had been hoping for, but the look of anxiety that suddenly spread over Jessica's face was not it. Her discomfort was unmistakable and Emily was sure that Inspector Moller had noted it too.

'It would be wonderful if that would help,' Jessica said, her voice as unconvincing as her expression. 'I just want this over with.'

'I'm sure you do, Mrs Stirhew,' Inspector Moller said. 'We all do.'

'Well, if you don't need me for anything, I'd like to go and lie down, or maybe I should go and take a walk . . . something . . .'

'Of course. I know how difficult this is and no, I don't need you for anything right now. Emily and I have some work to do. We won't be long, Annie. I promised Emily she would have time for a nap before the barbecue tonight.'

'Oh, tonight's the barbecue,' Jessica murmured vaguely before heading up the stairs. 'It's hard to think that just down the hill there's a whole different world going on.' Her voice trailed off to almost a whisper.

The mention of the barbecue seemed to stir Annie out of her malaise. 'That's right, the barbecue. Emily, how thoughtless of me! Have you heard anything more from Michael?' she asked solicitously.

'Not yet, but I'm counting on him arriving early this evening. I'm hoping we'll be able to go to the barbecue together. I've heard so much about it.'

'It's great fun, so you must come no matter what. But I'm sure Michael will be here by then. Now you better go do what you have to do or you won't get any rest.'

The door to the study had just closed when Inspector Moller turned to Emily with a look of deep concern on his face. 'I don't know if you caught the look on Jessica's face when she heard about your "progress."'

'I did. I couldn't take my eyes off her.'

'I have to tell you, Emily, that I'm deeply disturbed by her reaction. She seemed considerably more nervous than I would expect, under the circumstances.'

'It makes me feel so sad, really. I had hoped it wasn't Jessica. She's had such a tough life already. She doesn't deserve this.'

'I know how you're feeling. I feel bad for her myself. But before you start feeling too upset about this, remember this person is willing to hurt you to keep you quiet. Of course, one anxious look doesn't mean she's guilty . . .'

'I know you're right . . . and that's the one thing that keeps me from believing that Jessica did this. I guess I'm willing to believe that she killed Roger in a moment of rage or fear, but I just can't believe she would try to hurt me.'

'I've been in this business for a long time, Emily, and I've seen a lot of things you wouldn't believe . . . but . . . I take it you'd like to go back to your room now.'

'I would. Tonight is starting to lose its appeal, but maybe a nap will help. And who knows, Michael might even be here by the time I wake up.'

TWENTY-ONE

Before they headed back, Inspector Moller stopped at the office. The main house was quiet now. Nap time. Everyone resting up for the night's big event. While the inspector made a couple of calls, Emily once again stood on the terrace just as she had . . . My God, was it only yesterday?

'You're looking pensive, my dear,' Martin said, joining her at the low stone wall. 'It's been grueling, hasn't it?'

Emily was surprised. This was a much more subdued Martin than she had seen earlier. Like Annie, the toll of recent events was suddenly clear. 'You seem kind of drained yourself,' she said.

'Quiet moments like this, everything ready for tonight, everyone resting, nothing really to distract the mind. Moments like this make us face our demons. This is a sorry affair no matter how it turns out, Emily. Someone here is a killer; one life, no matter how unpleasant, is lost; others are a mess. It all seems to be coming undone, doesn't it? One could easily lose oneself in the tragedy. It would almost be comforting, in fact; part of the healing. Annie and I can't, of course . . . the guests. In some ways our lives are always lived on a public stage here. Maybe it's time . . . Ah, I must be getting old,' he said, a bit of humor returning to his voice. 'A touch of melancholy . . . dementia will be next. Now, can I get you something?'

'No, nothing. I'm just waiting for Thomas; he's on the phone in the office. Then I'm going to join everyone else here and take a nap.'

'Thomas is a good detective and a good man,' Martin said. 'I think he's worried about you, Emily. We all are. Do be careful.'

'All done,' Inspector Moller said, heading out on to the terrace. 'All set?'

'You bet. I'm exhausted,' Emily said, quite content to head back to her room.

'Thomas, I know we talked about this before but maybe we should revisit the idea of Emily staying at the rondoval. Maybe she should stay up here at the house. We have a lovely guest room on the first floor. It's quite private, has its own entrance. Don't you think that's a good idea, Thomas? Perhaps just for tonight?'

'I've thought about that, Martin,' Thomas answered, and for a moment he looked unsure. 'But I've just gotten word that her fiancé is booked on the six-thirty flight, so . . .'

'Oh how wonderful,' Emily exclaimed. 'How did you find out?'

'We've had our people checking the manifests for this evening's incoming flights. That was the call I got from headquarters . . . I can't tell you how relieved I am. I'll feel a lot more comfortable with Michael around. So shall we head back?'

On the way to her room, Thomas gave her a pep talk about their charade and assured her that he would have people watching out for her.

'Wouldn't it help if I knew who your people were? I think I'd feel more secure.'

'If this is to work, our target must believe you're vulnerable. Believe me, if you knew who my people were, you'd give it away. In fact, it would probably make you more nervous. You'd be looking for them, unable to concentrate on what was happening around you. And anyway, Michael will be here soon.'

'You're right. Michael being here will change everything.'

'I'm going to try to meet his plane at the airport,' Inspector Moller explained. 'I want to be able to let him know what's going on and I certainly can't do that here. Also, this way I'll be able to speed him through customs.'

'So Michael will actually make it for the barbecue? How wonderful.'

'I hope so. Once he's clear we'll have a taxi waiting to bring him here. Wouldn't do for him to arrive in a police car, of course.'

'I can't wait to see him. It's seems like so long since I last saw him. So much has happened.'

The news that Michael was actually arriving lifted Emily's spirits immensely. Once again, there was a refreshment tray in her hut, fresh fruit and cheeses, and a small bottle of champagne that she could not resist opening.

Champagne, how appropriate, she thought as she stripped off her cover-up and bathing suit. It's nice to have something to celebrate for a change.

Within minutes she had jumped into the shower to rinse the sand from her hair, wrapped herself in a huge terrycloth towel and poured herself a sparkling glass. She was certainly too restless to read her book, but she needed to settle her mind before trying to sleep, so she grabbed a local magazine and settled herself in the wicker chaise that sat by the window. This way she could lazily flip the pages and enjoy the ocean view.

The afternoon sun poured through her open shutters and in no time a relaxing languor settled over her. The day's events, both pleasant and unpleasant, had taken their toll and she was soon fast asleep. The sun set magnificently and a purple dusk came on, but Emily did not see it. In a deep slumber, she was oblivious to everything – the swish of the palm leaves as a gentle breeze blew by, the roll of the waves as the day's heat subsided, and the sound of soft footsteps and crunching pebbles directly outside her window. Nothing disturbed her peaceful slumber as dusk turned to night.

She woke slowly, stretching her arms and legs as she searched for her fallen towel. My God . . . Michael, she thought, a slow, secretive smile spreading across her face. Talk about sweet dreams. Unable to rouse herself immediately, she reached out a slender arm and switched on the nearby lamp. A soft glow lit the shadowed room as a content Emily lay musing, a perfect target for invasive eyes.

Blissfully unaware, she allowed herself these stolen moments, until thoughts of Michael's arrival spurred her into action. Wrapping the towel around her, she headed for the closet, suddenly intrigued by the idea of a costume.

A swirling black silk skirt, a black tank top, several scarves and all the beads she had brought with her. Perfect, she thought. And sandals that tie up the leg. No self-respecting gypsy would be caught dead without those.

Emily went about assembling her wardrobe until the sounds of footsteps on the path startled her. Looking out the window, she was relieved to see the nice young police officer patrolling the grounds. She was tempted to call out to him but knew she shouldn't. After all, as far as anyone knew, he was here for everyone's protection. But she went back to her preparations content in the knowledge of his presence.

It was a little after seven-thirty when the intercom on her night table buzzed. Emily, ready to meet the Parkers, picked it up immediately, sure that it was Michael calling from the main house, but she was surprised to hear Annie's voice.

'Emily, I just got a call from Inspector Moller at the airport. Michael's plane was delayed. Thomas will wait a while longer.'

'Any idea how long before it arrives?'

'Not for at least a half hour, maybe more. Thomas said to tell you to go ahead with your plan to meet the Parkers on the terrace. As a matter of fact, I just saw Nancy and Mark talking to Sarah. They're waiting for Jon to arrive. He's late and Sarah is worried. But Emily, why is Thomas at the airport? What's going on?'

'Nothing, really, Annie. He's just making sure Michael gets through customs quickly. I guess he's a little concerned.'

'I'm more than a little concerned myself after what happened this morning. Let me send someone down to walk you up? Nelson . . . Nelson . . .' Emily could hear Annie calling. 'Did Martin come back yet?'

'Not yet, Miss Annie.'

'He's been gone for a while. He should be . . . Oh, maybe . . . I don't know what . . .'

'Annie, Annie!' Emily yelled into the crackling intercom, trying to get Annie to hear her.

'Emily, I'm looking for Martin. He went up to the house to check on Jessica. I was worried there was something wrong up there. I couldn't rouse her on the phone. But he hasn't come back,' Annie said, her words sounding increasingly worried.

'No, Annie, please, that's not necessary. Really, I'm fine. As a matter of fact, I just saw that nice young policeman out on the path. I'll get him to walk me up if I get concerned.'

But Emily wouldn't have been so quick to reassure Annie

if she had seen the brief, violent episode that had occurred on the path just moments ago. The 'nice young policeman,' as Emily had described him, had slowly crisscrossed the walkways that led from the distant rondovals to the main house. His post was there, knowing that Emily would come this way to reach the terrace.

As he walked, he concentrated on the door to her rondoval. Occasional clouds blocked the bright light of the moon and he wanted to be sure that he didn't miss her. So focused was he that he never sensed the furtive figure that lurked behind a nearby tree or heard the *woosh* of the gun as it was swung through the air and hammered into his skull.

An unsuspecting Emily, still taken with the excitement of Michael's pending arrival and her costume preparations, never suspected that her protector had fallen. She put some final touches on her make-up, grabbed a small purse that could hold little more than her lipstick and tied a wildly patterned, red-fringed shawl around her waist. Perfect, she thought, taking a final look at herself in the mirror. She felt almost as wanton as she looked.

She was actually jaunty as she started out. The light outside her room illuminated her way along the beach path and as soon as she turned on to the garden walkway she could see the tiny, twinkling lights of the terraces in the distance. But she had taken only a few steps when all of the walkway lights suddenly went out, throwing the whole area into darkness.

Emily immediately stopped. She certainly wasn't going to continue on the darkened path. She would go back to her hut and buzz the main house. She could take Annie up on her offer; she certainly didn't see any sign of that policeman.

When she turned around, she saw that the light outside her rondoval was darkened too. All of the rondoval lights were. Maybe everyone had already left for the barbecue, she thought; after all, there were so few huts on this side of the resort.

Emily slowly made her way back, carefully opening the door to her rondoval and reaching in to switch on the inside light. Click . . . click . . . nothing. Using the bright silver light of the moon she groped for the night table and pressed the intercom's buzzer . . . silence . . . no steady hum or answering words. Dead. The intercom was dead.

Darkness, silence. Slowly, she reached her hand out again and this time the moon's light glinted off the ring on her finger. The ring . . .

Oh, God, she couldn't stay here. There was no one here . . . no one to help if . . . she had to get to the main house. She had to get to Thomas. They could reach him at the airport. She had to talk to him, to tell him . . . My God . . . the glinting in the sun . . . she'd remembered.

The candle. She'd use that to light her way. A match. Damn, this was what she got for quitting smoking – where could she find a match? It was then that she remembered picking up Jessica's stuff from the ground. Cigarettes . . . and matches! They must be in her beach-robe pocket.

Emily stumbled twice, rapping her shin on the corner of the bed and knocking over a tall lamp with a loud crash, but eventually she made her way to the closet and found the matchbook. It was in the glow of the candlelight that she first noticed the name on the cover . . . *Lago di Como*.

Emily quickly headed out of her room, the small glow barely lighting her way, but she had gone only steps when the wind blew the candle out. It was hopeless. She would have to manage in the darkness. But as soon as she started down the garden path she knew this way was impossible.

As she searched the darkness, she saw that there were a couple of lights leading up to the ocean path. I'll go that way, she thought. I've taken that path in the daytime. It's probably a little trickier at night, but it should be OK.

It was then that she heard the cries that seemed to be coming from further up the steep, winding path.

'Help me,' the voice pleaded. 'Please, someone, help me.'

She thought perhaps someone had fallen when all the lights went out, and she hurried to see what was wrong.

But the path was more of a struggle than Emily thought it would be – different than during the day when the uneven ground was easily navigated and the sound of the surf seemed more majestic than ominous. The wind howled up here, whipping her hair across her face. She could barely hear the cries up ahead. She had difficulty pinpointing where they were coming from. For a minute she thought they had stopped.

'Oh, God, someone please help me.'

No, there they were again. Her already sore hands and feet were taking a beating as she gripped jagged rocks to steady herself. But the urgency of the cries forced her on.

'I'm coming. Hold on, I'm almost there,' she called, hoping to calm whoever was lying injured up ahead.

She was at the top now. She could actually see part of the bay beach on the other side, but she was suddenly confused. There was no one there. Where was the voice coming from? She hadn't passed anyone lying in the crannies that lined the path. Surely if she had missed them they would have called out to her? Could they be further up ahead? Or on the downward path to the bay beach?

Is it possible I could have missed them, she thought. For a moment she thought of going back but her eyes were drawn to the lights of the bay beach. Move, she thought. She had to move forward. Too late, she realized something was terribly wrong as she felt the crushing blow to the back of her head.

For a moment everything went black, and then she felt her body being dragged along the rocky ground. Oh, God, the cliff edge – someone was dragging her toward the cliff edge. She tried desperately to think but her head was roiled with confused, broken images.

That voice . . . someone was talking. '*Sorry, Emily, but I can't take the chance that you'll remember.*' Remember . . . remember . . . Oh, God, remember . . .

'*I'm afraid you played a dangerous game.*' A game . . . a dangerous game . . .

'*Why couldn't you have just stayed out of it? It was none of your business. You hardly even knew him. I didn't want this to happen, but it's too late now. Everyone will think your fall was tragic, but the darkness, the slippery rocks and those shoes . . .*'

Rough stones battered her back and head . . . the sound of the surf was closer now. She had to do something. Scream, she had to scream. It was her only chance.

Emily struggled against panic. She waited for the momentary silence, that brief interlude between the roars of the rhythmic waves. Steady, she thought. Concentrate on the timing. Soon.

The next one. Now. But just as she opened her mouth, the stillness of the night was shattered by the opening salvos of the steel band . . .

Oh, God, no . . . no, not now.

'I never even saw you,' she said, desperately trying to play for time. 'It was all a ruse. I never even saw you. You're going to kill me for nothing . . . for nothing.'

'Nick, don't!' Jessica's tortured voice cried from the path behind them. 'I can't let you do this. Please don't make it worse. Please, Nick, people will understand. I'll stand by you; we'll face it together. They'll know that you did it for me. Roger's abusiveness, his rages, his drinking. They'll understand. But this . . . I can't let you do this, Nick . . . please, Nick, please stop. This is madness . . .'

'Can't let me do this . . . Oh, Jessica, you poor, poor thing,' Nick said, his voice cruel and hard. There was nothing relaxed about him now. 'You never did understand, did you? You give me too much credit. You were very pretty and fun. And it certainly did give me great pleasure to make a fool of Roger. He was so full of himself. Such a blowhard, really. But you? You weren't quite worth killing for. No, my dear, Roger's death was pure business. The foolish man thought he was invincible. I don't know how he found out about the restaurant and the money laundering but once he did there was no stopping him. I tried to convince him that some people would be pretty upset if he went ahead with his story – people who counted on me to launder their money; people who weren't used to taking no for an answer, but he wouldn't let go of it. He threatened to print it.

'Now, what to do with the two of you,' he continued. 'God, this gets more and more inconvenient. But perhaps not. Yes, I think this will work. Jessica, how desperate of you to kill Emily because she's discovered that it was you who killed Roger. And now, overcome with guilt, you have no choice. Tragic, really. Two lovely lives lost and for what? No one much liked Roger . . . Pity.

'Now, Emily, if you would just get up and stand there, close to the edge, I think. And turn. Your body will naturally fall over. On to the rocks, I'm afraid,' he said, motioning to her with the gun, and she saw his ring – the one that'd glinted in the sun that day. Tonight was the first time she'd seen him in his red shirt – he'd been too clever to risk it. 'And Jessica . . .'

But Jessica was not listening. Years of humiliation and rage finally exploded inside her and with one agonized wail she threw herself at Nick Marino. 'You bastard . . .!' she screamed, her voice lost in the night.

Nick, of course, was much too strong for her. Jessica was quickly losing the struggle on the ground. Emily knew she had only one chance, and a desperate one at that. Crawling along the ground she reached the edge of the bluff. She knew that it was not a straight drop. There were one or two spots where someone could hide among the crannies along the rock face. If she could just find a way. She would have to risk it, she decided, as she blindly lowered herself over the cliff.

Oh, God, she thought as she hung, dangling, above the jagged rocks and raging water. A foothold . . . if she could just find a foothold. Her arms were cramping and her hands had started to bleed.

Damn, what was I thinking? A dangerous game, that's what Nick had said. A dangerous game, and I've lost. I can't hold on any longer. She moved her legs back and forth, pawing at the rock face, but there was nothing. And as the sound of a gunshot rang out from above, Emily's tortured hands weakened and she fell into the void below.

Miraculously, the shawl which she had so jauntily tied around her waist only a short time ago caught on a jagged boulder a few feet down, breaking her fall. She was pulled up harshly and thrown to the side, banging her shoulder and scraping her face. But in spite of the pain she knew how lucky she was.

Below her, to the left she could see a narrow shelf and behind that a deep crevice. She knew the shawl would hold for only a minute; she had to move quickly. By stretching her leg as far as she could, she was just able to touch the end of the ledge and, grabbing on to the small outcroppings of rock, she lowered herself down. Another brief glance at the rocks and water below brought on a dizzying nausea as Emily crawled into the darkness of the crevice.

Thank God, she thought, tears starting to spill from her eyes and a muffled sob escaping . . . safety. Someone will come. Someone must have heard that shot. All I have to do is wait. I can lie here till morning if I have to. She lay quietly, trying to concentrate on every sound she heard, convinced that at any moment she would hear a friendly voice calling her name. Perhaps that young policeman, or Thomas. Thomas must be back from the airport by now – with Michael. They'd be looking for her. But except for the roar of the ocean, there was only silence. She wondered what had happened up above. Poor Jessica, she thought, what a desperate end. Used again.

It was then that Emily saw the light. A single piercing beam, coursing and probing, up and down the rock face. Certainly Nick must have fled by now, she thought. He must fear that someone will come and he'll get caught. Still, she pressed herself as far back in her crevice as she could, hoping that she would blend in with the rock. Oh, God, she prayed silently, please don't let that be him. Not now, not when she had almost made it. The light seemed to be coming closer. It was coming from below, as if someone were climbing the rock face, shining the light in every cranny. Searching. Searching.

Emily wanted desperately to close her eyes, shutting out what she now realized would be her death knell, but it was as if she was paralyzed. She watched horrified as the beam moved closer and closer, the light probing relentlessly. And then it found her.

'Thank God you're alive,' the sultry voice said as a black-clad figure pulled itself up on to the shelf. 'Moller would have had my job if you'd gotten yourself killed.'

At first Emily didn't recognize who it was, so overcome was she by the immediate, overwhelming realization that she was going to live. But there was no mistaking the lusty figure, dressed in a black bustier and black pants, a sash around her waist and a short dagger sticking out of a leather scabbard.

'Ms Turner?' Emily said incredulously. And then, remembering that afternoon's conversation in the beach bar, 'You were right, great costume!'

EPILOGUE

Emily was settled on the couch in Martin and Annie's living room. Once again, the resort's nurse had dressed her wounds and Martin had just brought her a piña colada in a frosted glass. 'Just one, to relax you,' he said. 'You've certainly earned it.'

Emily laughed softly, hardly able to believe she could. The night was finally quiet but no one had quite recovered from what had occurred. Between the police sirens and the flashing lights, the wailing of the ambulance and the throbbing of the steel band, Thomas had arrived in the midst of quite a scene.

'I'm sorry, Emily,' he'd repeated several times as they had assembled in Martin and Annie's living room.

'Michael?' Emily had asked as soon as she saw him.

'No. He wasn't on the plane. I checked with the airline agent. It seems he didn't make the flight in London. They didn't know anything more. I'm sorry.'

Emily just nodded. Deep down, she wasn't surprised.

'I can't believe it could have happened this way,' Thomas continued, shaking his head back and forth. 'Thank God I had Officer Turner covering Jessica. What if no one had seen her heading for that path? The two of you could have been killed and no one would have been the wiser. Maybe this was a mistake – too much of a chance to take. At the very least, I never should have gone to the airport. I thought I could get Michael through customs, let him know what was going on. I thought we had plenty of time.'

With those words, everyone turned to look at Emily. She ignored their sympathetic expressions. 'It doesn't matter, Thomas. You did what you thought was best. If Michael had . . .' But there was really nothing more to say.

'Well, I'm sure if you had any idea what was going to happen . . .' Sarah began from her comfortable spot on the couch, curled up next to Jon. Her hand held his and his arm protectively encircled her shoulders. 'But I'm confused. Did you know that someone was going to go after Emily? I thought you were waiting for the hypnotist? It seems like you had people staked out and everything.'

'I'm sure Inspector Moller was just being careful,' Nora joined in, unaware, as most people were, that a deliberate trap had been set and Emily was the bait. Nora set a tall glass and two small pills in front of Marietta.

'Thank you, Nora,' Marietta said, swallowing the pills and downing the drink greedily. 'You never do forget. Whatever would I do without you?' For a moment, Marietta paused, her eyes misty. 'It certainly was an exciting ending to a rather dreary episode,' she added, quickly returning to the events of the evening. 'Of course, it will be the focus of my column. You know, beautiful, sexy policewoman, daring rescue. Wonderful copy, don't you think? Thank God, as I just didn't know how I was going to write about Roger's death. And I couldn't just ignore it. This works out perfectly . . . I mean, seeing as how Roger had been killed and all that.'

Emily looked around the room as they talked. They made an odd picture – everyone dressed in some version of a pirate costume. Sarah wore a wildly swirled skirt and Jon sported a distinguished eye patch. Emily was still in her black skirt, now ripped and shredded, the beads half shattered and sandals, those damn sandals, torn and broken. Nora had on black harem pants and a red top with a frill at the neck. Even Marietta had dressed for the barbecue, albeit in a subtle, sophisticated manner. Everyone was too tired and spent to care.

It was just after two in the morning when Annie heard the phone ring. She answered quickly, sure that something else was wrong. 'Emily, it's for you,' she called quietly across the room. 'It's Michael. He sounds . . .'

Emily looked quietly down at the floor, then raising her head she answered, 'Tell him . . . tell him I'm not available, Annie.'

The mood in the room grew quiet. They had spent hours rehashing what happened and suddenly there was little left to say. After a few minutes, Annie urged everyone back to their rooms. 'I don't know about anyone else,' she said, 'but I'm exhausted and I want to head up and see how Jessica is doing. I think everyone could probably use some sleep. Especially you, Emily. But not in the rondoval.'

'Honestly, Annie, it's fine. You and Martin have had enough to—'

'Sorry, Emily. Martin and I insist. The guest room is lovely and you'll be quite comfortable there. We've already had your things moved so it's all ready for you. And it would be helpful to have you here in the morning . . . for Jessica.'

As the others said goodnight, Emily made her way out to the veranda. It was beautiful out there – a velvet sky with a million stars and a bright, round moon that lit up the night. On the horizon three cruise ships sat like glittering paper cutouts on a midnight sea. Most of the resort lights were out, save for the ones that dotted the paths.

'Emily,' Thomas stepped quietly on to the veranda. 'I'm so terribly—'

'No, Thomas, don't. There's no need to, really. I knew what I was getting into and if you hadn't been delayed, well . . . I'm fine. Although, I doubt if I can sleep.'

And so they had talked.

At first, Emily talked about life at Island Bluffs, the people she had met, their stories, their secrets. Thomas just listened, knowing that soon Emily would venture into the evening's dark events.

'Tell me Thomas, did you ever consider *me* a suspect?'

Thomas smiled. 'Well, naturally, in the very beginning. That's the way it is in my business. Everyone's a suspect, at first. And you had found the body – no one else was around, you know. But it didn't take me long to rule that out. Firstly, of all the people here, you were the only one who had no reason to kill Roger – I checked out your background, of course. And then, questioning you, it soon became clear that you were telling the truth.'

Emily was surprised at how relieved she was to hear him say that. 'You know, I never really believed I was in that much danger, Thomas. Not until the very end. I was pretty much convinced that someone was trying to scare me, but kill me? I couldn't think of anyone here who would do that. And of all people, Nick Marino. It wasn't until I remembered his ring. The day we went windsurfing . . . he had shown it to me. It was his grandmother's and it had glinted in the sun just the way it did on the day he killed Roger. But all along, he seemed like such a . . . I don't know, a lightweight, and so laid-back. You know, kind of like those old-time lounge lizards in B movies. Someone who fancies themselves: all smooth talk and slick moves, but nothing much behind it. But once I remembered the ring and then saw the matchbook, *Lago di Como*, the name of his restaurant . . . I knew he was no lightweight. I knew he had killed Roger.'

'Yes, well, from what we've found out there was a lot more behind Nick Marino than anyone knew . . . even Jessica. For the last eight years, Nick has been laundering money for a major crime family in Connecticut. A lot of it. His family has always had loose ties to organized crime, running numbers, making book. But Nick wanted more and, when some of his contacts were looking for a way to launder some money, he offered the restaurant. It obviously worked, but somehow Roger got wind of it. We don't know how but the Connecticut police and the FBI are all over this right now. We'll find out.'

'Poor Jessica,' Emily said. 'I feel so bad for her. She must have felt so violated by what Nick was saying out there on the bluff. So used. I think that was what made her attack him. She just didn't care anymore. She couldn't bear the thought that she had been so manipulated by him. That he didn't really love her as she believed – he was just the same as the others. What do you think will happen to her?'

Thomas joined Emily at the edge of the balcony. His presence so close to her was comforting. 'I can't be sure. I'm hoping she'll get probation. It seems she didn't actually know that Nick had killed Roger, just suspected. No wonder she was so devastated. Her husband dead and suspecting that her lover was the killer. She followed Nick tonight. She was going to confront him. She thought he'd killed Roger out of love for her. It seems that they had been having an affair for a little over a year. They had met at his restaurant one night that she and Roger had gone there. Roger was writing a review and, would you believe, he actually gave it a good one! Nick had been charming and was attracted to Jessica right away, but love? That was beyond him.'

'Jessica certainly did have awful taste in men,' Emily said sadly.

'Nick had come here intending to kill Roger. He and his contacts couldn't afford to have Roger reveal their secrets. Jessica should have told us about her suspicions. But she actually did save your life and put her own in jeopardy, so that should make a difference.'

'I remember speaking to Jessica after I was followed. She thought I should go back to New York then. What was it she said? "I would feel awful if anything happened to you, Emily, almost as if it were my fault." I thought she was being foolish at the time, but now I understand.'

'Thank God Turner showed up when she did,' Thomas said, his admiration for Officer Turner evident in his voice as Emily laughed. 'Did you suspect at all, Emily? You had spoken to her a couple of times. Any suspicions?'

'Not one. Amazing, isn't it? I knew you said you had people watching out for me, but I figured . . . like . . . guys. And with the way she dressed and acted, there was no way anyone would have caught on. Certainly Nick didn't. Every time I think of him standing with his arm around her that afternoon, I have to laugh. And when she told me about what happened up there on the bluff tonight . . . well, I just can't imagine. Actually, I think it was poetic justice that a female cop caught Nick. I would've loved to have seen his face when she shot that gun out of his hand. And then to have Jessica standing guard over him, with a gun in *her* hand. I'm surprised she didn't shoot him. I'll bet that gave him some anxious moments. I'm just so happy it's all over, Thomas.'

'What will you do now? I imagine you'll head back to New York.'

'No, I don't think so. Not yet. There's nothing there for me right now. And I can't face the snow and the cold. No, I think I'll stay on, maybe even try to extend my stay for a few days. With everything that's happened, I haven't really had a chance to see the island, get to know the people.'

'Maybe I could show you around. I'm off this weekend and—'

'That would be nice, Thomas,' Emily answered and smiled, even before he had finished.